The

BUG HUNTER

A Novel

by KEN DAVENPORT

Book design by The Frontispiece

ALSO BY KEN DAVENPORT

The Two Gates

To get updates on my writing and more
visit at *www.kendavenport.net*

"It is better to defeat the enemy by hunger than with steel..."

— **NICCOLO MACHIAVELLI,**
The Art of War

THE BUG HUNTER

PROLOGUE

Spring 2020
Helmand Province, Afghanistan

WIND RAN OFF THE MOUNTAINS and through the valley like a river; in the winter it froze the ears and made the cheeks hurt. In the summer it parched the throat and dried the eyes, blowing a fine dust that covered you in a cocoon, nestling in the crevices of your skin and bonding to it like a tattoo. And since you'd go for months without a shower, even the fairest would start to go native: a traditional scarf framing a face stained dark by dirt and dust with a craggy beard. Nobody was winning any beauty contests.

"God, I hate this place," said Adnan Mishner as he scraped at his eyelids, trying to unstick them. His contacts were acting like sandpaper. "Two more days and we are out of here."

Gabriel Marx glanced sideways at Adnan but said nothing. His attention was fixed on the fields in front of them, rectangles of color against a brown backdrop. Gabriel was amazed that anything would grow in these valleys; they were like barren craters on the surface of the moon. And yet thousands of square miles that ringed Helmand Province were among the most fertile in the world for growing poppy, a pretty plant that fueled the Taliban insurgency. "What's the wind doing now?"

Adnan held up a wind meter to the sky. "Thirty-two kilometers per hour from the northwest," he read out. "About right, and headed in the right direction."

"OK. Let's go," Gabriel said, turning to look at the marine company commander who was standing thirty feet behind them. His company, Bravo of the First Battalion, Fifth Marines, along with units from the Afghan National Army, the National Police's Poppy Eradication Force, and the American contracting firm DynCorp were spread out in a defensive perimeter designed to protect Gabriel and Adnan from an ambush. The two men would be totally exposed when they went out into the fields. Touching a button at his collar, Gabriel said, "Captain, we're moving out now. We will take the center route to the southern grid, release, and then double back to the east. Estimate about ninety minutes elapsed time."

"Roger that," came a metallic reply from the headset in Gabriel's Kevlar helmet.

Gabriel looked at Adnan and said, "Let's move. Step exactly where I do." He then took the lead, walking carefully along the perimeter of the first field. The poppies were vivid hues of pastel pink and purple, happy colors, incongruous with the mission at hand. Adnan kept his head down, his eyes fixed on Gabriel's footsteps, making sure to walk where Gabriel had last stepped. The trail had been swept for improvised explosive devices, but Adnan was taking no chances.

They walked deliberately for roughly twenty minutes until they reached the northeast corner of the field they'd chosen, the northernmost of the bunch. There were eight fields in all, each roughly one hectare in size. The location of the release had to be precise, so the wind would take the cloud in the right direction and spread it evenly, to ensure each field was properly seeded.

"This is good," Gabriel said, dropping down to his knees so they were hidden from view. Both Adnan and Gabriel removed their backpacks. Carefully, each unzipped the main pouches and pulled out large cylindrical canisters. At one end of each was a nozzle approximately two inches across, and at the other was a plunger that resembled an old-fashioned dynamite detonator. Without a word between them, they primed the canisters for release and donned their gas masks.

"On my mark. Three. Two. One. Go!" Gabriel said, and they twisted the plungers in unison, pointing the nozzles skyward. With a whoosh a pair of projectiles were shot into the sky, several hundred feet into the wind stream. When they reached the apex of their arcs, the projectiles released two plumes of white mist that joined and grew until the cloud was almost the size of a football field. Carried by the wind, the mist began to disperse itself over the fields, settling gradually onto the poppies like a blanket.

Though the mist was not technically dangerous to humans, Gabriel and Adnan kept their masks on as they retraced their steps back to where the marines waited. It was protocol to do so, and Gabriel liked to be extra careful with anything that was genetically altered to kill things. He knew the guys in Vietnam had been told Agent Orange was safe too, only to find out later that it was a toxic brew. He preferred to err on the side of caution.

Just as they reached the edge of the last field, Gabriel heard the .50 caliber heavy machine gun open up; the marines had started taking fire from a series of buildings across a canal that ran through the valley. And then came the shrill sound of mortars, and Gabriel knew that this was no random encounter with a few Taliban taking potshots from long distance.

Gabriel turned to yell at Adnan just as the first mortar hit, blowing a huge hole in the ground in the center of the marines' position and pelting Gabriel with rocks. He pulled Adnan to him and could see a look of terror in his eyes. Adnan was a civilian and had never been shot at before.

"Stay with me, and do exactly as I do!" yelled Gabriel. Adnan put a viselike grip on Gabriel's arm and nodded. There was a gap of about a hundred meters between where they were and where the marine MRAPs and other heavy vehicles were; they'd have to make a run for it.

Gabriel waited for the next mortar round to hit and then immediately ran out into the open. He zigzagged and tried to stay low, dragging

Adnan behind him. They managed to reach safety, diving headlong into the shadow of an armored truck. Adnan ripped off his mask and promptly threw up.

Bravo Company was fully engaged in the firefight by then, and the noise was deafening. As Gabriel sat back against the huge tires of the truck that was shielding them, he looked off into the distance and could just see the last bit of the mist they'd unleashed settling to earth.

※

Within an hour of their shooting off the canisters, the mist started working its destructive magic. Though it looked like a gas, it was actually a specially designed aerosol that carried thousands of Tubulifera thrips, a tiny winged insect with a needlelike mouth that fed on poppies by piercing their skin and sucking on their sap. This weakened the plant and destroyed vital cellular activity, reducing the yield but not permanently destroying the crop. Thrips were capable of asexual reproduction, and several thousand released into the air would in short order turn into a million or more. This alone would be a threat to the health of the poppy fields they were targeting.

But these weren't your ordinary garden thrips. These bugs had been genetically altered at the Biomedical Research Laboratory at George Mason University to carry a virulent strain of tospovirus, engineered specifically for this purpose to be immune to pesticides. Transmitted in the insect's saliva, this virus produced a fatal disease in the poppy plant that was both incurable and devastating. Within weeks the targeted fields would begin to whither and die; the only option would be to burn the poppies to the ground and start over.

The infected thrips had been shipped to Afghanistan aboard a military transport and delivered to Gabriel one week before. Since then they'd been unleashed on more than one thousand hectares of poppies all over Helmand Province.

Later that night at Forward Operating Base Eagle, Gabriel lay in the dark staring at the ceiling of the tent he shared with Adnan. The accommodations were terrible. The tents were made of cheesecloth and weren't waterproof. The floors were dirt and sometimes mud. Gabriel marveled at how the marine and army units in Afghanistan existed for months in these conditions. As a former marine who'd served in Iraq, Gabriel was used to roughing it. But Afghanistan was a particular kind of shit hole. The food was so bad that it wasn't a question of *if* you were going to get the runs but rather *when*; since arriving ten days earlier, Gabriel had been subsisting on power bars and bottled water. He was in a perpetual state of hunger, and it made him irritable and short-tempered.

Adnan came into the tent after his umpteenth trip to the head. He hadn't followed Gabriel's diet and was paying the price.

"My ass hurts so bad," Adnan said, falling onto his cot.

"I tried to tell you. But maybe you thought your blood would ward off the runs. Didn't work out so well."

Adnan grunted. "Apparently just because I was born in Cairo doesn't mean my stomach can handle putrid goat and rice."

Adnan Mishner had been born to an Egyptian mother and an American father; his parents had met in Alexandria when his father was assigned to the US Agency for International Development. Adnan was born in Cairo in 1992 and lived in Egypt until he was five, when his father returned to Washington, DC. He was a brilliant student who went to Yale and later got his PhD in entomology at Cornell University. He was recruited by the Department of Homeland Security to work on developing insects to be used as vectors and assigned to the Biomedical Research Lab based at George Mason University.

"When you were in Iraq, did you get sick like this?" Adnan asked.

"Everyone gets sick at first. But your stomach gets used to it."

Adnan thought for a moment. "When were you in Iraq?"

"In 2004 and 2006 Fallujah, Ramadi."

"Did you kill a lot of people?"

Gabriel paused. He'd been asked this question before but hadn't been expecting it from Adnan. This was the kind of question that civilians who didn't know anything about the military asked. It was a very personal question—perhaps the most personal—and Gabriel hated it.

"Why do you want to know that?" he asked.

"I don't know. Just curious, I guess."

"I did what needed to be done," he said simply.

"Does it bother you?"

"Not a bit. And unless you've been in combat, you'll never understand."

Adnan stared at Gabriel through the dark. "I hated the Iraq War. Terrible mistake."

"Nobody likes war, Adnan. And maybe it wasn't the right thing to do. But hindsight is twenty-twenty."

"You don't need hindsight to see that it was based on greed. The killing of Muslims in the name of oil—" Adnan caught himself, not wanting to anger Gabriel. They still had to share a tent, and he realized that the former marine had likely lost good friends in Iraq. "Anyhow, now we're still in Afghanistan—nearly twenty years after 9/11. It's . . . obscene."

"So if you hate what America is doing, why are you here now? You could have refused this assignment."

"Yes, I could have. But I don't like drugs, Gabriel. My brother died of a heroin overdose when he was nineteen."

Even after he'd spent many months with Adnan, this was new information to Gabriel. "I didn't know that."

"His name was Salman," Adnan said so softly it was barely audible. "It means blessing in Arabic. He was a sweet boy, kind and gentle. But he was also easily influenced. When he was seventeen, he met a girl who was into drugs. By the time he left high school, he was lost to my family."

Gabriel had seen his fair share of drugs growing up and knew the power of addiction. "What happened?"

"He overdosed," Adnan said simply. "They found him in an abandoned house with a needle in his arm."

"I'm sorry."

"The Taliban's opium is a source of heroin on the world market. So this is my way of fighting back for my brother."

"It's also a source of revenue for the insurgency. So you're doing more than just fighting the drug war."

Adnan considered that for a moment before replying. "Maybe so. But that's not why I'm here. And for my money, we should all pack up and go home."

Gabriel rolled over in his cot and thought about his own brother, wounded not by opioids but by an IED planted next to a road in a small village outside Lashkargah, Afghanistan. Chris Marx, a strapping Army Ranger, had lost half of his leg and part of his left hand to a homemade bomb in a milk jug and now rode a desk in the FBI field office in Chicago. He'd survived physically but had been emotionally damaged in a way that Gabriel thought might never heal.

So when the CIA had recruited Gabriel out of his viticulture graduate program at Oregon State, he'd felt he couldn't say no. He'd just finished his master's degree and had already accepted a position at a winery in Sonoma County. He'd studied viticulture so he could ultimately start his own winery; since he was a kid on his parents' farm in Michigan's Upper Peninsula, he'd loved growing things. After a trip to the Napa Valley in college, Gabriel had decided he preferred wine grapes to food crops. He immersed himself in the culture of wine, something unusual in rural Ohio, where he went to college. He ventured that he was the only subscriber to *Wine Spectator* within a hundred-mile radius.

Gabriel quickly found that his role with the CIA was complex and exciting. The agency was coordinating an interdepartmental effort—along with the army and Department of Homeland Security—to develop insect-borne pathogens to combat bioterrorism and to ultimately develop an offensive capability. Gabriel spent time working with Adnan at the Biomedical

Research Laboratory. The researchers there had trained Gabriel in the science of insect genomics and taught him how to handle insect vectors in the field. This mission with Adnan was the culmination of that training.

As Adnan began to snore, Gabriel counted the days before he'd be back home. He was tired of Afghanistan and tired of Adnan. Tomorrow they'd start their treacherous journey, escorted by an Afghan army unit, back to Bagram Airfield to fly back to the States.

Time to return to the wine, he thought as he drifted off to sleep.

†

The convoy taking them back to Bagram had been driving for more than an hour, moving slowly along unpaved roads rutted by recent rain. They had just passed through a small village of mud huts when Gabriel heard what sounded like a firecracker going off, followed instantaneously by the familiar ping of a bullet striking steel. At first it was sporadic, like someone shooting at tin cans for target practice. But then came the sound of automatic gunfire, and the driver of their Humvee veered off the road and into a ditch. Thankfully they didn't tip over.

Gabriel and Adnan sat pressed against each other in the back of the Humvee, unable to see anything through the dirty bulletproof glass. But they could hear shouting, followed by automatic gunfire and then high-pitched screaming. By the time they managed to get out of their vehicle, it was all over.

Adnan reached the little girl first; she was no more than eight years old, with jet-black hair. She wore a tattered yellow dress that was blackened by the growing stain of blood. She'd been shot in the stomach, the bullet ripping through her as if she were a rag doll, exiting her back and exposing her spine. Rolling her over, Adnan put his hand on her face and hopelessly felt for a pulse. Her brown eyes were open, but she was no longer there.

Gabriel put his hand on Adnan's shoulder, and after a moment, he let go of the little girl. He slowly stood and looked around. The Afghan army had decimated the village; there were bodies of old men, women, and children everywhere. "No, no, no!" he screamed.

"Adnan! We have to go! We are exposed here!" Gabriel yelled, grabbing him by the arm, pulling him toward the Humvee.

"They're all dead! Don't you see?"

"Yes, I see," said Gabriel, pushing Adnan into the vehicle. Gabriel got in after him and yelled at the driver to go.

Adnan sat looking at his blood-soaked hands and started to cry. "Murderers," he repeated over and over again.

PART ONE

Six Years Later

CHAPTER ONE

Argun, Chechen Republic

FROST CLUNG TO THE WINDOWS of the cinder-block house like cloudy white paint, and even sitting inside, perched on a rickety wooden stool set on a dirt floor, Abu Bakr al-Baghdadi could see his breath in the air. His hands cupped a mug of steaming hot tea, and he thought again about how much he hated Chechnya. "The shittiest piece of earth I have ever seen," he had called it when he first arrived. Coming from a man who'd spent years shuttling between cave-like bunkers in war-torn Syria, that was saying something.

"Is it all set?" al-Baghdadi asked, a note of skepticism in his voice.

"Yes," said Aslan Basayev, with more confidence than he felt.

Al-Baghdadi stared at the dim screen on the tablet connected to the dark web via a satellite link. The screen was open to a Tor browser connected to a highly encrypted blockchain network that was created at great effort specifically for this purpose. He had uploaded the final set of instructions and was ready to hit Submit.

Basayev was anxious. While the Russians were no longer patrolling the skies over Chechnya looking for communication signals to drop their five-hundred-kilogram bombs on, years of fear had left their mark. "Do it, Abu Bakr. Do it now," he pleaded.

For a man who'd personally sawed off the heads of many an infidel, al-Baghdadi was strangely nervous. This was a moment he'd dreamt about for so long; as the head of the Islamic State of Iraq and Syria (isis), al-Baghdadi had been in hiding for the past ten years. As Osama bin Laden had been, he was public enemy number one of the world's intelligence agencies and had a $100 million bounty on his head. As his armies had crumbled around him in 2017 and 2018, isis had been routed from its capital of Raqqa in Syria and forced into ever-smaller areas. By 2019 al-Baghdadi had taken refuge for a time in the hands of Chechen Islamists who had come to Syria to fight and kill Russian troops, but even that had been short-lived. With Russian-backed Syrian forces closing in, al-Baghdadi and a handful of top Chechen leaders had managed a harrowing escape into Turkey. From there they'd crossed through Georgia into Chechnya, where they'd been in hiding.

Chechen separatists had been in a decades-long battle with Russia over control of the Caucasus region. And though technically the Chechens and isis were fighting different battles, they shared a common goal of creating an Islamic caliphate. For the past several years, al-Baghdadi had been the guest of Aslan Basayev's Caucuses Province one of Chechnya's larger separatist forces. Basayev and al-Baghdadi had found common cause in bringing jihad to the West.

And now he was ready to strike back. As his finger hovered over the Submit button, al-Baghdadi said to himself in Arabic, "In the name of God, most merciful and most compassionate," and pressed his dirty index finger on the screen.

CHAPTER TWO

Russian River Valley, California

GABRIEL MARX'S DREAMS that night came fast and loose. They bounced from his boyhood home in rural Michigan to Fallujah to the poppy fields of Afghanistan to upstate New York, of all places. He'd never actually been anywhere in New York outside of Manhattan and had never met the grizzled old woman who told him that his father was in jail for murder. "Bullshit," he said to the woman. It wasn't that he thought his father incapable of such an act, only that he didn't think he'd be the kind to get taken alive. Gabriel's dad was a murder-suicide kind of guy.

Gabriel was about to ask the woman where the jail was when he awoke with a start; the clock beamed 5:15 a.m. in red numbers, and he realized it was morning. Or close enough. More sleep would mean more dreams and more images of things he'd rather not see. He had a good eighteen hours awake time ahead of him, in which life was often dull but didn't terrorize him.

That was something to be thankful for.

He carefully rolled out of bed so not to wake his sleeping wife, a beautiful woman named Claire who deserved better than him. He didn't know why she stayed, and he didn't ask; not knowing was better than hearing her reasons for loving him. He'd never be able to accept the reasons, and not knowing meant he could make up whatever he wanted. Maybe she was a sucker for veterans suffering from PTSD, or she had a savior complex, or she liked the way he sang in the shower. Whatever. She was there, and Gabriel had made a pact with himself that he wouldn't question her motives.

Pulling on his jeans, Gabriel moved quietly into the bathroom. The dim light from the small window cast a shadow across his face, making his beard look even darker than it was. He looked at himself in the mirror and didn't particularly like what he saw; his hair was too long and too gray, his eyes too puffy, and his teeth had taken on a faint reddish hue from all the wine he was drinking. "Red-wine smile," those in the industry called it, a common occupational hazard for those who made a living smelling, swishing, and spitting copious amounts of red wine. On the positive side, his body was still taut, his stomach flat, and his shoulders muscular. He looked like a thirty-eight-year-old former football player who was aging fast but still had a few yards left in him. He splashed water on his face, pulled his beard down to wring it out, and ran his fingers through his hair.

Satisfied that it was the best he could do at that hour without waking Claire, he slipped a sweatshirt on and headed for the kitchen, where the coffeemaker, a superautomatic machine from Italy that did everything but wash used coffee cups, stood on the counter, its Brew button blinking, beckoning him. As he passed by to open the kitchen door for his dog, Frankie, to go out and do his business, the machine's motion detector sensed Gabriel's presence and turned itself on. Frankie was a sweet old black dog with a white face, a lab that didn't fetch or swim but was always wagging his tail. Gabriel had gotten him from a shelter while in grad school. To the extent a human could own another living thing, he was one of Gabriel's oldest possession.

Coffee in hand, Gabriel walked outside into the chill to watch the sun rise in the east; the morning light cast shadows along hills filled with rows and rows of grapevines. His house sat at the top of a rise, a small plot of land owned by the winery he worked for. It was the assistant vintner's house, set aside for the second-in-command responsible for the growing operation of Landmark Estates. The house for the head vintner was up the road a mile, a large stone structure with a fire pit, a pool, and a hundred-bottle wine cellar. Ed Collier, the Landmark head vintner, had been there for twenty years and wasn't going anywhere. That house might just as well be on Mars, Gabriel had told Claire when he took the job.

Gabriel's own house stood adjacent to the plot of Pinot, and he and Frankie liked to walk it in the morning before the winery staff arrived. The dark earth crunched under his boots as he walked up and down the rows, looking at the leaves and grapes as he went. The Pinot grapes were Gabriel's primary responsibility; they were notoriously temperamental and difficult to grow and harvest. It took all of Gabriel's viticulture knowledge to ensure a healthy harvest of grapes for Landmark's Pinot Noir, its flagship product that had been rated ninety-eighth the year before in *Wine Spectator*'s Top 100.

For the first time in his life, Gabriel felt a sense of contentment. His life with Claire was as close to having a family as he'd ever had; his job was what he had long dreamed of. Even their house, which wasn't really theirs, felt like a home. And while he hadn't fully escaped the clutches of the government and still served as a consultant to the Department of Homeland Security in their Agroterrorism Division, for the most part, he'd been able to live his own life since returning from Afghanistan. And his job with the winery was perfect for him; it allowed him to pursue his passion for viticulture, and it gave him the tools and technology to do cutting-edge fieldwork on the vines they grew. And best of all, the winery's owners pretty much left him alone.

"You're up," he said as he came in through the back door. Claire was sitting at the kitchen table with a coffee, reading the morning news on her tablet.

She smiled and blew on her coffee to cool it down. "You didn't sleep well," she said. It was a statement, not a question.

He rarely slept well. But it had gotten worse since he'd dumped the sleeping pills the Veterans Affairs doctor had prescribed him. He hated the fog they put his mind in. "Yep," he said simply.

"The dreams again?"

"Yep," he said again.

"Same ones?"

"Mostly. Except this time some woman told me that my dad was in jail for murder."

"Hmmm."

"I know, right? Not sure what that's all about."

Gabriel had a troubled relationship with his father, who ran a family farm in western Michigan. It was a tough life, and he was a tough man; he rose early and worked late. Gabriel and his brother had worked the farm from the time they could walk; they had learned a lot, and it had imbued a work ethic in Gabriel that defined him to this day.

But farming was a boom-and-bust kind of business, and when it busted, as it invariably did, so did Gabriel's dad. Debt and pressure had a corrosive effect on him, one that caused him to drink too much and yell too much and fight too much. When Gabriel and his brother were little, his mom had taken the brunt of it. Later, when Gabriel grew up, he and his dad would face off on a regular basis. It taught Gabriel how to fight. But it also made him hate his father. Clearly, in Gabriel's subconscious, his father was capable of murder.

"Do you want to talk about it? Or anything else for that matter?" she asked.

He smiled at her. "No thanks, babe." He knew it wasn't the answer she wanted, but it was the answer she expected.

She nodded. "What's on for today?"

"I'm headed into the lab in a bit," he said as he poured a bowl of cereal and sat down beside her. "What's going on in the news?"

"God, don't ask. Let me read you a few of the headlines. 'US Now in Third Year of Recession.' 'Banks Worried about Cash Reserves.' 'Economic Pain Likely to Continue.' It's a nightmare."

Gabriel just grunted. He was living the headlines. Decades of profligate government spending had lead to an unsustainable national debt and crushing interest payments. Meanwhile a booming China was exerting its muscle all over Asia at the same time the Eurozone economy had been paralyzed by the breakdown of the Euro. The US was increasingly reliant on itself for everything from electronics manufacturing to food production.

When combined with climate change, this was a double gut punch for the wine industry. Not only were exports of American wines in the toilet, but also years of drought and intense heat in California, Oregon, and Washington had weakened the *Vitis labrusca* grapevines that were the backbone of the wine industry, making the vines more and more susceptible to disease. Just a year prior, a rare form of grape lice had reappeared for the first time since the late 1800s. The entire wine industry was running scared.

This was the real reason that Landmark had hired Gabriel. His background had hardly been textbook. Though Oregon State had an excellent viticulture program and Gabriel had scored at the top of his class, he had a past that made him an outlier in the moneyed world of wine. And it wasn't just his service in the Marine Corps, though that certainly made him an oddity. Gabriel had been a difficult teen and had run into his share of trouble. From the time he was a little boy, school had bored him. He was preternaturally bright and often knew more about the subjects he was learning about than the teachers who were teaching them. He left home at seventeen after one too many fights with his dad and promptly fell in with the wrong crowd. There were few ways of making a living in rural Michigan if you didn't want to be a farmer or work the counter at the ampm. It was a small-town economy where he lived, with a few corner stores and a Walmart at the edge of town. You had to be creative to put money in your pocket.

And Gabriel was nothing if not creative. He learned to survive by dealing small amounts of marijuana. He eventually earned enough to rent a room in a small apartment and buy a car. But he was always on the make, always looking, always dealing.

Ultimately, he dealt one too many hands, this time to an undercover cop, who busted him. But Gabriel got lucky. The cop had come from the same kind of hard background and could see himself in the undisciplined, bright kid he'd arrested. He decided to give Gabriel a break and charge him with possession of marijuana, a misdemeanor, rather than intent to distribute, which was a felony. The cop knew that a felony conviction would sink Gabriel's chances any kind of real future. So Gabriel did his community service and paid a small fine, avoiding jail time and a record that would have followed him for the rest of his life.

From the outside, the small metal building adjacent to Landmark's wine-pressing operation looked like any old storage shed; in fact, it was a state-of-the-art lab with a genomic sequencer and a large climate-controlled storage area that housed hundreds of bug samples collected from vineyards all over the United States. It was the kind of lab that any university would be proud to have and showed Landmark's commitment to using technology to protect its wine business.

Gabriel had been working for the past six months on a solution to the threat of grape lice—*Phylloxera vitifoliae*. The bug had a complicated history. It had once been the scourge of the global wine industry, destroying more than six million acres of vineyards in France alone in the late 1800s. It had eventually spread all over Europe and even to California, Australia, and New Zealand. It fed on European vines called *Vitis vinifera*, ultimately destroying them completely. Ironically, phylloxera had originated in America and infested Europe after stowing away on American vines bound for the Continent. These *Vitis labrusca* vines were naturally resistant to phylloxera but proved to be outstanding carriers that infected nonresistant European vines once they arrived. The result was a wine-industry bloodbath.

In the end, wineries were forced to pull up all the plants and start over at a cost of billions of dollars. And when they did, they used *Vitis labrusca* roots and grafted various varieties of *Vitis vinifera* on to them, creating a whole industry based on hybrid American-European grapevines that were phylloxera resistant.

It was a simple solution that had worked for more than a hundred years. But now phylloxera was back, with a new strain that was proving to be effective at damaging American vine roots that had previously been resistant. With Landmark's support, Gabriel was bringing twenty-first-century technology to bear on the problem.

Gabriel entered the lab to find his assistant, Meg Brown, hunched over a microscope.

"How did the test come out?" asked Gabriel.

"Looks good to me. Take a look."

Gabriel peered into the microscope. Minute larvae of phylloxera that had been genetically altered swam in a pool of tetracycline-laced solution. They were alive and active.

"Awesome! We can start the process of growing these now," said Gabriel.

The lab had created a climate-controlled hatchery to rear thousands of phylloxeras that had been genetically altered in a complex process that involved modifying the genome to carry a dominant lethal gene. This lethal gene was designed to kill young insects in the pupa or larva stage. Because it was a dominant gene, all offspring of the altered phylloxera would inherit it—meaning when released into the wild, the altered phylloxera would mate with other phylloxera, and their offspring would die.

The genius of the plan was the molecular On/Off switch—tetracycline turned off the lethal gene so the phylloxera could reproduce safely in the lab. Once outside of the lab, however, the absence of tetracycline would turn the gene back on, and they would become deadly sexual partners. The result would be a crash in the insect population and, over time, the certain eradication of the insect.

The plan wasn't without risk. But so great was the threat of phylloxera that Landmark and the other vintners wanted to be ready should grape lice attack the Landmark Vineyard. It was like having a silver bullet ready in the event the unthinkable happened.

CHAPTER THREE

Fairfax, Virginia

SPECULATION BEGAN ALMOST IMMEDIATELY after he arrived on campus. There was something off about the man, something rogue and vaguely threatening. The irises of his eyes were as black as night, emanating no light and no warmth. His face, while partly covered by a thick beard, was pockmarked as if peppered by shrapnel—a possibility that, over time, his students began to think wasn't out of the question. His attitude, particularly toward women, was as rough as his appearance and bordered on misogyny, leading more than one female student to file a complaint against him. Theories raged that he was a Palestinian refugee angry at his treatment by the Israelis (most popular), that he was an Iranian scientist who had been turned by the US but was unhappy about it, or that he was an Islamic fundamentalist here to start a terror cell (least popular). Guessing his true identity had become one of the most popular drinking games on campus.

Professor Abdul-Azim Bashera knew that he was the subject of gossip, but he didn't care. By the time any disciplinary action was taken by the university, he'd be long gone, and he knew that the American academy was loath to prosecute any complaints against a tenured professor who also happened to be a very devout Muslim. The faculty at George Mason University were so concerned about Islamophobia that they'd go out of their way to protect him. Praise be to God, he often thought. The Americans are so dumb!

Bashera arrived at his office that morning after a brisk walk across campus in the cool weather of early spring in Washington; even after many years in America, he was still not used to the weather and wore so many layers that his shirt was soaked through with sweat under the tunic he was wearing. The feel of sweat down his back reminded him of his days as a young man in Iraq, where he and his family had lived without air conditioning and had seen the heat and discomfort as signs they were doing Allah's work. Sitting down at his desk, he put on his Amazon Echo Glass, which projected his computer screen in a heads-up display. Moving his fingers in the air, he briskly swiped through his email.

"Alexa, appointments, please," said Bashera casually in Arabic.

"*As-salamu 'alaykum*," said his cheery digital assistant in British-accented Arabic. He'd been able to program Alexa to communicate in his native language but couldn't get rid of the accent, which was a continual source of irritation for him. He hated the British, whom he regarded as the original infidels to have occupied the Middle East. "You have an appointment with Dean Kroger at 1:00 p.m. in the administration building. Following that you have a meeting with the Islamic Students against Mideast Oppression at the Islamic Center of Washington. Shall I order you a car?"

"Yes."

The light on the Echo digital assistant flashed blue and then turned off. There'd be a self-driving car downstairs at precisely 3:00 p.m., and he'd be whisked away to sit in Washington, DC, traffic for ninety minutes. The Americans were amazing at technology, but the city was still gridlocked with cars.

Seeing no urgent emails, Bashera quickly moved his fingers to access a virtual private network on his computer. With a few swipes, he was into his Tor browser and on the dark web. He then quickly accessed a blockchain of his own design, one that offered the highest level of security by distributing pieces of information between users. While it wasn't impossible for the spooks at the NSA to access the information, the system made piecing together the bits of data into a cohesive picture that much more difficult.

Bashera was looking for a specific message, one that only he would understand. Finally, after months of waiting, he saw it. He then quickly picked up his iPhone and composed a text to his assistant, a strikingly beautiful graduate student named Haniya:

"We have our appointment in Samarra."

CHAPTER FOUR

Washington, DC

THE WEEKLY MEETING OF THE WASHINGTON CHAPTER of the
Islamic Students against Mideast Oppression (ISAMO) took place in the basement of the Islamic Center of Washington, a large stone-faced building with
a towering minaret. At the time of its opening in 1957, it had been the largest mosque in the Western Hemisphere. But those had been simpler times,
before al-Qaeda and before 9/11. Now the mosque was a continuous source
of protest and debate, sitting in the middle of Embassy Row on Washington,
DC's tony Massachusetts Avenue. The center had classrooms and conference
rooms in addition to the huge prayer area frequented by DC's Muslims.

As Bashera exited the car and walked up the front steps, he passed
a plaque on the wall that had been placed there in 2015 by the Muslim
Reform Movement. It called for Muslims to reject terror and to move
toward rights for women and gays and to end adherence to Shari'a law.
Bashera's ritual was to shield his eyes from the plaque as he passed and
recite to himself *"Allahu akbar"*—God is the greatest—over and over
again. It was his way of protesting the blasphemy that adorned what he
considered a great place of Islamic worship.

There were ten students and a few guests in attendance, and Bashera smiled when he saw his target sitting in the circle next to Haniya, her hand resting gently on his knee. He had been specially selected, a prize recruit with skills that would catapult Bashera into the pantheon of recruiters for the cause. This target was also older than the others, having come to the group with some real-world experience. He'd actually seen firsthand the terror of American bombs in Afghanistan when he had worked for the US government. Unlike the other students, who understood the war against Islam only from YouTube videos, Bashera's target had heard the screams and tasted the blood spilled by his fellow Muslims.

"*As-salamu 'alaykum*," said Bashera to the group. Peace be upon you.

"*Wa 'alaykum salam*," came the reply in unison. And unto you peace.

"Today we read from the Koran, verse ninety-five in Surat An-Nisa. This chapter is entitled 'The Women.' Is there a female here who would like to read out loud?"

A few hands went up. He chose a young woman in a blue hijab named Abeela. "Verse ninety-five: 'Not equal are those of the believers who sit at home, except those who are disabled, and those who strive hard and fight in the cause of Allah with their wealth and their lives. Allah has preferred in grades those who strive hard and fight with their wealth and their lives above those who sit at home. Unto each, Allah has promised good (Paradise), but Allah has preferred those who strive hard and fight, above those who sit at home by a huge reward.'"

"Thank you, Abeela. What does this mean to you?"

She thought for a moment. "I think it means that those who put their material wealth before the needs of Allah are hypocrites."

"Very good," said Bashera. "Anybody else?"

A young man with a scraggly beard raised his hand. "It means that those who are summoned and who answer the call are superior to those who don't."

"Exactly!" Bashera said. "That is correct. When called by Allah, you must go. And when you do, Allah has a reward for you. Those of you who don't answer the call, who sit at home in favor of material pursuits, are considered less worthy in Allah's eyes."

"Is Allah calling us now?" asked Abeela.

"That is a very good question," answered Bashera. "Who would like to answer?"

Bashera looked around the circle, his eyes settling on his target. A Muslim committed to their cause would not be able to resist this question; it was a fat, slow pitch down the middle of the plate.

But there was only silence for several long seconds until Haniya dug her nails into the target's thigh and he finally spoke. "We are being called by Allah, peace be upon him," he said softly. "Our...our brothers and sisters are being slaughtered in the name of oil. The Americans are helping to kill our men and our women. I saw...I saw it firsthand in Afghanistan. They are..." his voice trailed off.

"They are what?" Bashera pressed.

"They are dogs, Professor. Our Allah, peace be upon him, wants us to cleanse the world for our people."

The room was silent. A few of the students looked uncomfortable. Others were nodding and saying, "*Allahu akbar.*"

Professor Abdul-Azim Bashera was full of joy. "*Mashallah,*" he said quietly to himself. As God has willed it.

CHAPTER FIVE

Manassas, Virginia

BASHERA'S TARGET WENT TO WORK the next day as he always did, clad in a white coat and with all the requisite security badges to enter the high-security Biomedical Research Laboratory (BRL) run by George Mason University. It was one of thirteen regional biocontainment labs underwritten by the National Institute of Allergy and Infectious Diseases, and it was charged with doing some of the nation's most important research on emerging and potential biothreat agents.

The target worked in what was colloquially called the "Bug Wing," formally known as Entomology Vector Research. He was sitting at his desk looking over the results of a recent set of experiments when a BRL supervisor interrupted him.

"Got a minute, Adnan?"

Dr. Adnan Mishner desperately wanted to ignore the man standing in his doorway, but he couldn't. Not now, with things so far along. He could do nothing to jeopardize the mission. Putting on a fake smile, he said, "Sure, Mort. What can I do for you?"

"The administration has done another equipment audit, and we seem to be missing several of the advanced vector vessels." Vector vessels were self-contained carriers used to transport various insects into the field.

"Are you sure they weren't just misplaced? You know how this place is. Things seem to have legs—or wings—here."

Mort laughed. "True. But I told the powers that be that I would investigate it, so here I am." He stared at Adnan for a moment. When Adnan didn't say anything, Mort went on. "I'm going to poke around a bit and speak to the staff. Just wanted to let you know."

"No problem. Have at it," Adnan said with confidence. Nobody working there knew anything about the eight vector vessels that Adnan had removed from the lab over the past several months and that were now in a public storage unit outside of town.

CHAPTER SIX

Fairfax, Virginia

THE IMAGES WERE SURPRISINGLY SHARP, even if the camera, lodged inside the bedroom-ceiling smoke detector, didn't give him a clear view of her entire body. But he could see her bra and panties, the white lace material set off against her dark skin. Her full breasts moved as she swayed in rhythm to the electronic dance music coming from speakers next to her bed. It wasn't every night she did this, but it was frequent enough that he had come to crave it. Often he pleasured himself while watching her.

But not tonight; too many details were now in play, and Bashera was too preoccupied even for simulated sex. Sitting in his home office, a bank of high-res monitors arrayed in front of him, he silently watched Haniya finish her dance, click off the light, and get into bed. The darkness put the camera into infrared mode, and she lay there in a greenish hue, staring at the ceiling. He couldn't tell if her eyes were open or shut, but he could hear her quietly recite an Islamic prayer.

Bashera smiled at the prayer. If he saw any blasphemy in what he was doing—spying on a young woman in the privacy of her bedroom, watching her undress (often while touching himself)—he didn't show it. Without missing a beat, he clicked over to another set of cameras in Adnan's house. Flicking between the bedroom and the kitchen and the den, he found Adnan sitting in front of a huge flat-screen on which he was playing an Xbox game. He had a headset on and was obviously playing with someone over the web. Bashera couldn't tell which game it was, but it clearly involved car racing. The fact that Adnan couldn't even pick a game in which he killed people was irritating but not a surprise.

"*Jaban*," Bashera muttered to himself. Coward.

Bashera had known that Adnan was soft from the moment he found him. He had come to Bashera's attention when a search of scientists capable of vector genomics led him to a handful of options; Adnan, an American of Egyptian descent was his obvious first choice. After a deep search of Adnan's personal and professional history, Bashera knew he'd found someone he could turn against America.

☙

It hadn't been Bashera's first choice to work with Haniya, and he had initially resisted. He had thought she was nothing more than a honey-pot, a beautiful young woman designed to entice men into the service of jihad. ISIS used them effectively all over the world, and Bashera had had no doubt that she'd be effective in that role. Nonetheless, Bashera didn't like working with women in any capacity and had relented only when it was clear that he had no choice in the matter. He'd installed the cameras in her apartment to keep tabs on her. The naked dancing had been an added bonus.

And Bashera had to admit that Haniya was a true talent, someone as smart and cunning as she was beautiful who was thoroughly committed to the cause. When Bashera had raised the mission of turning Adnan, she'd been immediately resourceful, following him for several weeks and learning his routine. She knew when and where he parked every week when he came on campus to use the university credit union.

One rainy day she had watched in the shadows as Adnan ran from the parking lot, covering his head with his jacket. She timed her move perfectly, bumping into him just as he made it to the top of some steps. From there the conversation went like clockwork.

"Oh, I'm sorry!" he blurted out.

She stooped to pick up the notebook she'd dropped. Standing, she looked at him with her dark brown eyes flecked with gold. She was stunning. "It's OK," she said with a dazzling smile.

They stood staring at each other. Finally Adnan said, "You go to school here?" He wanted to slap himself for asking such a dumb question.

"Yes," she said. "And you?"

"Oh, no. I actually work . . . for the university."

"You're a professor?"

"Sort of. I'm actually a research scientist. I work off campus in a lab."

"Sounds interesting. What kind of research do you do?"

He laughed. "I work on bugs."

"Bugs? Like insect bugs?"

"Yes, like insect bugs."

She visibly shuddered. "I hate bugs."

He laughed again. "Most people do."

"My name is Haniya. Where are you from?" she asked, putting out her hand.

Adnan took her hand in his, feeling her soft warm skin on his. He felt a surge go through his body. "Ah, I'm from Virginia, not far, actually."

She smiled again. "No, where are you really from?"

"Oh," he said with a nervous laugh. "I was born in Egypt."

"Me too! Both my parents are from Alexandria. I was born there."

He smiled at her, transfixed by eyes so deep he felt he could fall into them. He was trying to keep the conversation going. Finally, he pointed at the flyers she was carrying. "What's that?"

Handing Adnan one she said, "They're flyers I'm putting up. I belong to this student group, ISAMO—Islamic Students against Mideast

Oppression. We meet once a week at the Islamic Center in DC."

Adnan looked at the flyer. It had the heading "Your Muslim Brothers and Sisters Are Being Murdered," underneath which it gave the location of the meeting and boldly stated, "Here's your chance to learn more about the Koran and how you can take action in the name of Allah." It was the kind of provocative poster that could be found only on a college campus.

"You should come. It's tomorrow," she said.

Adnan showed up at the ISAMO meeting the next day, just as Bashera had known he would, and Haniya was there to greet him. The relationship began slowly. At first, Bashera used Haniya to get Adnan to stay after the weekly meetings so Bashera could draw him into conversation. It worked brilliantly, and gradually, over a period of months, Adnan began staying after on his own and even meeting Bashera and Haniya for tea on campus. Adnan was opening up. It became clear to Bashera that Adnan was lonely and very angry about his brother's death. He needed to talk, and Bashera and Haniya became willing listeners.

One day over tea, the conversation turned to Adnan's brother.

"Do you believe it was *mashallah* that Salman was taken?" Bashera asked.

"Yes, I believe it was God's will," answered Adnan. "But I still wanted revenge."

"How did you find revenge? By finding the dealer who sold the drugs to him?"

Adnan looked at Haniya. "I went to Afghanistan and helped the Americans destroy the poppy fields fueling the Taliban insurgency. I can't tell you how. But I did it."

Bashera already knew how, of course. He had hacked the university's personnel system and had read Adnan's entire file. He knew about Adnan's childhood, his schooling, and his research and all about his temporary duty with DHS in Afghanistan. "Did it help you to feel better?" Bashera asked.

"It did for a time. But then some things happened in Afghanistan. Things that made me come to understand I had been used by the American government to hurt the Muslim people."

Bashera glanced at Haniya and encouraged her to push forward. "They've murdered so many of our people all over the Muslim world," she said. "They want to wipe our people from the face of the earth. Only a return to the Koran and Shari'a law can save us."

Adnan thought for a moment. "Are you saying it is us or them?"

"Yes, that is exactly what I'm saying. We are in a death struggle. Only one will win."

Bashera got up from his chair and went to his briefcase. He pulled out a thin book and handed it to Adnan.

"*Milestones* by Sayyid Qutb," Adnan read. "What is it?"

Bashera smiled. "It's our blueprint, Adnan. Read it, and we will discuss it next week."

CHAPTER SEVEN

Manassas, Virginia

ADNAN FINISHED READING *Milestones* in one sitting. It was obvious that the book formed the basis for radical Islamism, and thus he intellectually understood why Bashera wanted him to read it. But in many ways it was contrary to his worldview. *Milestones* was an indictment of the modern secular order where science and the scientific method are held dear; it argued for a return to the word of God through Shari'a law, a complete way of life based on subservience to Allah. According to Qutb, all beliefs and principles of art and science and the administration of justice were prescribed by Shari'a, and the Koran should be seen as a source of instruction for obedience and action.

To Adnan this felt like a rejection of everything he had worked for in his career.

The next day he met Haniya alone for lunch. He wanted to better understand her thinking and why she was so committed to Bashera, who seemed to have some kind of hold over her. Usually when Adnan was with her, Bashera seemed to be lurking close by, watching everything they did together. It was creepy.

"I read a lot of the book last night," he said, taking a bite of a sandwich. They were sitting alone in the corner of a campus deli. Haniya was eating a salad with pita bread.

"And?" she asked, excitement in her voice.

"I'm not sure I understand it," he said, deflecting. He wanted Haniya to tell him what the book meant to her. "I understand the words, but what does it really mean?"

Haniya sighed and tried to mask her disappointment. He always felt as if he was being tested by her, and this conversation was no exception. "What it means is simple," she said, her voice barely more than a whisper. "Muslims are under attack by Jahiliya, the unbelievers, the kaffirs who keep us from living a life of purity. *Milestones* is our treatise on how to destroy Jahiliya once and for all."

"Ja-hi-li-ya?" Adnan repeated, struggling to pronounce it.

"Yes. It describes the secular world, the world without Allah, without divine guidance. It's a world of ignorance, mistrust, fear, and conflict. Only by living fully by Islamic law and the Koran can you find true peace. That's what *Milestones* is all about."

Haniya spoke these last few sentences as if shooting them from a gun; they hung in the air between them, and Adnan could feel their weight. He knew she was completely invested in what she was saying and, by extension, what she and Bashera were working on. "And what about the professor? Does he feel this way too?"

Haniya laughed. "Oh, Adnan my sweet. You have no idea who you are working with! The professor is a true leader in our movement, a man who grew up in Iraq and who worked for al-Zarqawi himself."

Adnan took a deep breath. The name al-Zarqawi—the name of the man known as "the Butcher of Baghdad"—sent shivers down his spine.

"Bashera was with al-Qaeda in Iraq?" he asked.

"Shush," she said, looking around. "Yes."

Adnan sat back in his seat. The reality of what he'd gotten himself into was starting to sink in. He didn't doubt for a minute what she was saying about Bashera, whose menacing face and black eyes seemed as soulless as anything Adnan had ever seen. He suddenly realized that the anti-American and anti-Zionist protests he'd taken part in as an undergraduate were child's play compared to this. This was the big leagues.

"We are committed to fighting the infidel, Adnan. Do you understand that? It's vital that you do if our relationship is to continue," she said, grabbing his hand.

Butterflies in his stomach, brought on by her touch, overwhelmed any doubts he had in his head.

"Yes, I understand."

⁂

Over many weeks, Bashera connected seemingly disparate dots of Adnan's life into a full-throated indictment of the West and its morally debased culture, in which his brother's heroin addiction was due to the permissive and empty culture of America, one based on consumption and material wealth. "Your brother didn't have Allah, peace be upon him, as a guide," Bashera said to him one night after an ISAMO meeting. "Allah would have kept him safe," Bashera told him, "by giving him guidance and making him a warrior for Islam."

"And now you can be a warrior for Islam, Adnan," Haniya said. "Because we are creating an Islamic vanguard to free our brothers from the infidel."

Adnan nodded. He knew that *Milestones* called for the creation of an army to preach the power of Islam and then to destroy the infidel by force. "But how can this be done? The West is so rich and so strong. I've seen how powerful the American military is. It's not possible to defeat it."

Bashera smiled. "Yes, Adnan. They are very strong. So we won't defeat them by force. We will beat them down with fear, until they succumb to the power of our ideals. We are already doing it in Europe! We are weakening Europe from the inside, preying on their liberal values by slowly getting Shari'a recognized there. We attack them when we can, make them nervous and scared. And then we push for more accommodation. We claim they are Islamophobic, and they open up to our needs. Already we have huge swaths of Paris and Brussels and London that we control completely. The police are afraid to go there. We will do the same thing here in America."

Adnan looked unconvinced. "America is a superpower. And the NSA listens to every conversation, reads every email. It will be harder to do it here."

Bashera smiled again. Adnan didn't yet know about the blockchain network Bashera had set up that protected communication from the NSA. "Harder here, yes, but not impossible. I will teach you how we communicate in secret. America has become more vulnerable, more isolated. There are now opportunities to hurt it from the inside. And I'm not talking about simple martyrdom."

Adnan knew martyrdom meant suicide bombings or attacks using trucks or buses. These were the types of attacks that ISIS had been using inside the US to some effect. But while they sowed terror, they weren't particularly devastating and didn't have near the impact that 9/11 had. "So what are you talking about?"

"Targets of opportunity with big payoffs. Last year the US economy imported fewer agricultural products than it has in any year since 1960. Americans are more dependent than ever on growing, producing, and consuming their own food. And there are millions of acres of wheat, soy, corn, and citrus all across the country. In open fields, unguarded, just waiting for us."

"How could you possibly attack millions of acres of—" Adnan stopped in midsentence. He looked at Bashera and then to Haniya, who was sitting impassively, making a slight nodding motion.

Adnan now understood what they wanted from him.

"I can't do that!" he exclaimed. "It will never work. I would lose my job and everything I've worked for."

"No, Adnan. Actually you would be gaining everything you want," Bashera said, nodding toward Haniya. "And you only have to provide me the technology to do the job. I will do the rest."

Adnan took his meaning. If he didn't participate, there'd be no life with Haniya. Still, he was unconvinced. "The Americans are not stupid.

There are only a handful of labs that can engineer a vector to do this kind of attack. They will figure out where it came from. And I will spend my life in jail. Or worse."

Bashera smiled at Adnan and put his hand on the younger man's shoulder. "I will ensure your safety. If the Americans get close, I will get you out, back to where your parents came from, where you will be a received as a hero. You will have a beautiful lab at a university there. You can continue your research."

Adnan was silent for a moment. Was this really happening? "I don't know if I can do it."

As if it had been rehearsed, Haniya reached over and grabbed his hands, pulling them close to her face. She kissed them softly. "Adnan, my love. You must. For us to have a life together, this must be done."

He looked at this beautiful woman and thought about living with her in Egypt, where his mother had been born and where her family still lived. "We will live in Cairo?"

"Oh, my sweet," she said. "It will be wonderful. You will be someone special there, known as the one who brought America to its knees."

Adnan was silent for another long moment. He knew he couldn't say no to her. He wanted her more than anything else in his life. "OK," he said at last.

"*Mashallah!*" Bashera said.

Adnan was suddenly dizzy. "I—I need to use the bathroom," he said and quickly got up.

When Adnan had left the room, Bashera pulled Haniya close to him, grabbing her roughly by the arm. "He is your responsibility now. You must get him over the finish line."

She wrested her arm free. "It will be done," she said. "And never, ever touch me like that again."

CHAPTER EIGHT

San Francisco, California

THE CITY HAD CHANGED SO MUCH since Claire Marx lived there that it was almost unrecognizable. In the early 2000s, it had still had some grit left, reminiscent of its days as a working city, when its port had handled cargo ships and every neighborhood hadn't been taken over by overpaid tech-obsessed millennials.

"This feels more like Beverly Hills to me than San Fran," Claire said, walking past picture windows with fancy shoes and dresses on display."

Gabriel looked up at the gleaming condos that had replaced the row houses that had once made the city seem quaint. "Yeah, it looks sexy, but now it has no soul."

The wine bar on Hayes Street where Claire and Gabriel had met had long since shuttered, taken over by a Michelin-starred restaurant that was too expensive for even a special occasion like their tenth anniversary. When they met, Claire had been working at the wine bar as a waitress after graduating from UCLA, thinking that she wanted to become a sommelier.

"God you were clueless about wine," Gabriel said laughing.

"Hey! I was learning," she said, slapping his arm. "You were so smug too. I remember you came in and started peppering me with questions about the vintage, the oak in the barrels, the grapes, whether the women had washed their feet before crushing them. You were such a pain in the ass!"

Gabriel laughed again. "It was my pickup technique. And it worked!"

"How it worked I'll never know. But somehow you wormed your way in."

Gabriel had come into Claire's wine bar after interviewing at a few vineyards in Napa. He had been killing time before meeting a buddy from college and had taken a seat in Claire's section. "Come on. You thought I was adorable."

She smiled. "You were cute all right. But you really didn't make an impression on me until you started talking about bugs. That's when I fell in love."

"Does it every time."

"After you left that night, my friends referred to you as 'bug boy.'"

"Seriously? You never told me that!"

"Most of them still do."

"Funny girl. Come on. Let's eat."

﹡

Dinner consisted of steak au poivre for Gabriel and Dover sole for Claire, accompanied by a bottle of Landmark Chardonnay. Red went better with steak, but Gabriel drank white because it paired better with Claire's fish. It had been a light evening thus far, the kind that seemed less and less frequent, but the conversation then turned more serious.

Claire looked at her husband and saw a tired man. It hurt her to see him struggling like this; she knew that he wasn't sleeping and that his dreams were really nightmares that wouldn't leave him be. His two tours in Iraq were now a part of their marriage and their life together; she hadn't had much success getting him to open up to her. It was a problem that many spouses of combat veterans faced. Maybe tonight, with the wine flowing and the laughter they were sharing, would be a different story.

"You know how much I love you, right?" she asked.

He smiled. "Should I be worried about what comes next?"

She laughed. "No. I just want you talk to me. You don't sleep, babe. And when you do, it's like you are fighting for your life. It's gotta be . . ."

"Exhausting?"

"Yes," she said and waited. She knew it was hard for him to talk about it, but she hoped he'd say something. Anything would be better than nothing. She stared at her husband and knew every fiber in his body was to grin and bear it. Showing weakness was not something a marine was ever taught to do.

"I'm fine," he began. "OK, I'm not fine. I'm screwed up, actually. I'm angry and frustrated by the smallest things. I get super irritable when I shouldn't. Yesterday I wanted to punch the wall after an experiment we were working on didn't go as planned. I . . ."

She looked at him and reached over for his hand, which was clammy. "It's OK, babe."

He nodded but said nothing.

Claire was beginning to panic; she'd seen him go down this path before, and it had taken everything she had to pull him back from it. And that was at home, not in a crowded restaurant in a city they didn't even live in. She waited a moment and then saw the warmth return to Gabriel's eyes. It had passed.

"How can I help?" she asked. "There must be something . . ."

"You're doing it."

"Really? I feel helpless."

"I need to talk about it," he blurted out, the words passing his lips before he could catch them.

She watched her husband and waited. "It's OK, Gabe. I'm here."

He nodded again. He wasn't sure how to explain it to her. It wasn't a simple thing, a moment in time that he could point to. Rather, it was a million moments that separately didn't amount to much, but together were a mosaic of hyperadrenalized fear. "Combat is weird. It's not like the movies," he began. "In Iraq, we weren't fighting to take territory like in World War II. We were fighting an insurgency, an enemy that was everywhere and nowhere. It was hard to tell the good guys from the bad, so you were always on edge. Always scanning. Always pumped up. I lived in a constant state of fear until we made contact with the enemy. Then there'd be twenty minutes of adrenaline. And then more fear."

"Must've been hard being up and down so much."

"It wasn't at first. It was a blast, to be honest. We were trained to do a job, and we were unleashed to do it. We kicked ass. Killed a lot of bad guys—" He stopped. He'd never talked to his wife about killing. He didn't want her to see him differently. But she had to know that's what marines did, right? "Anyhow, we were very good at it. But over time it wore on me. It got to the point that I couldn't come down, couldn't relax. I was used to the adrenaline of combat and came to crave it. That's when I bought the crotch rocket." Gabriel had owned a Ninja-style motorcycle when he and Claire had met.

"Don't remind me. I hated that thing."

He smiled. "Yeah, I know. But it was the one thing that made me feel normal. When I got back after my second deployment and got out, I really struggled. Besides the motorcycle, school was the only thing that helped. I attacked studying like it was al-Qaeda. I crushed it. But after school . . ."

"You met me," she said, smiling.

"Yes, I met you. What a gift," he said, meaning every word of it. "And we settled down and life got to be something close to normal, or what I imagine normal to be."

"But Iraq came with you. To live with us."

"Yeah, it did. It will always be with me. And us. I lost good friends there. Saw them die. I saw women and children die violent, horrible deaths. It will never not be there."

"And it haunts you?"

"Well, it haunts my subconscious. I don't think about it during the day. But at night it comes and visits me, and I can't seem to stop it. The only time it didn't was when I was in Afghanistan with the CIA. I didn't dream there."

She nodded and was silent for a moment, taking it all in. "What does that tell you?"

"I'm not sure," he said, without conviction.

"Really? I know what it means. It means you were back in your element."

"Maybe," he said. "But I want to live a normal life. I don't want to have to be in Afghanistan to feel normal."

"I know," she said after a pause. "But there must be something we can do, besides drugs, to make you feel better, so you can sleep and really rest. You look so tired all the time."

This he knew. He hated the way he looked, the way the years had piled on him like a ten-car wreck on the interstate. He loved the vineyard and the research he was doing, but it wasn't enough. He needed something more. But what?

That he did not know.

⁂

Stirred by their dinner discussion, his dreams that night were particularly violent.

I'm trapped in a building, looking desperately for a way out. Moving from room to room, my M4 at the ready, I see only women and children huddled in fear. Then an insurgent appears behind them, clutching a child as a shield. He raises his AK at me. I have a split second to react. I fire two rounds in quick succession. The child falls to the floor screaming. Blood is everywhere . . .

Awakening with a start, Gabriel began to get out of bed. Claire reached up to him and pulled him back down. She put her arms around him and buried her face in his chest; she could hear his heart pounding. He put his hands through her hair and started to softly cry. She crawled completely on top of him and pulled her shirt off so her bare breasts pressed against his hairy chest. She was trying to get as close as she could to him, to become one with his body. He wrapped his strong arms around her, and together they went through a silent emotional dance. No words were spoken, and none were needed.

It felt like the first night of the rest of their marriage.

CHAPTER NINE

Manassas, Virginia

HANIYA'S LONG BLACK HAIR FELL in Adnan's face as she writhed on top of him; her eyes were closed, and she was moaning softly, as if in a trance. He peered through the darkness at her beautiful body, her dark skin gleaming with a slight sheen of sweat. He still wasn't sure if she was there because of Bashera and the "mission" or because she really loved him.

At this very moment, he didn't really care.

Later, after they were finished, Adnan lay staring at the ceiling, waiting for his pulse to come back down to normal. Haniya lay next to him, one leg draped over his. "Why is it that just as you get what you want, life makes it impossible to really enjoy it?" he asked.

"What do you mean?" she asked.

"I mean the future. The life we could have now if we weren't . . ." he said, his voice trailing off.

"Weren't what?"

Adnan wanted to say, "Weren't becoming terrorists," but demurred. Instead he just said, "Working on this mission."

She sat up and looked at him. "Adnan, this is the life that I want. I live for Allah. There is no future for any of us if we don't destroy our enemies."

He suddenly was scared that she would doubt him, that she would get up and leave and tell Bashera he was not worthy. He quickly changed the subject. "Why did your parents come to America?"

She sighed. She was worried about his devotion and knew that it was her responsibility to keep him focused. She would have to work harder. "My parents? They ran a business in Egypt, one they inherited from my grandparents. It was a good business, a carpet and rug shop. They mostly imported from Afghanistan. My grandfather was the main buyer and spent a lot of time in Kabul and Kandahar. After the Americans invaded, he stopped going. It was too dangerous. Many of his suppliers were killed or put out of business."

"That's too bad. What happened to the store?"

"Eventually they had to shut it down. My aunt had come to America before 9/11, and she helped my parents get a visa for us to join her. That was in 2002."

"Where did you live when you first came here?"

"Brooklyn. We all lived in a small two-bedroom apartment there for a year. Two families with six kids altogether. It was very cramped."

"I bet," he said, waiting for her to continue.

"We moved to the DC area when my dad got a job at a carpet company. That lasted eight years. Then he got laid off. So they gave up, and we moved back to Egypt, this time to Cairo."

"But you came back."

"I was sent here."

"Sent here? To go to GMU?"

"Yes. I was sent here by Daesh to help the professor attack America," she said, using the Arabic term for ISIS. "I went to school at a madrasa in Cairo, where I learned the Koran and the history of our people. How we were exploited and murdered by the infidel. My brother joined the resistance after he left school. He was killed in Afghanistan by the Americans in 2012."

"So is that when you joined Daesh?"

"At first they wanted to use me to have their babies, like the other girls they conscript into domestic servitude. But I wasn't having any of that. I convinced them that I was more valuable if I used my education and my looks to infiltrate the enemy. It took a while but they eventually agreed."

Adnan was quiet. "It's hard to imagine you as a member of Daesh. You seem so liberal, in your dress and your actions . . ."

She laughed. "You mean because I don't cover my face and I have sex with you even though we aren't married?"

Adnan blushed. "Well, yes."

"I'm here to do a job. It's not possible for me to do that without integrating to a certain degree. I'm using American values against America."

"So sleeping with me is part of your job?"

"No, my love. Sleeping with you is my choice. I do it because I want to."

Adnan smiled. He was relieved. "Good."

"So you also lost a brother to America." He said it as a statement but meant it more as a question.

"Yes. And it makes me hate everything America stands for. And you must too. Or this will never work."

Adnan wasn't sure whether she meant the mission or their relationship. "I hate many things about this country," he said after a moment. "I hate its hubris, its imperial foreign policy. I hate its sick culture, full of porn and drugs . . ."

She looked at Adnan and knew he was referring to his own brother. "Good," she said at last. She then got up out of bed and started to get dressed. He watched transfixed as she slipped on a pair of thong underwear and a lacy bra.

Suddenly aware that she was getting dressed, he said, "What are you doing, my love? Come back to bed."

She laughed. "We have work to do! I have to go home and pack, and you have to go to the lab and finish preparing the bugs. Is that what I should call them? Bugs?"

Now Adnan laughed. "Technically the scientific name is Insecta. But in this case they are properly called vectors."

"Vec-tor," she said slowly. "I like that better than bugs. Doesn't sound so . . . creepy."

After she finished dressing she went to the mirror to adjust her hijab, framing it perfectly around her face. In the mirror, she could see him staring at her, and she took an extra moment to make sure he got a nice look.

"I'm going to miss you while you're gone," Adnan said.

Haniya looked at Adnan with a mix of curiosity and pity. He was so emotional. "Oh, love, I'm only going to be gone a few days."

"I know. But still . . ."

"Up, Adnan!" she said as she left the bedroom.

॰

As Adnan badged his way into the Bug Wing inside the Biomedical Research Lab, he was relieved to see that it was empty that Saturday afternoon. He passed through the double glass doors and studied the wall of vessels that held the lab's insects. There were Mediterranean fruit flies, olive fruit flies, whiteflies, thrips, various types of mosquitoes, and diamondback moths.

His work at the lab was focused on the genetic modification of insects to kill off populations of vectors that damaged crops and/or had the capacity to harm humans. It was at the leading edge of entomological science. The process involved sequencing an insect's genome and using an advanced version of the CRISPR (clustered regularly interspaced short palindromic repeats) technique to edit the insect's genetic code. Adnan would inject a Cas9 enzyme—a modified, highly accurate genetic scissors—into a cell to cut the DNA at a desired location and then remove an existing gene while adding a new one to the chromosome that carried a dominant lethal trait for a bacteria or virus. This then made the insect a delivery vehicle for disease. This was essentially the same process Adnan had used to engineer the thrips to carry the tospovirus that destroyed the poppy fields in Afghanistan.

Only this time Bashera had something different and potentially more deadly in mind. It was a modification he had pushed Adnan to pursue, and after many weeks of work, Adnan believed he was on the verge of perfecting it. He'd told Bashera that they would need to test the concept before unleashing an attack on a bigger scale. But if it worked they would have a vector that could truly devastate America.

CHAPTER TEN

Central Florida

HANIYA WAS TOO SMALL for the truck she was driving and strained to see over the steering wheel of the silver Ford F-250 pickup. She wore a plaid shirt and a dirty mesh ball cap that covered her long black hair, which she'd twisted into a bun; her dark skin meant that at a distance she looked like one of the thousands of Hispanic fieldworkers who crisscrossed the state during the citrus growing season. She drove along US Route 41, careful to not go above the speed limit, peering through the gloom for the turnoff at mile marker 22 and the entrance to the Rockford Citrus operation.

Rockford, a family farm that had opened for business in 1922, had more than a thousand acres of orange trees and had been chosen specifically for this operation. Its main customer, Tropicana, was a wholly owned subsidiary of PepsiCo, the global beverage behemoth. Unlike many of the oranges picked for Tropicana, which ended up in frozen concentrate, Rockford's Hamlin variety oranges were used only in the company's fresh-squeezed juice products. Meaning the juice from these oranges was going to end up in restaurants and stores within a week or so of their being picked.

Haniya pulled off the highway and turned right onto Orange Blossom Road. Heading east, she could just make out the very faint glow of the sun rising somewhere over the Atlantic. Looking at her watch in the dim glow of the dashboard lights, she knew she was on time. "Don't rush," she'd been told over and over. "Those who rush make stupid mistakes."

Just as she passed a shuttered Esso gas station, she made a sharp right turn onto a dirt road that ran along the south edge of the Rockford farm. She drove slowly, careful not to disturb the cargo in the bed of the truck. About a mile down the road she turned off her headlights and took a sharp left onto a slender access path that ran between tree groves. After about ten minutes of driving, she stopped and shut off the engine. Sitting in the cab, she heard nothing but her own breathing and the ticking of the hot engine as it cooled down.

After a moment she got out of the cab and softly closed the door. Moving to the bed of the truck, she unstrapped a pair of cylindrical containers and moved quickly into the groves. In just a few minutes, she was in the middle of a block of more than a thousand trees full of small Hamlin oranges.

She carefully put on a mask to cover her face and bent down, placing one of the containers on its side. She then carefully twisted the cap off. She slowly pulled out the inner tray that contained a sugar-based substance; on it were thousands of Mediterranean fruit flies. Once the tray was out of the container, she walked along a path between two lines of trees, dispersing the flies into the air. After a few minutes, the tray was empty. Moving five hundred yards to the middle of another grove, she repeated the same process with the second container. In less than ten minutes, more than a hundred thousand fruit flies had been deposited in the middle of Rockford's trees to wreak their havoc.

PART TWO

Three Months Later

CHAPTER ELEVEN

New York, New York

KIRK LARSEN WAS AT THE BEGINNING of a career that promised to make him one of Wall Street's wolves. A thirty-two-year-old investment banker with an MBA from Harvard, he was tall with a powerful build from years of CrossFit and a shock of blond hair that framed a handsome face.

He was also paralyzed.

Lying in the wreckage of what had been his 2023 Tesla Model SE, he could see the night sky. There was a cacophony of sound and a blur of activity around him, but he was having trouble making sense of it all. Then suddenly a man's face appeared over him. The man wore a helmet, and his breath smelled vaguely of onions and peppers.

"Can you hear me?" he yelled over the din.

Kirk tried to speak, but no words would come out. He then tried to nod, but found his head wouldn't move. So Kirk moved his eyes back and forth. The man in the helmet seemed to get the message.

"OK, good. I'm a paramedic. You've been in a serious car accident. We are preparing to transport you to the hospital. Can you move your arms?"

Kirk wanted to scream, "No, I can't move my fucking arms!" but his tongue was stuck to the roof of his mouth. Instead he just blinked a few times.

The paramedic shook his head and then yelled over to someone Kirk couldn't see. "We need a cervical collar and backboard over here!"

Cervical collar? Backboard? What was going on? Everything around him was moving frenetically. He could sense hands on him even though he couldn't feel their touch. He could see open sky, trees, lights, and then the ceiling inside of an ambulance.

And then nothing but sirens.

❧

By the time the paramedics contacted Manhattan's Mount Sinai Hospital to report that Kirk Larsen was on his way, Dr. Eve Simmons was already sensing that something was seriously amiss. As head of the Emergency Medicine Services, Dr. Simmons was used to crazy Saturday nights full of car crashes, gunshots, and other forms of violence. But tonight the pattern of activity was different. Several patients had presented themselves with stroke-like symptoms, including facial drooping, slurred speech, and partial or full paralysis. Several more had come to the emergency room complaining of severe nausea, blurred vision, and difficulty speaking. The department was quickly being overwhelmed with patients.

Simmons walked into her small office and picked up the phone. She dialed the number of one of her colleagues at NewYork-Presbyterian Hospital.

"Stan, Eve Simmons here over at Mount Sinai. We've got some strange stuff going on—"

Before she could finish, Dr. Stan Lombardi interrupted her. "It's strange all right. We have two dozen cases of paralysis and what looks to me like toxic poisoning. I just got off the phone with Merrill Hodge at Beth Israel. Same thing there."

"Jesus Christ. What the hell is happening?"

"Not sure yet. But we are activating our disaster protocol. My guess is that there is some kind of poisoning going on—accidental or intentional, I have no idea. But this feels like the beginning of a public health crisis."

"OK, we'll do the same. Have you contacted the CDC yet?"

"That's my next call. I'll keep you posted."

Down in Atlanta, the director of the Centers for Disease Control and Prevention, Dr. Ken Smythe, was at his desk in his home office. He and his wife had been entertaining friends when the first call came in from the CDC's field office in New York. That call—and others from states up and down the Eastern Seaboard—had come into the CDC's emergency response line. The volume and pattern of calls immediately set off the CDC's alarm bells.

His wife poked her head in. "Ken, are you coming back to the party?"

Smythe sighed. "Don't think so, I'm afraid. Sorry," he said with fatigue in his voice.

She frowned. "OK. Anything I can do?"

"Bring me a scotch and soda?" He laughed. She knew he was kidding. Picking up his iPhone, Smythe said, "Call Tim Manley."

After a few rings, Manley picked up. "I'm one step ahead of you, boss."

"Good. I don't like the look of this. Let's activate the full EIS response." The Epidemic Intelligence Service was the CDC's "disease detectives," a quick-reaction force that responded to outbreaks of natural and man-made epidemics. Tim Manley was its director.

"You got it. I've already dispatched agents to hospitals in New York and Newark, and they'll also be in Charlotte, Richmond, and Philly within the next several hours."

"Good. I'm heading back up to Washington first thing in the morning. Keep me posted."

Dr. Eve Simmons stood over Kirk Larsen and checked his oxygen levels. His lungs had shut down, and he was breathing only with the help of a ventilator. He was still conscious, and Dr. Simmons could see the terror in his eyes.

"Kirk, we are doing everything we can for you," she said. "We believe you've been poisoned, and we aren't one hundred percent certain what it is. My suspicion, based on your symptoms and those of other patients here, is that it's botulism. I've given you an antitoxin, which should help. We'll know more once your blood work comes back."

Kirk blinked a few times. He couldn't believe what was happening to him. Botulism? He thought about what he'd done that day. It'd been a pretty normal Saturday. He'd gone to the store and picked up eggs, bacon, and fresh squeezed orange juice for breakfast, which he made at home while binge-watching Netflix. He'd then gone out for a late lunch with his girlfriend and spent the rest of the day in Central Park. Was she now sick too?

As if reading Kirk's mind, Dr. Simmons said, "We found the emergency contact number in your wallet and have called it. A young woman is on her way."

A small tear formed in Kirk's left eye and began to travel down his cheek. Dr. Simmons reflexively scooped it up with her gloved hand. "I'm sure she'll be here soon," she said.

By early the next morning, Tim Manley and a team of EIS agents were standing in the very busy trauma department at Mount Sinai Hospital. They wore black windbreakers with "CDC" stenciled on the backs. Like accident investigators at a crash site, they were there to conduct an epidemiological emergency response. This would involve reviewing medical records and interviewing patients, family members, and friends.

"Dr. Simmons, I'm Dr. Tim Manley from the CDC. Do you have a moment?"

Eve Simmons looked exhausted, her white coat stained with vomit and blood. Even so, she managed a smile and put out her hand. "The cavalry has arrived!"

Manley smiled back. He looked into Eve's blue-gray eyes and placed her age at around forty-five. She wore her long blond hair in a ponytail, and even without a hint of makeup, she was a striking woman. "Is there someplace we can talk?"

"Sure," Eve said, and led the way into her small office. She moved some papers off a chair so Manley could sit down.

"You look beat."

"We've known each other for five minutes and already the flattery?"

They both laughed. "Touché," Manley said. "What I mean is it's obviously been a long night."

"That's putting it mildly. As of now we've had twenty-three cases of botulinum toxin poisoning. Among those we've had two deaths and ten patients who are suffering from full or partial paralysis."

"So you've validated that it's BT?"

"Yes, blood work has just come in," Eve said, pulling up test results on her tablet. "At first I thought it might be myasthenia gravis. But no such luck."

"Myasthenia gravis?"

"Sorry, I figured you for a medical doctor."

Manley smiled. "Nope, just a run-of-the-mill PhD in epidemiology."

"Myasthenia gravis is a neuromuscular disease with symptoms that look a lot like BT—weakness and paralysis in skeletal muscles, particularly in the face and neck."

"Isn't that pretty rare?"

"Yep," she said. "So you probably won't be surprised to hear that the blood work for every patient shows the presence of botulinum toxin."

"Definitely not surprised. Have you had time to detail any patient histories over the past twenty-four to forty-eight hours?"

Eve nodded. "Fortunately we activated our public health emergency response protocol last night. It doubles the trauma staff and requires us to document every detail we can about where the patient's been and where and what they've eaten."

"Great. Can you show me?"

Sitting side by side in Eve's tiny office, they started by reviewing the records of the least sick and progressed to those who were more seriously ill. Manley took out a pad of paper and began making a list of everything that had been consumed by each patient since dinner the previous day and where it had been purchased. After ninety minutes a pattern had emerged.

He handed over the list to Eve. "Notice any common denominator?"

She scanned the list, and it quickly became clear that every patient had consumed only one common food. "Orange juice. Huh. I didn't think that bacterial toxins could survive in high-acid foods."

"That's a common misperception. If the juice is unpasteurized—like a lot of fresh-squeezed juice—then it can transmit botulism, *E. coli*, and other bacteria."

"I didn't know that. Is there any pattern in where they consumed it?"

Manley looked at the list and came up with four common locations where patients had eaten: Tribeca Market, Tavern on the Green, the Boathouse and the Plaza hotel.

"That's quite a list," she said. "Some of the better-known establishments in the city."

Manley nodded and brought up Google Maps on his iPhone. "It's time to pay these fine establishments a visit."

⁂

Tim Manley presented his ID to the hostess at the Tavern on the Green in Central Park as a detective would, his wallet open to his ID card and a small silver badge that said, "CDC Inspector." The badges had been a recent addition, giving more heft to EIS agents' requests for access to various establishments as they looked for clues.

"May we speak to the manager?" he asked.

The hostess looked at the badge and said, "One moment, please." She then walked into the back, where the kitchen was located. After thirty seconds a young woman came out.

"I'm the manager on duty," said the slightly overweight woman in black pants and a crisp white shirt. She had flaming red hair that was rolled into a bun. She looked suddenly nervous as she surveyed the men in front of her. "Can I help you?"

"We're from the Centers for Disease Control and Prevention, and we'd like to ask you some questions."

"Disease control? Yikes. That doesn't sound good." The manager then looked around and said, "Will you follow me, please?" She led the group into a small vestibule off the kitchen, out of earshot of any customers. "What's this about?"

"A number of people who ate breakfast here over the past twenty-four hours have come down with botulinum toxin poisoning," Manley said.

"Oh my God!" she said, her hand flying to her mouth. Nobody in the restaurant business ever wants to hear the words "toxin" and "poisoning" in the same sentence. "Seriously? Here?"

Manley looked at the other investigator who accompanied him. "Seriously," Manley said. "What kind of orange juice do you serve?"

"Orange juice? That depends. For weekend brunch we serve a particular kind, a fresh-squeezed variety," she said, moving into the kitchen. "For all other times, we serve a garden-variety filtered juice."

"We're interested in the brunch juice," Manley said.

Looking at one of the kitchen staff, she said, "Oscar, can you bring me the brunch orange juice?"

Oscar disappeared into the cooler and came out carrying a glass bottle. It was almost empty. Manley took the bottle and read the label out loud. "Natural One, fresh squeezed from Florida's finest oranges." He then turned the bottle over and read the back. "Bottled fresh by Tropicana in Sarasota. Unpasteurized." The bottling date was just three days before.

"We have this flown up from Florida every week. It's kind of a specialty thing we do just for our weekend brunch menu."

"Do you know any other restaurants that do that?"

"A few that use the same supplier we do. Let's see, the Boathouse here in Central Park, the Plaza, and I think a few upscale markets or two."

Manley nodded. It was starting to add up. "How much of this do you have left?"

"That's it," Oscar said, motioning to the bottle Manley was holding.

"How many brunch diners do you have on a typical weekend?"

The manager thought for a moment. "Five hundred or so, sometimes more."

"OK. We're going to take this bottle with us and have it tested. In the meantime, you need to rewash all of your glasses and do a complete cleaning of the kitchen. Make sure you use hot water."

"OK. What should I tell the restaurant owner?"

Manley nodded to his colleague. "Henry here will fill you in. We have a protocol that covers this. With any luck you should be back in business in a few days."

᠅

By the time the CDC had finished visiting the other locations in New York, it was clear where the toxin had originated, and within hours EIS investigators had descended upon Tropicana's production facility outside of Sarasota, Florida.

CHAPTER TWELVE

Washington, DC

WHITE HOUSE CHIEF OF STAFF SARAH WITT STOOD on the South Portico waiting for her soon-to-be ex-husband to arrive for an emergency meeting with the president of the United States. Standing next to her was Special Assistant to the President Kate Russo.

"God, I need a smoke," Russo said, taking a pack of cigarettes out of her jacket pocket. "You won't tell, will you?"

Sarah laughed. "I won't tell, but you know the president has a nose like a bloodhound. She's going to smell it on you."

"Shit," Russo said, reluctantly sliding the cigarette back into its pack. The White House under President Jennifer Cooperman had a strict no-smoking policy. "So, what's going on with you and Jason?"

"The paper's are filed. Just waiting on the court now," Sarah said. "Honestly, I feel kind of shitty about it all."

"Well, you fell in love with someone else. That's not your fault."

Sarah sighed. "I know. But Jason has been in a meat grinder since taking over at DHS."

"Really? He's a cabinet secretary! What I wouldn't do for that job!"

"God, Kate, you can be so naïve sometimes. You know what it's like being a male in this administration? Under a female president and with women occupying more than half the cabinet positions? Poor guy has to check his balls at the door every time he comes over here."

"Damn straight he does!" Russo said. "The #MeToo movement ain't over by a long shot. Thank God for President Cooperman and our band of merry feminists."

Sarah was about to reply when a black SUV pulled up to the curb. A Secret Serviceman opened the door, and Secretary of Homeland Security Jason Witt emerged. He wore a tailored blue suit over his six-three frame with a white shirt and maroon patterned tie. Sarah had bought him that tie on a trip they'd taken to Italy one summer before their son was born.

"Hello, my dear," Jason said with genuine warmth.

"You're late," she said, turning on her heels and moving through the door the marine sentry had opened for her. Russo followed quickly behind.

"So nice to see you too," Jason said to her back.

"Sorry, Jason," Sarah said, turning to face him just on the inside of the doorway. "But we're getting hammered today. The networks are all over us. People are starting to panic over these illnesses." Just outside the Oval, she stopped and faced him again. Her piercing blue eyes were offset beautifully by the dark green suit she was wearing. She was as beautiful as the day they had met back at the University of Chicago. "The president is not in a good mood today. So I hope you have some answers."

"Answers? I'm not even sure what the questions are yet," Jason said. "Who else is going to be in this meeting?"

Sarah entered the Oval without knocking and without answering Jason's question. There they found President Jennifer Cooperman, CIA Director Anne Maddox, and the director of the Centers for Disease Control and Prevention, Dr. Ken Smythe, sitting across from one another on the couches that framed the Oval Office's wood-burning fireplace.

Cooperman looked up as Sarah and Jason entered. The president didn't get up and didn't offer a greeting. She was deep in conversation and looked annoyed at being interrupted.

"Madam President, I got here as soon as I could," Jason said, sitting down next to Maddox, who offered him a smile and a nod.

"Jason, I've asked Dr. Smythe to fill you in," Cooperman said.

"Secretary Witt, the CDC has been tracking a series of reports about an outbreak of botulinum toxin poisoning in various locations up and down the eastern United States. As of this morning, there have been three hundred reported cases and ten deaths."

"Wow, that's a lot," said Jason.

"CDC's Epidemic Intelligence Service has been on the case since Saturday night. They were able to quickly determine that the toxin is linked to orange juice produced by Tropicana and sold into stores and restaurants in North Carolina, New York, New Jersey and part of Virginia. This juice was processed in the Tropicana bottling plant outside of Sarasota, Florida."

"So you found the source?" Jason asked.

Smythe sighed. "Yes and no. We know the contaminated juice came from that plant, but the source was actually the oranges themselves. We've since traced the oranges back to their point of origin, which is the Rockford farm"—he paused to check his notes—"about forty miles south of Gainesville. The owner reported to us that the groves had been attacked by this." He held up a vial with a single fly in it and tossed it to Jason.

"A fly?" Jason asked incredulously.

"Not just a fly, Jason," the president said. "A Mediterranean fruit fly."

Jason was trying to make sense of what he was hearing. He knew the medfly was a dangerous pest that could cause agricultural devastation. But that was a long way from spreading a toxin. "So you believe the medfly caused a botulinum toxin outbreak?"

"We think so," Smythe answered. "EIS suspects that there is some link between the medfly infestation and the outbreak of the toxin. The farm managed to destroy the medflies through the use of pesticides, but not before they laid their eggs in thousands of oranges that ended up in Tropicana's products."

Jason held the fly up to the light. "And you want my bug hunters to look into it?"

"Yes," said the president. "Customs and Border Protection has the most advanced insect detection capability in the federal government."

Jason looked at Smythe and asked, "If this is the culprit"—Jason held up the fly—"then what you are really saying is that this may be a deliberate attack using insects as vectors—in this case the medfly—to spread the toxin?"

"Yes."

President Cooperman looked at Jason and then glanced at CIA Director Maddox. This conversation had suddenly taken an unexpected and alarming turn. "Wait a minute," the president said. "Insect vectors? Are you shitting me?"

"No, ma'am," Jason said simply.

"Jesus, that's all I need!" She took a deep breath and tried to calm herself. "OK, let's work through the problem," she said more for herself than the others in the room. "Have we seen this before?"

Jason glanced at Maddox, who gave him a slight nod. "Yes, at least in part." Knowing that this answer would make Cooperman crazy, he quickly continued. "What I mean is not as a terrorist plot. But the CIA, in partnership with the US military and DynCorp, executed a campaign to eradicate the Afghan poppy fields using vectors—in that case a tiny winged insect called a thrip—that had been genetically altered to infect the poppy crops with a fatal virus."

"And it worked?"

"Yes, it worked," chimed in CIA Director Maddox, wanting to take credit for that win. "In fact it was so effective that it permanently altered the poppy economy. The bugs that were used carried a disease that is harmless to humans but devastating to poppies. And they are so prolific at reproducing that the insects have stayed active. The Taliban have been unable to replant their crops. It's totally devastated the insurgency."

Cooperman let that sink in for a moment. "So, *we've* done it. Do we know of any other country that has tried it?"

The director of the CIA took the question. "Ma'am, this technology is spreading rapidly as gene-sequencing capabilities are advancing. We have intel that the North Koreans and the Chinese are working on advanced genomic testing and experimentation of all types, so we can't rule it out. But we don't have any evidence that they—or any nonstate actor—has used genetically modified insects as a terror tool."

The president nodded absently. The litany of intelligence failures was long and distinguished, and she had little more confidence in the accuracy of the CIA's intel than had her predecessors. "If this is an attack by a terrorist—domestic or foreign—it represents a whole new threat to the country. I don't even want to think about the ramifications for the food supply if terrorists can use insects to poison us."

Jason knew that Cooperman was on the brink of going down a rabbit hole on the political ramifications of what this all meant for her and the Democrats, and he didn't want to be in the room for that. "Ma'am, we need to first verify that this is what we're facing," he said, again holding up the medfly.

Cooperman looked momentarily relieved. "Yes, that's right. Maybe we're wrong. We definitely need to verify it."

Jason paused for a moment. "If this vector has somehow been modified to spread botulinum toxin, there are a number of labs that are capable of such work. I don't want to alert any of them by bringing this in for analysis. But I know of a private lab that can test this for us. It's run by one of the men who did the Afghan operation. He's a former marine."

The president looked at Jason. "Can we trust him?"

"Yes, ma'am."

"OK," said Cooperman, looking at her watch and signaling to her chief of staff that it was time to wrap up. "Jason, I want to be updated on this daily. Coordinate with Sarah," the president said with a slight smile. She knew how uncomfortable that would make Jason. "Are we clear?"

Jason glanced at Sarah, who was staring at him impassively. "Crystal," he said after a moment.

⁂

Later that night, Jason Witt was dropped off at his home in Alexandria. His son Nate was home from college and was staying with Jason for a few weeks. He was happy to have the company; since he and Sarah had separated, the house had seemed so empty. He didn't even really like the house, a faux colonial that had been built in the 1960s. But he had gotten stuck with it when Sarah decided to move in with her new girlfriend. Every time he thought about what had happened, he was reminded of the joke "What should a lesbian bring on a second date? A U-Haul." It still wasn't very funny to him.

"I saw your mom today," he said to Nate, popping open a beer. It was an IPA from Latitude 33 Brewing out in San Diego, Jason's favorite craft brewer. It was ice cold, and he was suddenly very thirsty. Looking at the clock on the oven, he realized he'd not eaten anything since breakfast.

Nate didn't respond to his dad's statement; Jason knew that since his mom had left, Nate had been struggling to come to terms with their split. "Cool," he finally said.

Jason looked at his son and felt pangs of guilt that his son no longer had both his parents under one roof. Jason knew from experience that divorce—at any age—was hard on kids. His own parents had split when he was sixteen. He and his older sister had been left with their mother, a well-meaning but clinically depressed woman who was never satisfied with what she had. His dad had worked as a cop in the town they grew up in; deep down Jason knew his father was a good man and believed he had tried hard to make the family work. But in the end he hadn't been able to and had ultimately given up.

"I also spoke to your granddad today," Jason said. "He says he emailed you and never heard back."

"I've tried to get him to not use email. I never check email. But he's old school."

Jason laughed. "He's definitely old school."

"What did he want this time? Does he need money?"

"Actually, no. I called him."

"Really? That's a change. What about?"

"Well, I can't really say. It's DHS business."

"Granddad isn't a cop anymore. He's been retired for twenty years!"

"Yeah, I know. But I needed some information from him."

Nate looked at his iPhone and noticed a text from his girlfriend. "Cool, Dad. Talk to you later," he said and quickly went upstairs to his room.

Earlier in the day Jason had placed a call to his dad, Travis.

"Jason, how're those feminazis you work for?" Jason's dad was a devout Rush Limbaugh listener.

"Still listening to that garbage, Dad?"

"Hell, I tried to make you a Rush baby. I must've made you listen to a thousand hours of Rush in the car. Pity it didn't take."

"Well, you tried. But I prefer NPR."

"National Progressive Radio? Don't remind me of my wasted tax dollars."

"Honestly that's the least of the government waste you should be worried about, Dad."

"Probably. So to what do I owe this call? You must be very busy counting all the Mexicans crossing the border." As always he laughed heartily at his own joke.

"Actually, I am very busy. And I'm calling about something important. I can't tell you what it is, but I need a favor."

Jason's dad was suddenly serious, his law enforcement background kicking in. "Shoot."

"You remember last year we were talking about Gabriel Marx? That you had gotten an email from him and that he was now living in California working at a vineyard?"

"Sure, we've kept in touch for a long time, ever since I helped him beat that marijuana rap."

"Right. Well, you also told me that he was doing cutting-edge genetic stuff on insects and that his vineyard had built a high-tech lab for him."

"Correct."

"I need to get in touch with him, Dad. We're dealing with an important national security issue, and I need his help."

Jason's dad was silent for a moment. "I know better than to ask what it is, though I would love to know."

"I wish I could tell you, Dad. But you know the joke: Then I'd have to kill you."

"Funny," he said without mirth. "Do you want his number?"

"Actually, no. What I'd like to do is have you call him and tell him I'm coming to see him."

"When?"

"Tomorrow morning."

"Seriously? That fast?"

"That fast."

"OK. I have his address someplace here if you need it."

Jason smiled. "I know where he lives, Dad. Thanks."

CHAPTER THIRTEEN

Russian River Valley, California

GABRIEL STOOD AT HIS KITCHEN SINK and watched the string of black Suburban SUVs wind through the valley below. He knew from experience that the secretary of homeland security would be in the third vehicle. That was the way the feds did it: two in front and two in back with the VIP in the middle.

Gabriel took a final sip of his coffee and poured the rest down the sink. Just at that moment, Claire came up behind him, putting an arm around his waist as she kissed his cheek. She had planned on taking an early yoga class in town that morning but had canceled when Gabriel got the call from Travis Witt. It wasn't every day you got to meet a cabinet secretary. And besides, she was curious as to what the government wanted with her husband.

The call from Travis had been cryptic—not because he was withholding, but because he didn't know much. His son was coming to see Gabriel, and it had something to do with national security. Gabriel had no idea what that could mean and what he could do to help. But he was about to find out.

Gabriel and Claire stepped out onto the front porch as the caravan pulled up. Six large men exited the third vehicle simultaneously, all wearing dark suits and sunglasses. The one who had exited the front seat opened the rear door, and out stepped Jason Witt.

Gabriel didn't move, preferring to wait until Witt approached him; he'd learned long ago that it was wise not to make any sudden movements with so many armed men around.

Witt smiled as he walked up. You look just like your picture," he said to Gabriel, proffering his hand. They shook, and Gabriel looked into Witt's eyes.

"And you look a lot like your dad," Gabriel said after a moment. "This is my wife, Claire."

"Nice to meet you, Claire. And my apologies for this intrusion," he said, looking quickly back at the caravan of SUVs now taking up their driveway. "They don't let me travel light."

"Not a problem, Mr. Witt. Nice to meet you," Claire said.

"Please, call me Jason."

"Well, all right then. Jason, would you like some coffee?" Claire asked.

"I'd love some." They walked into the house and were immediately greeted by Frankie, who gave Jason a sniff and promptly leaned into him, looking for a scratch behind the ears. "Beautiful place you have here. And the view is spectacular."

Claire placed a cup of piping hot coffee down, and they sat around the kitchen table.

Gabriel got right to the point. "Your dad says that you need some help. Not sure what I can do for you, but he asked me to meet with you, and I'd never turn down a request from Travis Witt. So here we are."

"Yes, here we are. I'm happy to finally meet you, Gabriel. My dad has been talking about you for years. It's nice to put a face to the name."

"Your dad saved my life," Gabriel said simply. He figured that Jason knew the story and didn't see the need to elaborate.

Jason smiled and nodded. "Well, I appreciate you meeting with me." He looked at Claire. "I'm afraid I need to talk to your husband in private,

Mrs. Marx. You see, what I'm about to discuss with him is classified, and he still holds an active security clearance."

"Of course, I understand," she said, standing. Witt stood too as a sign of respect, and Claire reached down and kissed her husband. "I'll be in the study if you need me, babe." She shook Witt's hand and left the room.

"She's lovely. You are a lucky man."

"Yes, she is," Gabriel said. "And yes I am. You married?"

"I used to be," Witt said with a tinge of sadness in his voice. He then reached into his pocket and pulled out a vial with a half-dozen flies in it. He handed it over to Gabriel.

Gabriel held it up to the light. "*Ceratitis capitata*. Nasty bugger. Where'd you get them?"

"What I'm about to tell you must be kept in complete confidence. It can't be shared with anyone, including Claire. OK?"

Gabriel nodded. "OK," he said after a moment.

"Have you been following the orange juice contamination scare on the East Coast?"

"More than a scare. A few people have died. That's some pretty strong *E. coli*," Gabriel said with a bit of a raised eyebrow, showing that he didn't believe what was being reported in the media.

"That's because it's not *E. coli*. It's actually botulinum toxin."

Gabriel looked at Witt and then looked again at the flies. "And you think that these"—he shook the flies—"are the source of it?"

Witt nodded. "These flies infested a citrus farm in central Florida, contaminating thousands of trees. We traced the affected juice to oranges produced by this farm during the time that the contamination was in full bloom."

"*Ceratitis capitata* usually kills the fruit and eventually the trees; the infestation must have happened at just the right time for the oranges to make it to harvest. That was bad luck."

"Or good planning."

"If these are what you think they are," Gabriel said, again holding the vial up to the light, "and for the record, I'm skeptical that they are, then you are dealing with an Alpha Vector."

"Alpha Vector? Shit, that doesn't sound good," Witt said.

"In the entomology world, it's pretty much the doomsday scenario for bioterror. It involves modifying a vector to carry a disease or compound that is fatal to humans. That's the bad news."

"Does that mean there's good news too?"

"Maybe. Creating an Alpha Vector involves some pretty heavy genetic engineering and also requires access to toxins that are difficult to acquire. It can only be done in a few places. So that narrows things down some."

Since Witt knew that already, it hardly qualified as good news. "I figured that."

"Why not have them tested by taking them to the Biomedical Research Lab at George Mason or to Plum Island off Long Island? In fact, I once knew a guy who worked at BRL. We did a mission in Afghanistan together. He may still work there. I can put in a call—"

Witt interrupted Gabriel in midsentence. "I can't do that. If these flies are the source of the botulinum toxin, they may have been engineered in one of those labs. I can't take the chance of tipping them off that we are on to them." Gabriel nodded. That made sense. "So what do you want from me?"

"My dad tells me you have a state-of-the-art lab here," Jason said, gesturing to the property surrounding them. "The kind of lab that might be able to verify what we're dealing with here. Is that true?"

"Yes, that's true. I have the equipment to sequence the genes and see if these flies have been altered to synthesize botulinum toxin."

"And I also know that you are capable of doing that kind of work."

Gabriel knew that Witt was referring to Afghanistan. "I can do it," Gabriel said.

"Will you do it?"

Gabriel hesitated for a split second. Of course he was going to do it. But he didn't want Witt to think him too eager, because once you gave the government an inch, they would always take a mile. He took a slow sip of coffee, letting the tension rise. Finally he said, "OK."

Witt looked relieved. "Great. How long will you need?"

"Twenty-four hours."

Witt looked at his watch. "Then I'll be back tomorrow."

"And what happens if this turns out to be an Alpha Vector? What then?"

Witt shrugged. "Then we have a big fucking problem on our hands."

CHAPTER FOURTEEN

Russian River Valley, California

FOR SEVERAL HOURS GABRIEL WATCHED THE SHADOWS gradually recede as the light of a new day filtered through the lab's windows. He'd been working all night and was about to look at the final results of the gene sequencing he'd done on the flies Witt had given him. Now it was time to see what they were really dealing with.

The Illumina gene sequencer flashed a message on its screen indicating that the results were complete. Gabriel quickly scanned the output, a four-color chromatogram graph that looked something like an EKG. Each color corresponded to a specific base that makes up the double helix of the DNA: black for guanine, blue for cytosine, red for thymine, and green for adenine. He looked for abnormalities in the peaks and valleys of the data, which at first glance appeared negligible; he found minimal noise that distorted the results and no mis-spaced or double peaks.

So far, so good.

Gabriel then loaded the raw data file into his computer and ran a program that compared the genetic sequence he'd just run to the known normal sequence of *Ceratitis capitata* in InsectBase, a publicly available database that contained more than 12 million sequences of over 150 insects. This comparison was designed to quickly tell Gabriel whether the medflies that Jason had given him had been genetically altered or not.

After a few minutes, the comparison was complete.

By the time Jason Witt showed up at the lab, Gabriel had showered and changed into jeans and a light jacket.

"How'd it go?" Witt asked as he came through the door. A man in a suit carrying a large satchel followed him closely. He was slightly taller than Witt, about thirty pounds heavier, and twenty years younger. Something told Gabriel that this man was not part of Witt's normal security detail.

"It's done," Gabriel said after a moment.

Witt waited for Gabriel to continue. When he didn't, Witt said, "And?"

Gabriel nodded at the man with the satchel. "Who's he?"

"This is Lee Jensen, a special agent in our Homeland Security Investigations unit. Lee, this is Gabriel Marx."

Jensen stepped forward and put out his hand, which Gabriel took; Jensen's grip was like iron. His eyes were steel blue, and Gabriel instantly knew that this was a warrior. "Marines?" he asked.

"Army Special Forces, actually," Jensen said. "You?"

"Marines. I was with 3/5 in Iraq in '04 and '06."

"No shit. I was in Ramadi in '06." Jensen and Gabriel were having one of those instant bonding experiences between veterans that civilians don't really understand. They were both independently reliving their years in Iraq, and though one was army and the other marines, they had seen the same things and chewed the same dirt.

Gabriel, deciding that Jensen passed his test, instantly switched gears. "Follow me." He turned on his heels and walked to the bench where his computer was set up. He moved the mouse to wake the computer up, and the chromatogram immediately appeared.

"What's that?" asked Witt.

"This is basically a map of the DNA of the flies you gave me. It's the sequence of chemical base pairs that make up the DNA molecule. By looking at the sequence of the bases—the A, C, G, and Ts—we can determine a lot about the organism, including whether or not it's been mutated or altered to synthesize botulinum toxin."

Witt nodded. "OK, I got it."

"Without getting into the weeds, here's how it works: We use a DNA sequencer to scan the DNA and pull out all these bases in their specific order. That leaves us with a code of millions of letters strung together. The whole process of mapping the genome was essentially assembling a machine to break this code by identifying the specific genes that these letters make up."

"So these letters correspond to different genes."

"Yes and no," answered Gabriel. "A gene is really a small section of the DNA that contains instructions for a specific protein molecule. The human genome is made up of more than twenty thousand of these protein-coded genes. In fruit flies it's usually something around fourteen thousand. But not all of these letters correspond to genes. They also correspond to instructions and other information that determine how the genes function."

"How do you find the genes in all these letters?"

"Fortunately, genetic sequence technology has continued to improve, and it's a lot easier than it used to be. We use annotation pipelines to mark where known genes are in the sequence, using proteins and start and stop codons as markers. . . ." Gabriel looked at Witt and Jensen and knew he'd lost them. "In English, we use a combination of technology and manual review of the sequences to find the genes."

"Got it," Witt said, relieved.

"Good. So what you are looking at is the result of the process I've just described. What I did next is take this genome and compare it to the known genome of medflies from a public database that stores sequence data. This process allowed me to find out whether this genetic sequence had been modified or mutated using CRISPR/Cas9 technology."

"What's a crisper?"

Gabriel laughed. "CRISPR/Cas9 is essentially a biological scissors that can be used to cut and splice new genetic code into the sequence. It's how genetic alteration takes place at the cellular level. Make sense?"

Both Witt and Jensen nodded that it did, though Gabriel wasn't sure they understood. But in the end, the details mattered less than the results. "So, was it altered?" asked Witt.

"Yes," replied Gabriel, pulling up the chart of the comparison chromatogram he'd run. "A string of code was inserted in the sequence here." Gabriel pointed to a section of the graph. "It corresponds to a gene sequence found in the database GenBank that instructs a protein to synthesize a variant of *Clostridium botulinum*—"

"Shit," Witt said before Gabriel could finish his sentence.

"—toxin. Only there's a problem."

"I'd say we have a problem all right," Witt said, his voice rising. "A big fucking problem—"

"Mr. Secretary," Gabriel said loudly. "Please, listen."

Witt gathered himself. "Sorry. Go on."

"This genetic sequence doesn't match any of the known sequences that produce botulinum toxin. There are currently eight families of botulinum toxin—named A to H—on record. This appears to produce a new one—type I—and that poses additional problems."

Witt stared at Gabriel and motioned with his hands for him to continue.

"How did those sickened by the orange juice on the East Coast react to treatment?"

"Not well. They were all given antibodies provided by the Centers for Disease Control and Prevention to try and combat the poison. But none of them responded well to them."

"I'm not surprised. The CDC would only have antidotes for versions A through H. This version has no antidote."

Witt tried to comprehend what he was hearing. "Jesus, this gets better by the minute."

"Take a look at this," Gabriel said, handing Witt a printout of an article from the *Journal of Infectious Diseases*. "Apparently type I was identified three years ago by scientists at Berkeley after a child got sick and died after receiving known antidotes. The scientists sequenced the bacterial DNA and found it was a new variant."

"So why doesn't that show up in the database you used?"

"Good question. Because there is no antidote, the scientists decided it was too dangerous to make the sequence public, fearing that someone might use it as a weapon. They did the same thing with Type H when they discovered it back in 2013 – the sequence wasn't published until 2017 after the antidote was developed."

"So if I understand this correctly, you are saying that not only do these flies produce botulinum toxin but also it's a variant that has no known treatment."

"That's what I'm saying."

"This is worse than I thought," said Witt. "And if this news gets out to the public, there's going to be a panic that will make 'The War of the Worlds' look like child's play."

Gabriel and Jensen both had confused looks on their faces.

"Orson Welles? Alien invasion?" Witt looked at them each and then said, "Never mind."

"Oh, that. I saw the movie. Tom Cruise. It sucked. But I take your point," said Jensen.

Witt went over to a stool and sat down heavily. He looked frazzled; he'd not slept much over the past few days, and his suit was wrinkled. He desperately wanted to lie down. For a moment he put his face in his hands and rubbed the stubble and tried to slow his mind so he could see a clear path forward. Finally he looked at Jensen. "OK, Lee. Any suggestions?"

"Yes, sir," Jensen said. "We have a genetic sequence that was never published but has ended up in the hands of someone with the knowledge and technology to genetically alter a fly to secrete a deadly toxin. So I suggest that we first pursue the source of the type I sequence. If we find that, we will have a better chance of finding out where the genetic engineering on the fly was done. And hopefully that will lead us to who did it."

Witt thought for a moment. "You have any thoughts on the matter, Gabriel?"

"I think that makes sense. I have a contact at UC Berkeley—one of my mentors teaches there—so you could start by seeing who had access to the type I sequence."

"You?" Witt said. "You mean 'we,' right?"

Gabriel looked at Jensen and then at Witt. "Sorry?"

"I need you, Gabriel. You are still technically on contract with DHS, and I want to assign you to work with Jensen on this."

"Mr. Witt, I appreciate the offer. But I'm a vintner now. I'm not sure I'm the best person to help. . ."

"Actually, you are the *only* person. My dad told me about your service in the Marine Corps, and I know what you did in Afghanistan. But more important, I need your brain. This guy," he said, looking over at Jensen, "is tough and smart, but he doesn't know a gnat from a butterfly."

"That's true," Jensen said with a smile.

Gabriel was immediately uncomfortable. While he looked strong on the outside, he felt crippled inside, a prisoner of his dreams and of his mind. He didn't know if he could do it and wasn't sure he wanted to find out. He needed to stall for time. "Can I talk to my wife?"

Witt nodded. "Yes, but I need an answer today. In the meantime, I'll need to brief the president and see if I can contain this before it blows wide open."

CHAPTER FIFTEEN

Berkeley, California

GABRIEL SAT NEXT TO LEE JENSEN as he drove down Interstate 580 toward Berkeley in a government sedan. Jensen had the self-driving mode on and was looking at the *Wall Street Journal* on a heads-up display that projected the "paper" onto the car's windshield. The lead story was President Cooperman's upcoming visit to Beijing to discuss the growing trade war between the US and China.

Gabriel looked out the passenger window and watched the miles slip by. He was feeling better since they'd left the vineyard, and a calm had come over him. Maybe Claire was right that he needed to be on a mission to feel like he was normal. He went over the brief, cryptic conversation he'd had with her before he left.

"Secretary Witt wants me to work on this . . . project."

"Great!"

"It's going to require me to be away for a bit. It's an investigation . . . into something I can't really talk about."

She'd laughed. "Go."

"Really? What if . . ."

"Gabriel, go. It will be good for you."

Maybe she knew best, he thought. Maybe he needed to face down his demons, and having a mission again would still his mind. Claire had no doubt he could do it and that it would be good for him. He had reservations, but he put his trust in her.

Jensen flipped the pages of the *Journal* by tapping a button on the steering wheel, while he simultaneously played with the buttons on the satellite radio. He was in perpetual motion. Finally finding a song he liked—"Mr. Brightside" by the Killers—he started drumming the steering wheel to the beat. "I love this old stuff! They don't make them like this anymore!"

Gabriel smiled and realized that Jensen was typical of former Special Forces operators. He was driven, always thinking, always in motion, always doing three things at once. Gabriel also found out quickly that Jensen was fond of peppering his speech with movie lines. Sometimes they were spot on, and sometimes they were corny. But they were proving to be pretty entertaining.

"Where'd you grow up?" Gabriel asked.

"Ever heard of Hope, Arkansas? As in a 'place called Hope'?"

Gabriel thought for a moment. "Nope."

"You follow politics?"

"Not if I can help it."

Jensen smiled. "Yeah, me too. But this is old stuff. When Bill Clinton got the nomination for president 1992, he began his acceptance speech by saying, 'I still believe in a place called Hope.' He put the town on the map. But it's really just a small town in southwestern Arkansas."

"Did you know him?"

"Clinton? Nah. He was long gone by the time I came along. He and Hillary left Arkansas after he became president and never came back, except to build their library in Little Rock."

"Hillary didn't seem like an Arkansan."

"Shit, you can say that again. She couldn't get out of there fast enough."

"I take it you're not a fan."

Jensen just smiled. "I joined the army right out of the University of Arkansas. That was right after 9/11. I spent the first few years studying to be a corpsman and then got the opportunity to do the Q Course. They needed medics then, just as Iraq was cooking off. And the rest, as they say, is history."

"How long were you in?"

"Sixteen years. After a while I'd had enough. The Obama years were tough for Special Forces. We were kept on a short leash. And giving back Iraq to the hajis was really, really depressing. We got good at snatching defeat from the jaws of victory."

Gabriel thought about Iraq and the friends he'd lost there. It had been a painful chapter for him. "Yeah," he said simply.

"What about you? You like living in California?"

"It's a love-hate kind of thing. I love the wine country. And I love the vineyard. But the idiots in Sacramento have taxed and regulated the shit out of everything. When the tech bubble burst again a few years ago, the bottom fell out of the economy. Now the state can't pay its pension obligations, and the tax base has gone to shit. It's a mess."

"Forget it, Jake. It's Chinatown."

Another movie quote. "Sorry, must've missed that one."

"*Chinatown*? Jack Nicholson? Man, you need to do some streaming! It means it's the way things are and the way they will always be. California has jumped the shark. There's no fixing it."

As they entered Berkeley from the north, they passed through tony neighborhoods and noticed more cop cars than Gabriel could remember seeing in the past; the last several years had seen a resurgence of the demonstrations all around the university which had returned to its counterculture roots but in a more aggressive and less idealistic way than in the 1960s. Student groups protesting everything, from climate change to Israel to capitalism, had become the new Greek system; fraternities were out and social justice armies were in.

As they passed through a line of police cars setting up a barricade on Solano Avenue, they noticed a line of cops in riot gear and a group of student demonstrators, many dressed in black and others carrying vividly painted signs, massing in the distance. "Reminds me a bit of Ramadi, only without the smell," Gabriel joked. "Let's hope this GPS doesn't put us in the middle of Indian country."

Gabriel instinctively slouched down in his seat, trying to make himself a smaller target. He watched the map on the center display and knew they'd soon be at the gates of the sprawling campus. While it had once been an open public university, it was now cordoned off into security zones. Only students and registered visitors could drive onto the campus, and every inch was covered by high-definition cameras and/or high-speed drones. How sadly ironic, Gabriel thought, that this bastion of liberal arts education and free speech had been reduced to an armed camp.

As the car approached the gate at the top of Center Street, a burly uniformed officer wearing a helmet and armored vest put up his hand, motioning for them to stop. Jensen took control of the car and rolled down the window to show the officer his badge.

"We're here to see Professor Lassiter," Jensen said.

"Where's he work?" the officer asked.

Jensen looked at Gabriel, who answered the question. "In the synthetic biotech department."

The officer scanned their car's VIN into a handheld device; when it came up clean, he said, "Do you gentlemen know where you're going, or do you require an escort?"

"Depends on the escort," Jensen said with a straight face. When the officer didn't crack a smile, Jensen said, "We're good. Thanks."

Jensen rolled up the car window, and they were waved through. "That guy needs to lighten up," Jensen said. "So what's synthetic biotech?"

"It's basically a mash-up of engineering, computer science, and biology. Its goal is to create new and better life-forms by modifying what nature gave us."

"New and better? Seems like it can also create new and worse."

"Like a lot of technology, in the wrong hands, it can be dangerous."

As they approached the synthetic bio building, there was no spot out front, so Jensen just parked by a red curb. He put a DHS "Official Business" placard in the window, and they got out of the car.

Walking into the building brought back a flood of memories for Gabriel; he'd collaborated with students from Lassiter's lab on a paper entitled "The Frequency of Genetic Mutations in Fruit Flies," and he'd spent several weeks working from this location. It had been a good experience, one of Gabriel's first real research projects. It had even gotten published in the *Journal of Synthetic Research.*

They reached Lassiter's office door, and Gabriel knocked several times. There was no answer. He was just about to check and see if Lassiter was in his lab when he heard a voice from down the hall.

"Office hours are tomorrow from one to three."

Gabriel turned to look and found himself face-to-face with Professor James Lassiter, one of the world's foremost experts on genetic engineering in insects.

"You look familiar," Lassiter said, looking at Gabriel. "Were you a student here?"

"Not really. I'm Gabriel Marx, Professor. I did a research project . . ."

"I remember you! Oregon State, right? When was that? God, my memory is failing me."

Gabriel was pleased that Lassiter had remembered him at all. "That was ten years ago at least. Great to see you again, Professor," he said, holding out his hand.

Lassiter was in his midfifties and wore jeans and an old "Obama for President" T-shirt. He had wild gray hair and wire-rim glasses and looked like a cross between John Lennon and Warren Zevon. He shook Gabriel's hand and then looked at Lee Jensen.

"I'm Jim Lassiter," the professor said, offering his hand.

"Lee Jensen. Nice to meet you."

They stood for a moment looking at one another. Finally, Lassiter said, "What can I do for you guys?"

"I take it your secretary didn't give you the message that we were coming?" asked Gabriel.

"She probably did, but I don't always pay attention. It's a flaw, and I admit it. My wife hates it too."

Gabriel smiled. "Is there someplace we can go to talk in private?"

"Sure," Lassiter said, opening his office. "Come on in." They entered and found a surprisingly clean, tidy office.

"Have a seat," Lassiter said, motioning to a pair of chairs in front of his desk.

Lassiter sat down at his desk, pulled his iPhone out of his pocket, and laid it facedown on the desk in front of him. He folded his hands in front of him and waited for somebody to start talking.

Gabriel kicked things off. "Professor, I'm here at the request of the Department of Homeland Security—"

"DHS?" Lassiter asked. "What do they want with me?"

"They—we—need information about some research that came out of one of the synth-bio labs a few years ago."

Lassiter looked confused. "You'll have to be more specific than that."

"We will be, Professor. But first I need to have you sign this federal nondisclosure form," Jensen said, pulling out his iPad. "By signing—"

"Who are you?" Lassiter asked.

Jensen stopped in midsentence. He reached in his coat pocket and pulled out his badge. "I'm a special agent in DHS's investigations unit."

Lassiter took the badge and studied it. He then handed it back. Picking up the iPad, he read the NDA. Satisfied that he understood the secrecy he was committing himself to, he signed it by putting his thumbprint on the screen to be scanned and matched to its record and handed the iPad back to Jensen.

"Thank you, Professor," Jensen said. He quickly uploaded the NDA to the cloud and nodded to Gabriel that they were good to go.

"Three years ago you ran the DNA on feces from a small boy who died from botulinum toxin," Gabriel said.

"That was done in Lab B under the direction of Dr. Sam Attisha," Lassiter said. "The boy's name was Samuel Billings. He was five years old. He contracted it from soil that touched an open wound. His parents couldn't figure out what was wrong; over a period of twelve hours, he'd stopped eating, couldn't sit up, and couldn't talk. Eventually the toxin paralyzed his respiratory system, and he literally suffocated to death. Terribly sad."

"That's the case," Gabriel said.

Lassiter sat for a moment deep in thought. "I remember it like it was yesterday. We did a DNA test because the hospital in Fresno ultimately suspected it was a case of BT and gave Samuel an antidote. But it failed to work. So they were curious if this was a new type of toxin they hadn't seen before. And it was."

"Right, we read the article you published on it. Type I."

Lassiter looked at Gabriel. "Are you here because it's come up again?"

"Yes, we believe it has," Jensen answered.

"But not organically, Professor," Gabriel said. "We believe that the type I strain was sequenced by someone using medfly larvae. We also believe that it's from Samuel's sequence."

"Can't be. We never published that sequence. In fact, it's locked away in a highly secure account with military-grade encryption. There's no way an outsider . . ." Lassiter stopped himself in midsentence. "You think it's possible it came from inside this lab?"

"Yes, we think it's possible. Maybe even probable," Jensen answered.

Lassiter, in disbelief, repeated what Gabriel had just told him. "Someone genetically altered medflies to secrete type I botulinum toxin."

"Yes, Professor," Gabriel said.

"Does this have anything to do with the outbreak of sickness surrounding the Tropicana juice on the East Coast?"

Gabriel glanced at Jensen before replying. "Yes."

Lassiter pondered what he was hearing. "I have a lab to teach in a few minutes. What do you want from me?"

"We would like to examine the list of students, interns, employees, and anyone else who worked on the Samuel Billings case specifically and also anyone who had access to your lab's computer system over the past three years."

Lassiter checked his watch. "I'm afraid I'm out of time. You'll have to take that up with the university's legal department. Personnel records are confidential, as I'm sure you understand. They'll make the call on whether or not to provide all that to you." With that, Lassiter stood, indicating the meeting was over. "Good luck, gentlemen," he said as he ushered them out of his office.

Jensen and Gabriel stood and watched Lassiter walk down the hall toward his lab. When he was out of earshot, Jensen said, "No soup for you!"

Gabriel looked at him quizzically.

"*Seinfeld*, man!"

"Whatever. All I know is that Lassiter just lawyered up."

"Let's call Witt and get some pressure on the university. It's going to take a lot more firepower than we can bring to bear."

CHAPTER SIXTEEN

Washington, DC

JASON WITT HATED BEING ON HOLD. He paced back and forth behind his desk and listened to some awful elevator music playing over his speakerphone. He looked at his watch for the fifth time in the last two minutes and swore under his breath. Wasn't anyone taking this seriously?

After a moment his soon-to-be ex came on the line. "Jason, I'm trying to get in to see the president, but she's in a meeting with the Joint Chiefs and the SecDef. Something's brewing in the South China Sea."

"Jesus, Sarah. Something's brewing all right, but it's in our goddamn backyard! I need to speak to the president as soon as possible."

"I'll call you right back," she said, and hung up.

Witt swore and punched the Off button on his speakerphone; he missed, and the phone fell to the floor. "Goddamn it!" he yelled, loud enough that his secretary popped her head in. "I'm fine, Susan, thanks," he said to her with some embarrassment. Picking up the phone, he replaced it gently on the desk and plopped down to wait for the phone to ring.

He'd spoken earlier to Lee Jensen, who'd recounted the conversation with Professor Lassiter. Witt felt as if there was a bomb ticking, and now they'd have to run the gauntlet of the University of California's lawyers unless Cooperman could put pressure on the UC president to allow them access on national-security grounds. Witt was skeptical that she could because the politics in California—particularly on a university campus—were hostile to government data mining and surveillance; the progressive intelligentsia was deeply opposed to the NSA and the deep state and still had people like Chelsea Manning and Edward Snowden on a pedestal. Witt had no illusions that this would be an easy battle.

After five minutes the phone rang. "This is Witt," he said.

"Hold please for the president," the White House operator said. After a few seconds, Cooperman came on the line.

"What's so urgent?" the president asked without pleasantries.

"Madam President, you asked me to keep you briefed on the Florida attack investigation. We've made progress and have a very good lead that requires us to access personnel data in the University of California system. There is a lab at Berkeley that may be the source of the strain of botulinum toxin used in the Florida attack."

"Good. So what's the issue?"

"The issue is that my investigators went to Berkeley to interview the head of the lab and got stonewalled. They want us to get a court order."

"Shit. Have you spoken to Justice about it?"

"Yes, that's in process. But this is extremely sensitive, and the last thing I want is to march in the front door with a federal search warrant. That would certainly alert those who smuggled out the toxin's sequence if they are still at the university. So I was hoping you might bring some pressure to bear so we could get access more quietly."

The president thought for a moment. "Look, I'm an old friend of the UC president. We went to law school together. I can call her and see what I can do."

Witt smiled and pumped his fist. "That would be great, ma'am. Thank you."

UC President Justine Acevedo answered her cell phone on the third ring.

"Justine, how are things with Sam and the kids?"

"Fine, Jennifer—oops, Madam President," she said laughing.

"Oh, you can call me Jennifer when it's just us. We've known each other since we were practically kids ourselves!"

"I'll say. Back to when you were dating Matt Blumenthal!"

"Matt Blumenthal. I haven't thought of him in ages. I wonder how he is."

"He's dead, actually. Sorry to say. Died of a heart attack two years ago."

"Oh, what a shame. I still remember those blue eyes and dimples," Cooperman said wistfully. "Sorry to hear that."

"We aren't getting any younger; that's for sure. Anyhow, I know how busy you are, Madam President," Acevedo said, putting particular emphasis on the *M* and the *P*. She then laughed a bit. "How can I be of service to the most powerful woman in the free world?"

"Oh, Justine. You haven't changed a bit," Cooperman said with a laugh. "I actually need a favor. And it's a big one."

"Name it."

Cooperman told Acevedo the outline of the situation at Berkeley and what they needed. When Cooperman was done, there was silence on the other end of the line.

"Justine? Are you there?" Cooperman asked.

"Yes, I'm here," Acevedo said after a moment. "That's a very big favor."

"I know. And I wouldn't ask unless it was absolutely necessary. This is a major threat to the United States, and we need to move quickly."

"I understand. But I'm afraid I can't help you. I'm sure you can get a court order to compel us to open up our records. But I can't order that to be done."

"Can't or won't?" Cooperman asked.

Acevedo hesitated before answering. "Technically I can, but I won't. I . . ."

"You don't want to take the heat, correct?"

"I'll get absolutely killed if it gets out that I voluntarily aided the federal government in an investigation that involves UC staff or students. And it will get out."
Cooperman knew that Acevedo was correct about this. "Look, I'm sympathetic to your predicament. But this is not about you, Justine. This is about the security of the American people. Surely you can see that."

"I can see that from your vantage point, Madam President. I really can. But I live in a different reality. I can't risk what this will do to my ability to lead this university. I'm sorry. I wish I could help."

Cooperman was shocked. She had known that it wouldn't be easy for Acevedo, but Cooperman had also thought that their friendship—and the fact that the nation was under real threat of attack—would win the day. It clearly hadn't. "Goddamn, Justine."

"I'm sorry. I really am. But I can't help you. Please get a court order. I will ensure that we comply with it immediately."

"Thank you, Justine. Good day." She disconnected the line. "What a bitch," Cooperman muttered to herself.

CHAPTER SEVENTEEN

Berkeley, California

LEE JENSEN THOROUGHLY ENJOYED the deer-in-the-headlights look on Professor James Lassiter's face when he, Gabriel, and a pair of plainclothes DHS agents descended on the synthetic biotech department. Lassiter was conducting office hours when they barged in, apparently doing his best to bedazzle a blond co-ed with his knowledge of genetics.

"Just a minute here!" he exclaimed when Jensen and Gabriel came in. "You can't—"

"Actually, we can," Jensen said, handing Lassiter the warrant. "Miss, will you excuse us please?" The young woman quickly fled the office, but not before being admonished by one of the accompanying agents to not speak about what was happening there or "face the consequences of violating a federal nondisclosure agreement the university is a party to." Whether that deception would work or not, they didn't know.

Jensen was attempting a low-key search that didn't include the army of federal agents they'd normally deploy in a situation like this. Witt was hoping that they could avoid it becoming a spectacle that would attract the media. He'd ordered Jensen and the agents to dress in casual clothing with no markings. "Blend in as much as you can," Witt had told them. That was easier said than done; only Gabriel, with his jeans and beard, looked as if he truly belonged on a college campus.

"Professor," Jensen said, "We need access to all of your lab's personnel files, including those of the staff that worked in the lab at the time of the type I discovery."

Lassiter sat staring at the warrant. "Just a minute," he said finally. Picking up his desk phone, he punched in the number for the Berkeley chancellor's office. "This is Professor Lassiter. I need to speak with Chancellor Jimenez immediately. Yes, I'll hold."

After a minute, Jimenez came on the line. "Jim, I think I know why you're calling," she said.

"Dr. Jimenez, I have federal agents here—"

"Yes, and I have received word from President Acevedo that we are to cooperate fully and provide whatever information they require."

"You can't be serious? We aren't going to even fight it?"

"I understand your frustration, Jim. But you are to provide them whatever assistance they require. Is that clear?"

"Yes," he said with reluctance in his voice.

"Good. I am sending over a representative from my office now to be there to assist. Thank you for calling, Jim." She promptly hung up.

Lassiter hung up the receiver, hit a button that connected him with his lab's administrator, and asked her to come to his office. After a few minutes, a middle-aged woman appeared in his doorway. She looked surprised to see the five men crowded into the small space.

"This is Ms. Brandt," he said. He then said to her, "These gentlemen are here to execute a federal search warrant. You are to provide them whatever they want."

"Yes, sir," she replied.

"Ms. Brandt," Jensen said in his most officious voice, "Would you please take us to a computer where we can access the lab's personnel files."

"Right this way," she said.

Jensen and one of the two accompanying agents, a computer expert, followed Brandt to her office. That left Gabriel and the remaining DHS agent alone with Lassiter, who sat glumly in his desk chair.

"You're really helping this investigation, Professor," Gabriel said.

"That's nice," Lassiter said with sarcasm.

Gabriel didn't understand Lassiter's attitude. "Thousands of lives may be at stake. Maybe more."

Lassiter stared at him. "Yeah, maybe. But there's one life I'm certain is going to be destroyed. Mine."

"Jesus Christ," Gabriel said louder than he intended. He looked at the agent. "I'll be outside." He then got up and left the room.

Later that day, Gabriel, Jensen, and the two DHS agents were working out of a pair of rooms at the Rose Garden Inn on Telegraph Avenue. They had left the synth-bio lab with two boxes of files and a thumb drive.

They began sorting through the files by date, segregating the files for people who had worked for the lab on the type I sequencing process. That had run for two weeks in September of 2023 and involved approximately ten people. Gabriel and Jensen then took half of those files and the two other agents the remainder. They agreed to put aside anyone who looked suspicious in any way, whether because of family origin, occupation, or association with outside groups.

Gabriel was enjoying the hell out of himself. He'd never been in an investigation like this, and he felt as if he were playing a part in an action movie. But he was also in a totally new element and had no idea what he was doing. After they finished laying out their plan, Gabriel asked, "So, what are we looking for?"

"Ah, grasshopper," Jensen said. "We're looking for anyone who has a link to the Middle East, Indonesia, North Africa, and any other known Islamic hot spots. We also want to flag Russian, Chinese, or North Korean connections and anyone with radical environmental, antifa, white-na-tionalist, or far-right political activities. Those go in any of those buckets placed over there," Jensen said, pointing to a spot on one of the room's two double beds. "We'll then dig deeper into them."

They got to work. They quickly eliminated Professor Lassiter, Ms. Brandt, and several graduate students who had been assigned to the proj-ect but didn't have direct access to the lab. Three others—lab attendants and administrators—were deemed too junior to have the technical knowl-edge needed to access and compile the sequence.

But two other files caught their interest. One was for a Dr. Omar Madiya, a professor of biochemistry who had emigrated to the US from Saudi Arabia in the 1990s. The other was for an Ahmed Sahid, a Somali national who was getting his PhD at Berkeley in applied genomics. Both of these names were uploaded to the National Security Database, and a full security profile for each was developed and downloaded within a few minutes.

"OK, here's what we got," Jensen said, starting to read from the first file. "Madiya has lived in the US since the early 1990s. Did his under-graduate work at Stanford and his PhD at UC San Diego. He's married with three children. Lives in Richmond. Says here he has only been abroad once, to London, and has no known associates in the Mideast or Asia. He's also a member of the First Methodist Church of Oakland. Probably not our guy."

"What about the other guy?" Gabriel asked.

"Sahid came to the US about five years ago as a graduate student. Went to university in Dresden, Germany. He's single. He hasn't been abroad since he left Germany. And he's also a member of the Berkeley gay men's choir." Jensen laughed. "Probably not the typical radical profile."

"You mean there are no gay jihadists?" Gabriel asked.

"There may be gay jihadists. But no gay jihadists who sing in a gay choir. That's a pretty surefire way to get your head—both heads—cut off."

Gabriel laughed. "Hadn't thought about that."

"So we need to go deeper now. Let's review all employees and students in the lab during that same period, whether they worked directly on the type I sequence or not."

They again went to work, dividing up the forty-five files that fit the criteria between the four of them. After three hours they had whittled that pile down to four names. They agreed to review each one's security profile as a team.

"Antonin Lebedev," Jensen said. "Twenty-eight years old. From Grozny in Chechnya. Entered the United States on September 1, 2019, on a student visa. He was a graduate student studying computer science. Specializes in genetic modeling. No travel history to the Mideast. He reported that his brother was in the Russian army and was killed in Chechnya by Islamic terrorists."

Gabriel looked at Jensen. "Pretty unlikely he'd be helping Islamists, if that's who we're looking for."

"Maybe. But I consider Russia one of our enemies, so I don't want to rule him out just yet," Jensen said. He read on. "Lebedev was employed by GenomeX, a biotech in Redwood City, up until a week ago."

"Where'd he go to school?" Gabriel asked.

"He did his undergraduate work at George Mason University. His . . ."

Gabriel's alarm bells were suddenly ringing. "George Mason? Let me see that." Jensen handed over the file. "He was a computer science major. Looks like he graduated with honors. Did his thesis on blockchain technology and genomic-sequence networking under a professor named Abdul-Azim Bashera. Wow, this may be our guy."

"How do you figure?" asked one of the DHS agents.

"GMU runs the Biomedical Research Lab, one of the nation's top sites that works on synthetic biology, including genomics and insects. It's one of the few places in the country where Mediterranean fruit flies could be made to synthesize and transmit botulinum toxin."

"That's pretty circumstantial," the agent said.

"Yeah, but we don't have anything better at this point," Jensen said. "Let's dig into this guy."

The two agents and Jensen opened up their tablets and connected to various databases in the federal government. They searched the immigration records to learn more about Lebedev's application for entry into the United States, searched IRS records to track his employment at GenomeX, and looked at Virginia state and police records. One of the agents did a public records search that included newspapers, published documents, and any other media, using the CIA's extensive database of global media resources.

After a few minutes, one of the agents found the nugget they'd been looking for. It was a Russian newspaper article dated June 5, 2019, that covered a terrorist attack against Russian forces at their headquarters in Grozny. Eight Russian soldiers had been killed when a Russian officer turned against his comrades in a suicide attack and detonated a grenade.

"Take a look at this," the agent said, handing his tablet to Jensen.

Jensen quickly read the news summary. "Bingo! Lebedev's brother was killed in Chechnya all right. Only he wasn't a victim of terrorism. He was the terrorist."

CHAPTER EIGHTEEN

Redwood City, California

"TOTO, I'VE A FEELING WE'RE NOT IN KANSAS ANYMORE." Lee Jensen looked wistfully around the soaring steel and glass atrium that served as the lobby of GenomeX. Behind the reception desk was a huge wall of monitors displaying a mesmerizing double helix of various colors floating in deep space. The receptionist was a striking brunette with lips the color of pomegranate.

"May I help you, gentlemen?" she asked in a lovely British accent.

"Yes, Miss, we're here to meet with a Dr. Nomura," Jensen said.

She rolled her eyes as if dealing with an imbecile. "It's 'Mix.,' not 'Miss.'"

Jensen was confused. "Excuse me?"

"Mx. As in M-x. It means I identify as gender neutral."

Jensen laughed at first, but then saw the receptionist was deadly serious. "Ah, OK, Mx.," he said after a moment.

"Do you have an appointment?"

"Not exactly," Jensen said. He took out his DHS inspector badge and showed it to the receptionist. "Can you tell him the Department of Homeland Security would like a minute of his time?"

The receptionist stared carefully at the badge and the picture of Jensen on the accompanying ID card, glancing at Jensen's face a few times. The picture was ten years old, and Jensen had clearly aged. "It's me; I promise," he said with his best smile.

The receptionist gave no reaction at his attempt at humor. "Just a minute, please. Will you gentlemen mind sitting over there?" The receptionist pointed to a bank of spare leather and wood armchairs in the corner. "I'll see if Dr. Nomura is available."

Gabriel and Jensen walked over to the chairs and sat down. "Mx.?" Jensen said. "Jesus. Only in the Bay Area."

"Well, she definitely looks like a woman to me," Gabriel said.

"I'm just glad I'm not dating these days. Everything's so damn complicated."

"How long you been married?"

"Twenty five years. Good woman. We raised two kids together. One's at West Point. The other works at Amazon."

"Eventually we're all gonna be working for Amazon."

"Not me. My job isn't something Amazon would—or could—do."

"Maybe. But I thought that about health care too. And now they practically run the whole hospital supply chain."

Jensen and Gabriel spent the next twenty minutes in silence; fatigue was setting in for both of them. They had spent the previous day combing through Lebedev's past. He had graduated from Berkeley with a master's degree and immediately gone to work for GenomeX, where he spent two years in its genetic sequencing division under Dr. Nomura. By all accounts he'd been a rising star at the company. But then a week ago he'd suddenly quit and disappeared, without even collecting his final pay, which the company remits in a paper check. A search of the ICE records told had them he'd returned to Russia, flying through JFK on an Aeroflot flight. Given what they suspected of Lebedev's role in smuggling out the type I sequence, they were now very interested in what he'd been working on at GenomeX.

Finally, an Asian man in a lab coat walked up to them. "I'm Dr. Nomura. Can I help you?"

Both Gabriel and Jensen stood. "I'm Lee Jensen from Homeland Security. This is my colleague Gabriel Marx." Jensen and Gabriel had agreed that if anyone asked, Jensen would refer to Gabriel as a "colleague" or an "associate" in the hope that more explanation wouldn't be needed. It wasn't a lie because Gabriel was technically still an approved contractor for DHS, even if he didn't carry a badge.

"I can assure you gentlemen that my immigration papers are in order. I have a valid green card—"

"Dr. Nomura," Jensen interrupted. "We aren't here about your immigration status. Please, just relax."

Nomura's expression visibly lightened, and a smile crept across his face. "Well, that's a relief. I know friends who are legal residents who have been through ICE investigations that made a proctology exam seem like fun."

Jensen knew this was true; over the past decade ICE had conducted increasingly frequent raids on companies, looking for people who'd overstayed their visas. It had prompted IRS-style investigations of suspects' lives that were time-consuming and stressful. "We're here to ask you some questions about a former employee of yours. Antonin Lebedev."

Nomura's face darkened again. "Oh, I see. Is he in some kind of trouble? That might explain why he just up and quit last week."

"We're not sure if he's in trouble or not. That's part of the reason we're here. Is there someplace we can talk?" Jensen asked, looking around the very public space they were in.

"Yes, of course. Let's get you badged in, and we can go to my office," Nomura said, moving over to the reception desk, where the beautiful gender-neutral receptionist awaited them. Nomura instructed the receptionist to create visitor badges for them and then escorted them through the massive automatic glass doors into the building's core.

"We built this building just last year to house our labs and administrative offices," he said as they walked through the hallways on the first floor. Pointing to a huge door that looked like the entrance to a vault, he said, "This area houses our IT operations and servers. As you can see, we run a very tight ship. We keep a record of everyone who goes in and out and also track their movement in the building. It's why we don't use Amazon Web Services or any other third-party server farm."

"Is this where Lebedev worked?"

"No, Antonin worked in my lab. He worked on our most complex genetic modeling."

They rode the elevator up to the fifth floor; the doors opened to a lobby area with a panoramic view of the San Francisco Bay. "This is where my lab is located. It takes up this entire floor," he said as he walked through a pair of walnut double doors to his office, a room as large as some houses in San Francisco. "Please sit," Nomura said, gesturing to the chairs in front of his desk.

"What's your role here, Dr. Nomura?" asked Jensen.

"I'm the chief science officer," he answered with pride. "I'm in charge of our research and drug discovery lines, as well as our contract work with the US government."

"What kind of contract work?" Gabriel asked.

"I'm not at liberty to discuss, as I'm sure you can understand. But it's around genetic mutations of biological agents, work on antidotes, and things like that."

"Interesting," Gabriel said.

"Dr. Nomura, we'd like to know more about what Antonin Lebedev was working on during his time at GenomeX," Jensen said.

"Well, let's see what I can tell you. He worked on the team that is researching new approaches to eradicating Gram-negative bacteria—the so-called 'superbugs' that are resistant to antibiotics. These bacteria carry a gene for antibiotic resistance that rides on a small fragment of DNA called a plasmid. The plasmids enable the bacterial genes to move over to other bacteria and to different species of bacteria, breeding resistance to antibiotics and transforming these bacteria into potentially untreatable superbugs. We are using a variety of approaches to this, including genetic sequencing to develop a deeper understanding of how the superbugs work. Antonin developed computer models to help us focus our research on the most promising approaches."

"I've read a great deal about antibiotic resistance. It's a major health issue," Gabriel said.

"Indeed, it is. And a massive market opportunity," Nomura said. "For years, drug companies ignored antibiotics because the revenue potential didn't merit the investment. Now that more than ten million people a year are dying from bacterial infections, there's great interest in finding new antibiotics. Unfortunately, it's a very complex problem and requires a great deal of technology."

"Can you tell me what Lebedev worked on?" Jensen asked. "What project specifically?"

"I can," Nomura said. "But first I'd like to know why you want to know."

"I can't tell you that," Jensen said without elaboration.

Normura wasn't used to people not answering his questions. "Well then, I'm not sure I can help you."

"That's too bad," Jensen said, glancing at his watch. "I'm sure I can have ICE in here today to start an audit. Won't be terribly inconveniencing. It'll just take a week or two."

Nomura and Jensen stared at each other. They were taking each other's measure. Finally, Nomura blinked. "Antonin was working on our CRE program."

Jensen waited for Nomura to elaborate. When he didn't Jensen said, "Look, Dr. Nomura. Let's not play twenty questions here, OK?"

"CRE stands for carbapenem-resistant Enterobacteriaceae. The CDC refers to them as 'nightmare bacteria.' They're basically resistant to any known drugs. If you come down with a CRE, you basically have a pretty good chance of dying."

"Can you provide some examples?" asked Gabriel.

"Yes," Nomura said. "*Klebsiella pneumoniae* carbapenemase and *E. coli*, among others."

"You mean KPC?" Gabriel asked.

"Yes, that's right. KPC."

"And when you say he was working on this, what does that entail?"

"It means he ran the genetic sequencing database, ran the tests, compiled the data, and provided reports to the scientists."

Gabriel knew where this was going, and he didn't like it. He knew KPC was a deadly enzyme produced by drug-resistant bacteria that several years prior had killed several hundred people in the New York City area when there had been an outbreak at one of the hospitals there. If Antonin had access to the genetic sequence that could synthesize KPC, this was going from bad to worse. "Can you do an audit trail on the access to the KPC sequence files?"

"We can. But I can assure you those, and the sequences for more than a hundred other viruses and bacteria, are safely tucked away in our database. We require a double-entry system, much like an old safety deposit box at the bank. It takes two keys from two different identification cards to access the database. It's pretty foolproof."

In Jensen's mind nothing was foolproof. "Humor us, Doctor," he said.

"Very well." Nomura picked up the phone and called his head of data security. "Please run an audit report for"—he paused to reference his computer—"project code 23244, and get it to me right away. Yes, do it now."

He put down the phone. The room was silent except for the hum of the AC unit that circulated the air in the huge office. Gabriel studied the view while running through the possibilities in his mind. None of them were good. After several minutes, there was a ding that signified a new message had arrived in Nomura's inbox.

Nomura opened the report. "It says here that the last access to the KPC file was three days ago from an employee with ID number 3545 and an employee with ID number 7699. Obviously, neither of those ID numbers match Lebedev."

"And what about Lebedev's ID number? Can you check if and when he last accessed the files?"

Nomura keyed some strokes on his computer and brought up Lebedev's ID number. Comparing it to the list, he found three instances, all earlier in the current year. "Once in February, once in March, and the last time just a week ago," he said.

"Just before he disappeared," Jensen said.

"Yes. Let me see who else accessed the file with him." Nomura cross-referenced the other ID number and read off a name. "Alex Fleming," he said with a confused look on his face. "That name is familiar, but I can't place the person," he said.

Gabriel laughed. "The name should be familiar. Alexander Fleming?"

Nomura's face went slack. He had suddenly comprehended what had happened. "Oh, shit!" he exclaimed.

Jensen was confused. "Who the hell is Alexander Fleming?"

"The man who invented penicillin. In 1928," Gabriel said.

"Houston, we have a problem," Jensen said.

CHAPTER NINETEEN

Washington, DC

DHS SECRETARY JASON WITT had spent the past twenty-four hours working fervently to keep control of the investigation into what was now being referred to in the media as the "Toxic OJ Scare." That DHS had the case at all was owed to the fact that bugs were involved; DHS was at every airport and point of entry inspecting cargo and luggage for stowaways into the US that could harm domestic agriculture. DHS was, for all intents and purposes, the first and last line of defense against insect vectors.

Over the past decade, DHS had also developed a robust ability to carry out investigations into criminal and terrorist activities, which meant it was increasingly playing on the FBI's turf. Some of this was out of necessity, given the nature of the threats related to both immigration and border security.

So far at least, Witt had been able to keep the FBI at bay. He'd been able to convince President Cooperman that stealth was critically important to the investigation and that getting the FBI involved was akin to broadcasting the investigation live on national TV during the Super Bowl. The FBI was great at many things, but doing things quietly was generally not one of them. Cooperman was incredibly nervous that what the public thought of as the "Toxic OJ Scare" would turn into the "Attack of the Deadly Insects" and felt that DHS should be given a bit more time to quietly work its investigation.

But Witt was under no illusions; he didn't have much time. If they weren't able to break the case open in the next few days, he was sure Cooperman would bring in the FBI, if only because the president would feel compelled to do whatever was necessary to protect the nation. Witt knew that the only thing worse for the president than calling in the FBI would be not calling in the FBI and having the US attacked again. That would be politically unsurvivable.

Witt's desk phone buzzed. "Mr. Secretary, I have Special Agent Jensen and a Gabriel Marx here to see you."

"Great. Send them in, please."

Gabriel and Jensen looked worse for wear. Jensen had a day's stubble on his face, and Gabriel's hair was as unkempt as his beard. They'd flown in on a red-eye and had come straight to DHS Headquarters.

"You guys look like crap," Witt said, shaking their hands.

"Yes, sir. Thank you, sir," Jensen said with a laugh.

"OK, give me the update," Witt said.

"Sir, we believe that we are dealing with a massive potential threat—even greater than we'd previously thought," Jensen said.

"We? You mean you and Gabriel?"

"Yes, sir," Jensen said. Gabriel sat quietly on the couch in Witt's office as Jensen recounted the events of the past few days: the second visit to Berkeley, the stolen type I sequence, the link to Antonin Lebedev, and the trace of Lebedev to GenomeX.

"What do we know about this Lebedev?"

"He's a computer scientist who emigrated to the US six years ago and did his undergraduate work at George Mason. He grew up in Grozny—"

"Chechnya?" Witt said, his alarm bells ringing.

"Yes. He also has an older brother who was an officer in the Russian army. He was killed in Chechnya during one of the flare-ups in 2019."

"Huh. If Islamic separatists killed him, then he'd likely not be a jihad-ist, correct? That would mean we are dealing with something different. Possibly a Russian-sponsored government plot?"

"That's the rub, sir. The reports we have are that Lebedev's brother was killed after attacking Russian soldiers in a suicide attack."

"A blue-on-blue attack?" Witt said. "So this may have links to the Caucasus Province, or some other Islamic extremist group in Chechnya. Where is Lebedev now? Do we know?"

"He flew to Moscow a few days ago. That's all we know."

"We need to find out everything we can about this guy. I'll alert the CIA and the NSA, and we'll see what they can find out from the Russians. Though don't hold your breath. Putin is likely going to take pleasure in whatever pain we're experiencing over this."

"Sir," Jensen said, "there's more. Lebedev used a fake ID to defeat the security system and access the database that houses GenomeX's genetic sequence data, which includes a host of nasty and very dangerous bio-logical agents." He left the rest unsaid.

Witt finished the thought. "And you think he may have provided one or more of these to whoever is behind the orange juice attack."

"Possibly, yes," Gabriel answered. "Lebedev had access to the sequences for a number of deadly antibiotic-resistant bacteria—so-called superbugs."

"That doesn't sound good," said Witt.

"It's not," Gabriel said. "A superbug killed a bunch of people in New York City several years ago. The hospitals were powerless to stop it, and no drugs could arrest the spread of the bacteria."

"Jesus! I remember that. Is that what we're talking about here?"

"Yes."

Witt thought for a few moments. "So walk me through how it would work."

Jensen nodded for Gabriel to take the question. "Well, it would work a lot like the medfly and the botulinum toxin, only the target would be people and not crops. How they'd do it depends on what vector they chose to transmit the bacteria. I'd probably use mosquitoes, which can be engineered to synthesize the bacteria and transmit it to people when they bite them—a direct line to the bloodstream. Once these people are infected, they become carriers themselves and can spread the bacteria to those around them. Voilà, an instant epidemic."

"Fuck!" Witt said, his mind racing, contemplating all the heinous possibilities. "What if this guy smuggled that sequence into Russia? Will they be able to use it against us?"

"Yes and no. Yes, the sequence can be lethal in the wrong hands. But it takes a sophisticated technical capability to use a genetic sequence in an insect that can deliver it. I'd guess there isn't that kind of technical infrastructure in Chechnya. Now, if it turns out that Lebedev is working for the Russian government, it's a different story. I'd be surprised if they didn't have this capability."

Witt nodded. "So let's say one of these superbugs gets unleashed. What would the damage be?"

"Well, as I said, there are no known effective antibiotics against these bugs, so the mortality rate would be above fifty percent, maybe higher. The CDC would be able to give you better numbers on that. The health care system would quickly be overwhelmed. Once the bacteria gets moving, it spreads pretty quickly through human contact, so it will be very hard to quarantine. The damage ultimately depends on how big the initial attack is and in how many different locations."

Witt knew he'd need to brief the president on this. The question was when. He hoped he could hold off for a bit until they knew more. He looked at Jensen. "What's the next step?"

"First we want to pick up the Lebedev trail at George Mason," Jensen said. "That's where he went to school, and I want to learn what we can about his time there. Gabriel knows a scientist who works at the Biomedical Research Lab—a guy he was in Afghanistan with. He'll reach out to see what he knows."

Witt looked at Gabriel and asked, "You think BRL is where the medflies came from?"

"It's certainly possible," Gabriel said. "As I said earlier, there aren't many labs where this work can be safely done at scale—and the Florida attack required a pretty substantial testing and growing operation. And the link between Lebedev and GMU can't be coincidental."

"I don't believe in coincidences," Jensen said.

Witt liked the plan. "Just be damn careful, OK? I don't want to spook the bad guys. And the president wants to keep this under wraps until we have a better idea of what we're dealing with."

"Mum's the word," Jensen said.

CHAPTER TWENTY

Moscow, Russia

FOR THE PAST FEW DAYS, Antonin Lebedev had been in and out of consciousness. His dank cell in the bowels of the Soviet-era Lubyanka prison had no window and no light other than a single bare bulb that burned 24-7. The only way he could tell that time was passing was from the putrid food pushed through a slit in the door three times a day; though since it was always the same—a hard roll and some indeterminate brown slop—it was impossible to tell what was breakfast or lunch or dinner.

Lebedev had known it was risky to return to Grozny, but he'd really had no choice. It was his home, and he'd promised his brother before he left that he'd provide not only the sequences he'd stolen from GenomeX but also the knowledge necessary to utilize them. His brother had martyred himself, after all. This seemed like the least Lebedev could do.

Unfortunately, Lebedev had been picked up as the bus he was riding crossed the Chechen border on its way to Grozny. He'd managed to slip through customs at the Moscow airport and had picked up the bus at the main terminal in the city. He had been dressed like most students, with a backpack and a beanie, and had avoided smoking or doing anything else that would draw attention to him. Everything had gone smoothly until the bus approached the Russian side of the Georgian border. As soon as the bus was directed off the road into a search area, he knew he was in trouble.

It was clear from how his arrest went that they knew he was coming; they made little pretense of searching the other passengers. When Lebedev stepped off the bus, a huge guard carrying a PKM submachine gun grabbed him by his backpack and flung him backward onto the ground. Within seconds he was zip-tied and thrown into the back of a van, headed to the airport for a direct flight back to Moscow on a plane graciously provided by the Federalnaya Sluzhba Bezopasnosti (FSB), the Russian state security service.

Now, as he fluttered his eyes open, he tried to focus on a face hovering inches from his own; he could smell garlic and onion on the man's breath and thought for a moment he might get sick. "Good, you are awake," the man said in a deep, cigarette-stained voice. He grabbed Lebedev by the collar, placing him effortlessly onto a chair at the center of the small cell.

Lebedev looked through the glare of the single light bulb and assessed the man in front of him. He was squat, not more than five feet, five inches tall, with a face as flat as a pancake and ears that looked like saucers. He wore an ill-fitting black suit made of cheap wool rather than the bespoke Savile Row suits of the men in Putin's orbit. It was a sign of his status or lack thereof; he was a midlevel bureaucrat, charged with doing the dirty work. He pulled another chair over and sat in front of Lebedev.

"There are two ways we can do this," the man said. "The first way is that you can tell me everything I want to know, and we can get this over with. I'll put you back on the bus, and you can get on your way." It was a lie, of course, but one that had fooled many a prisoner who was hungry and sleep deprived. "Or, you can decide not to cooperate, in which case I'll have to try and convince you. And I must say, I am very convincing." Again, that cigarette-stained voice, followed this time by a deep, gravelly laugh.

Lebedev's brain was trying to process what he was hearing. His throat was dry, and his head throbbed. He was near panic. "What do you want from me?" he managed to sputter out.

"I want to know why the Americans are so interested in you."

"The Americans? I don't know what you are talking about."

"No? The American embassy seems very concerned about you, Antonin. They've been asking about you for the past few days. They would like to talk to you. Why?"

Lebedev swallowed. "I don't have any idea. I'm just a student."

Igor Alexandrovich Popov shook his head in resignation. "Oh, Antonin. Such a shame."

The man with the pancake face and saucer ears was the third deputy director of the FSB's counterterrorism directorate. Popov was a grinder, a man with little tact and even less ambition to move up the ranks. He enjoyed his role immensely, allowing as it did for him to partake in the gratifying violence of interrogations and intelligence gathering. It also meant he didn't need to negotiate the hyperpoliticized bureaucracy of the "new" Russian state. Popov was a holdover from the KGB days, when disagreements had been less tolerated and more easily dispensed with, and backstabbing had been more literal than figurative.

The case of Antonin Lebedev had ended up on Popov's desk in a most unusual way. A call had come in several days prior from his boss's boss, the first deputy director, who had been called by the director himself. The Americans were inquiring about a Russian citizen who'd emigrated to the United States to attend college and who they believed was on his way back to Russia. He was wanted for questioning in a crime they refused to disclose. That in and of itself would have set off alarm bells within the FSB. But when the US ambassador had divulged the surname of the suspect, he had become of even greater interest.

Lebedev. The name was well known inside the FSB. Vasily, Antonin's older brother, had been a true enemy of the state, a Russian army officer who had turned on his comrades in a suicide terrorist attack that killed a dozen of his fellow soldiers. After the attack, the parents of Antonin and Vasily, knowing they were in the cross hairs of the Russian state, had disappeared. And the younger brother? He had been in America when the attack occurred, a lucky break that had put him out of reach of Russian security.

But no longer. Now he was in Popov's capable hands. His orders had been to extract from Lebedev the reasons the Americans wanted him so badly. Fortunately, Lebedev's laptop had been seized with him and offered a treasure trove of information. IKSI, the FSB's tech division, had spent twenty-four hours dissecting the hard drive and the telltale crumbs from his web activity. Besides the porn and a proclivity for online gaming, they found Lebedev's encrypted folders from his time at GenomeX and UC Berkeley, which thus far they'd been unable to crack open.

Popov knew that, whatever they had found, it would have something to do with Lebedev's work on genetics. Popov didn't really understand what that work entailed and had no idea whether it could be important to the Russian state. So, like a good bureaucrat who understood that his job security was directly linked to taking as few risks as possible, Popov brought in an expert to assist him.

That expert was Dr. Mikhail Sokolov, professor of genetics at the prestigious I. M. Sechenov First Moscow State Medical University. Sokolov, the son of a former KGB agent in the old Soviet Union, was often consulted by the FSB on the use of bioterror agents and had proved particularly useful in Syria, where Russian troops occasionally ran into chemical toxins used by the Assad regime against its own people.

"Dr. Sokolov, thank you for coming in," Popov said, pouring tea into silver-ringed glass cups.

"Igor Alexandrovich, it is my pleasure. My father had an office on this floor, and as a boy I loved to come and visit him," he said, his voice trailing wistfully off. "Those were simpler times."

Popov grunted his agreement. "Speaking of simple, I have something to show you that my simple mind cannot understand," he said, reaching for a folder on his desk. "Take a look."

Sokolov opened the folder and started leafing through the pages, which included metadata on work that Lebedev had done at GenomeX. "Where did you get this?"

"It comes from a detainee who worked in America on genetics of some sort."

"Igor, this is not just genetics," Sokolov said, holding up some of the pages. "This is work being done at one of the world's leading genomic engineering firms in Silicon Valley."

Popov stared at Sokolov, his flat face showing incomprehension. "And?"

"And we've been trying to do this kind of science for the past several years with only moderate success," Sokolov said. He looked again at files. "GenomeX does this kind of genetic engineering work on different bacteria, viruses, and toxins. Among other uses, these can be used to genetically create new weapons for transmitting them."

Popov was again confused. "Weapons using bacteria and viruses?"

"Yes, Igor," Sokolov said, trying to calm himself. "They can be used to modify insects to carry disease, to poison crops or people. It's cutting-edge technology!"

It suddenly dawned on Popov that if what Sokolov was telling him was true, how he handled Lebedev could make or break his career. While he had no aspirations to climb higher in the ranks of the FSB, he certainly had no interest in losing his current position.

"I want to know more about this detainee," Sokolov said. "There is no telling what he knows. He's a potential gold mine!"

"Perhaps you want to join me in questioning him, then?"

Sokolov had no stomach for the rough stuff and was not interested in seeing pain inflicted. He knew how the FSB worked. But at the same time, he was salivating over the information he might learn. It could make his career and catapult him into the top echelons of Russian science. He swallowed hard. "*Da*," he said finally.

CHAPTER TWENTY-ONE

Moscow, Russia

ANTONIN LEBEDEV SOON REGRETTED HIS DECISION not to answer any of Popov's questions. Before he went to America, he'd gone through a terror group's version of boot camp, which was nothing like that of a modern military. There he'd learned to fire an AK, perfected a few self-defense moves, and done a lot of calisthenics. But he hadn't gotten any help in knowing how to resist a determined interrogator.

Now he stood naked in the center of his cell, his arms above his head, wrists shackled by a chain to a pair of eyebolts anchored in the concrete ceiling. The temperature in the room had been cooled to seven degrees Celsius; the Soviets had learned through testing that being cold was more uncomfortable than being hot, and that naked prisoners in temperatures below ten degrees Celcius tended to crack much more quickly than they otherwise would. Lebedev had long ago lost feeling in his hands, and his knees were shaking, both from the cold and from fatigue. Standing on his tiptoes, he could briefly alleviate the pressure on his arms. How long he'd be able to keep it up was anyone's guess.

Popov's interrogation plan for Lebedev was to walk a fine line; he wanted to break Lebedev but not kill him. Based on what Sokolov had told Popov, the prisoner was a resource that could be extremely valuable to the Russian state. If something were to happen to Lebedev—if he were to suffer brain damage or paralysis or even death—Popov would have failed.

"Wake him up!" Popov yelled to the guard.

The guard walked over to Lebedev and threw ice water on his face, attempting to get him out of his stupor. The cold liquid braced him and caused him to flinch, which in turn shot sharp pains up his arms. He opened his eyes and attempted to spit on the guard, but his mouth was dry, and spittle ended up on his chin.

"Let's try this again," Popov said with a hint of pleasure in his voice. They'd slowly extracted information about Lebedev's work at GenomeX and confirmed that the files on his laptop were genetic sequences for a variety of viruses and bacteria. But they still didn't know whom he was working for.

"What were you going to do with the information on your computer?" Popov asked.

Lebedev didn't respond, so Popov nodded at the guard. With a swift motion, the guard pulled down on the chain, lifting Lebedev off the ground. He screamed in pain before the guard let him back down.

"Answer me!" Popov shouted.

In an instant, as if a switch had been flipped in his mind, Lebedev knew it was over. He'd done his best to resist and knew that Allah would forgive him. He'd have preferred they just kill him, but he knew they weren't going to do that.

"I—I was taking it back to Chechnya," Lebedev sputtered.

Popov laughed. "*Da*, we know that. Whom are you working with?"

Lebedev could feel the pressure mount on his arms as the guard slowly, inexorably pulled on the chain. "Baseyev," Lebedev said, his voice almost inaudible.

Popov knew the name all too well. Aslan Baseyev, terrorist, leader of the Caucasus Province, and enemy of the Russian state. "And what was Baseyev going to do with the information?"

Lebedev swallowed hard. "I don't know."

Again, pressure on his arms increased until his toes were barely touching the floor. The pain was excruciating. "OK! He was going to use it against you."

Popov looked back at Sokolov, raising one of his caterpillar-sized eyebrows. Sokolov then walked forward from the back of the room.

"Perhaps they were working with another government, maybe North Korea or China. But they couldn't do this work from Chechnya," he whispered to Popov. "It's too sophisticated."

Popov nodded. "How was Baseyev going to use it against us?"

Lebedev was hyperventilating. "I really don't know! He said that he had found a way. Al-Baghdadi had found a way."

The name al-Baghdadi sent shockwaves through the tiny cell. Popov pounced on it. "Is al-Baghdadi working with Baseyev? In Chechnya?"

Popov nodded at the guard, who again put a slight bit of pressure on the chains binding Lebedev. "Yes!" Lebedev shouted. "Please stop! He's in Chechnya. They are working together!"

"*Da*, good," Popov said, nodding again to the guard, this time signaling him to release the tension. "Would you like a drink of water?"

Lebedev nodded. He was so thirsty. Popov motioned for the guard to give Lebedev water from a cup; he drank it hungrily. "Why did you leave America?" Popov asked.

"Because our plot was in motion, and they would have found me."

"Plot?" Popov asked. "What plot?"

"Orange juice," Lebedev rasped. And suddenly the pieces began to fall into place in Popov's simple mind.

"The toxic orange juice in Florida?"

"Yes."

Popov smiled. This was getting very interesting. The Americans were under attack from a weapon that he now potentially held the blueprint for. And he was going to be able to tell the director of the FSB that the leader of ISIS was now operating right in Chechnya. This would be a feather in the cap of the FSB and a great pretext for President Putin to launch another strike on Chechnya.

"OK," Popov rasped. "Let's get you some food. That's enough for now."

CHAPTER TWENTY-TWO

Manassas, Virginia

THE BUG WING INSIDE BRL had always been a place of refuge for Adnan Mishner; it was behind secure doors, a place where access was permitted for only a select few and where he could work in solitude. His only companion was his ever-present music—on this day a techno dance mix—pumped into his brain by custom Bluetooth headphones. The beat of the bass put him into a trance that enabled him to block out other noises inside his head. Those noises, like fingernails on a chalkboard, were starting to drive him crazy.

It had been several months since he'd provided the first of the vector vessels to Bashera for use on the Florida citrus fields. Adnan had at first viewed that task with clinical objectivity; he'd been more concerned about the flies themselves than the people they were going to poison. But then people started getting sick, and a few even died. Suddenly it didn't seem so clinical any longer. But he felt trapped, committed to a cause he'd convinced himself was worth sacrificing everything for. Committed to a woman who had no reservations about her mission and who looked at it as central to their life together. Theirs was a relationship bonded by her passion; it was seductive to Adnan in ways he couldn't fully comprehend and felt powerless to resist.

Adnan's work on their mission was now largely done; the last of the vectors he'd created were in Bashera's hands. He often wondered what would happen to him once his usefulness was over; his heart told him that Haniya wanted him for who he was and not what he could do for her. But his head was less sure.

"Dr. Mishner, there's a visitor here for you," came a voice over the loudspeaker in the lab.

When Adnan didn't answer right away, a message was sent to his computer screen. When that failed, a runner was sent to enter the airlock and bang on the inner glass door of his lab. Finally, Adnan saw the movement outside the door and removed his headphones. He walked to the door and pressed the intercom button. "Yes?"

"We have a visitor for you in reception."

Adnan looked at the clock on the wall. It was already late afternoon. "A visitor? I'm not expecting anyone."

The young girl, an intern from GMU, looked at Adnan through the green-tinted glass and shrugged. "You have a visitor," she repeated.

"OK," he said. "I'll be right there."

He removed his glasses and smoothed out his hair. He then left the Bug Wing and headed for the front desk. As he opened the door, he saw a man wearing jeans and a brown corduroy coat. He looked vaguely familiar.

"Can I help you?" Adnan asked.

The man approached him. "Hello, Adnan."

The voice was familiar. Recognition slowly dawned on him. "Gabriel Marx?"

"In the flesh," Gabriel said, holding out his hand. "It's been what? Six years?"

Adnan's stomach was suddenly in his throat. "What do you want?" he said. It came out more brusquely than he'd intended.

Gabriel was a bit taken aback. "Nice to see you too."

Adnan gamely tried to recover. "Sorry, I meant what are you doing here? In Virginia."

"I was in DC on some business and thought I'd come by. You know, to see my old haunt."

"Oh," he said. He wasn't sure what else to say.

They stood staring at each other. Finally, Gabriel said, "Can we grab a cup of coffee?"

Adnan looked at his watch. "I actually don't have time right now. I'm on a deadline," he lied.

"No problem. I'll be in town for a few days. How about tomorrow morning?"

"Sure, I guess."

"Nine o'clock OK?"

"Sure, I guess."

"OK then," Gabriel said, nodding at Adnan. "See you tomorrow."

Adnan watched him walk out the front door, his eyes following Gabriel all the way to the parking lot. There he met a man in a suit and tie. They talked for a few minutes and then got in a car. The man in the suit was driving.

"Fuck," Adnan said under his breath. He watched the sedan until it left the parking lot and then walked quickly back to the sanctity of his lab. He fumbled with his key card and slammed the airtight door behind him.

"What the fuck is he doing here?" he yelled at the top of his lungs. He paced quickly back in forth. His mind was racing. Gabriel had been a contractor for the CIA and had also done work for Homeland Security. Adnan hadn't seen him since they'd returned from Afghanistan, and they hadn't gotten along well when they were there. They weren't friends.

Adnan instinctively knew something was very wrong. He sat down at his computer and realized that he might end up having to leave in a hurry. He spent the next hour and a half getting everything he needed out of his office.

By the time he got home that evening, Adnan was in a state of panic mixed with anxiety. He looked around his house and realized he was ill prepared for this moment. Where to start? What to take with him? He cursed himself for not putting together a list of the things he and Haniya would need to start their new life in Egypt.

He looked at his watch and knew he had a half hour before Haniya came over for dinner. He went into his study and uploaded a single file from a thumb drive to his Amazon cloud account. Once that was done, he signed off and walked into the kitchen. He put the thumb drive in the microwave, set it to run for thirty seconds, and turned it on. Sparks flew and smoke filled the inside, and when the thirty seconds were complete, the plastic case was nothing but a melted glob. He then went to the bathroom and flushed it down the toilet.

Adnan was in his closet rifling through his clothing when Haniya arrived. She poked her head into the closet and was shocked at the mess he'd made. "Adnan, what are you doing?"

"I'm packing! We must get ready to go."

"What are you talking about?"

"They're on to me! To us! We must go now to Egypt like we planned!"

Haniya was trying to comprehend everything she was hearing. "Wait, wait. What? Who's on to us?"

"The government. Homeland Security. The FBI. I'm not sure which one. But I know they know!"

"Adnan, my sweet, come sit down," she said, leading him to the bed. "Calm yourself, and tell me what's going on."

Adnan took a few breaths. Just having Haniya there was making him feel better. "I got a visit from an old friend today. He came to the lab."

"Oh? What friend is that?"

"His name is Gabriel. He and I were in Afghanistan together."

"Really?" Haniya asked. "What did he do in Afghanistan?"

"He and I worked with the vectors. He worked for the CIA then. Now I'm pretty sure he's working with the government."

Haniya was now clearly getting agitated. "What did he want?"

"I didn't talk to him. We are meeting tomorrow morning at 9:00 a.m. But I think he wants to talk about the medflies."

"How do you know that, Adnan?"

"I don't know. It's just a feeling I have. He knows this is work I've done in the past. He's figured it all out."

"*Ya Allah!* You can't really know that! Maybe he just wanted to see how you were doing. Maybe it's just a social call."

"No, it's not social, Haniya, my love. We aren't friends. He was there with another agent. I know he wants to talk about the medflies."

"But how? How can that be?"

"I don't know!"

Haniya's mind was racing through the possibilities and the risks. "Adnan, why don't you meet with him and tell him nothing? Just be pleasant. Talk about Afghanistan . . ."

Adnan started to shake at the mere suggestion that he meet with Gabriel. Haniya looked into his eyes and could see panic. She knew at that moment that it was hopeless. "My sweet, are you packed for our journey?"

Adnan smiled. "I think so. I'm not sure what to bring."

"Just what you can carry. Bashera will take care of us."

"When will we leave? Now?"

"No, my love. Not now. Let's have dinner and get a good night's sleep. We'll leave first thing in the morning. I'll text Bashera and let him know to put our plans in motion."

Adnan suddenly relaxed. "There's leftover lamb in the refrigerator. We can heat that up."

Later that night as Adnan slept, Haniya lay awake, her mind racing. What was she feeling? She didn't really know. She looked over at her boyfriend, a man she'd professed her love to and agreed to be with forever, and felt nothing. Love? Hardly. Pity? Some. Contempt? Absolutely. He was weak. A man who crumbled under pressure. A man she could never respect.

Haniya rolled over to Adnan and spooned him in a soft embrace and whispered sweetly in his ear in Arabic. "Our Lord, forgive us our sins and anything we may have done that transgressed our duty. . . ."

And then, with a practiced stroke, she dragged a blade across Adnan's throat, pressing deeply into sinew and bone. By the time he could react, she'd cleanly severed his carotid artery; with every beat of his dying heart, he spilled a river of blood onto the sheets. Within a few seconds, his heart became still. Haniya stared at him through the darkness and waited until she was sure he was dead. She then kissed him on the forehead and softly said, "*Allahu akbar.*"

CHAPTER TWENTY-THREE

Manassas, Virginia

LEE JENSEN PULLED INTO THE BRL PARKING LOT at precisely 8:55 a.m. Gabriel hadn't slept well the night before, and he was sipping his third Starbucks coffee out of a paper cup. He'd gone over the list of questions he was going to ask Adnan and had practiced the casual way he was going to ask them. This was to be, in Jensen's words, a "noninterrogation interrogation." Gabriel looked nervous and clearly didn't want to blow it. They knew this would be their best chance to get information about what was going on at BRL before the FBI came and dropped a huge hammer on the investigation.

Jensen looked at Gabriel and gave him a thumbs-up. "You good?"

"I think so," Gabriel said, taking a final swig of his coffee. He unhooked his seat belt and opened the passenger door. Before getting out he asked, "Any final thoughts?"

"May the Force be with you," Jensen said.

"Funny," Gabriel said, smiling.

He entered the BRL lobby and smiled at the receptionist, the same one whom he'd talked to the previous day. "Good morning," he said. "Can you ring Dr. Mishner and tell him Gabriel Marx is here for him?"

"Of course, though I don't think that he's in yet. Let me check," she said, picking up the phone. It rang a dozen times with no answer. "Do you want to have a seat? I'll let you know as soon as he gets in." Gabriel knew that employees entered through a separate entrance at the side of the building and that he wouldn't know when Adnan arrived unless he was told.

"OK, thanks," Gabriel took a seat in the lobby area and looked at his watch, an Omega Speedmaster that Claire had given him as a birthday present the previous year. It was 9:05 a.m. From the coffee table in front of him, he picked up the *Washington Post*, one of the few daily newspapers that still published a hard-copy edition, and read the headlines: "China Blockade of Taiwan Entering Second Week," "Cooperman to Visit Beijing as Crisis Grows," "Unemployment Remains Steady at 8%." He tossed the front page aside and reached for the sports section. The last thing he needed now was to get his mind wrapped up in geopolitics.

After more than an hour had gone by with no sign of Adnan, Gabriel stepped outside and walked into the parking lot. It was a hot summer day with high humidity, and by the time he got to Jensen's car, Gabriel was already sweating.

Jensen, who was sitting in his car with the AC on listening to a podcast of TED Talks, rolled down the window and asked, "What's up?"

"He's a no-show. I wonder if this is a sign."

"A sign of what? That he doesn't like you?"

"Funny. Yes, and maybe he's got something to hide."

"How long do you want to give it?"

Gabriel again looked at his watch. It was 10:25. "Can you get his home address?"

"Is the pope Catholic? I work for Homeland Security. I can get anyone's address," Jensen said, punching Adnan's name into his iPhone. After a few seconds, it came back with an address. "He lives on Dean Park Lane in Manassas. It's less than ten minutes from here."

Gabriel went around to the passenger side of the car and got in. "Let's roll."

As Jensen pulled out onto Wellington Road, Gabriel noticed a sign for the Manassas National Battlefield Park, the site of the First and Second Battles of Bull Run during the Civil War. He wondered how many men had died on the land surrounding the BRL; how ironic, he thought, that they were now chasing a weapon made up of DNA-altered insects on the hallowed ground where men killed by black powder guns and steel swords.

Adnan's house sat on a tidy street full of ranch-style homes with picket fences. They pulled up to the curb, and Jensen turned off the ignition. There was a car in the driveway.

"Let's run the plate and see if it's Adnan's," Gabriel said.

"You're getting the hang of this cop stuff, my friend," Jensen said. He punched in the car's Virginia plate number, and it came back instantly. "It's his," Jensen announced.

Gabriel nodded. "Now what?"

"We knock on the door."

They walked up the brick drive and approached the front door. Jensen took out his DHS badge and moved to the left of the door to look through the picture window. The inside was dark, and he couldn't see much. He stayed to the side of the door and rapped his knuckles hard on the wood.

"Homeland Security!" he yelled. "Open up!"

They waited for a few moments, and Jensen repeated the drill. There was no answer. Gabriel then put his hands on the doorknob to see if the door was locked. To his surprise, it gave way. Pushing the door open with his foot, Jensen again yelled, "Homeland Security! Anybody home?"

When there again was no answer, Jensen stepped into the foyer. He looked at Gabriel. "We're on thin ice here. We don't have a warrant and really should back off now and get one. But if you are a friend who is concerned about his welfare, we can call this a welfare check. Are you a friend concerned about his welfare?"

Gabriel nodded with a slight smile. "Yes I am."

Jensen stepped farther into the house and repeatedly called out, "Homeland Security!" They moved through the living room and checked out the kitchen. There were dirty plates on the counter with food still on them. They then moved down the hall to the bedrooms.

Jensen was in the lead and pushed open the door to the master bedroom. He could immediately see a form in the bed lying on its side. He yelled, "Hello! Homeland Security!" There was no movement. He flipped on the lights and stepped in.

"Uh oh," Jensen said. They approached the bed and found Adnan staring blankly toward the ceiling, his head twisted grotesquely in a way that accentuated the gaping wound in his neck. Blood had soaked the sheets and the mattress and had dried a deep shade of purple.

"Jesus Christ!" Gabriel blurted. He'd seen a lot of dead bodies in Iraq, but this was different. Bile quickly rose up from his stomach.

Jensen instinctively knew Gabriel might get sick. "If you're gonna hurl, do it outside and not in the bathroom. I don't want to be accused of contaminating the crime scene!"

Gabriel nodded and ran from the room and out the front door. He promptly dropped to his knees and threw up on the front lawn.

Jensen followed him out and handed him a handkerchief. "Don't feel bad. Happens to everyone who isn't used to seeing crime scenes. And that was a particularly nasty one."

Gabriel wiped his mouth and stood. He started to hand the handkerchief back to Jensen, who quickly said, "It's a gift."

After a moment, Jensen said, "Well, this is going to change things, my friend. We're going to have to call this in. It's gonna be a murder investigation. If we're lucky, we'll only have to deal with the local cops. But eventually the Fibbies are gonna get involved."

"Fibbies?"

"G-men. Feds. FBI."

Gabriel nodded. "Listen, I don't want to put you in a tough spot here, but before you call this in, I want to go back in there and see what we can find. Maybe he's left notes, paper work, laptop. If we leave it for the police, we'll never get a crack at it."

Jensen looked around, noticed that the streets were fairly empty. "I like the way you think," he said. He pulled out a pair of disposable gloves and handed them to Gabriel. "Here, put these on."

※

Within the space of two hours, the house on Dean Park Lane was a hive of police activity. Yellow tape cordoned off the house, and a uniformed Manassas police officer was guarding access to the crime scene. Gabriel and Lee Jensen stood just outside the tape, leaning on their car. They were waiting for the local head of homicide to show up.

Just then Jensen's phone buzzed. "Go," he barked.

"I just got off the phone with the president," Jason Witt said. "She's willing to hold off on the FBI for another day or two."

"Got it," Jensen said. "So we've got what? Thirty-six hours?"

"Tops. You need to get going on this as fast as possible."

"I need two things. Can you get us a warrant to search Adnan's lab without creating a ruckus?"

Witt sighed. "I've got a judge who owes me a favor. I'll see if he'll keep it under seal. What's the second thing?"

"I need a computer expert assigned to me. Can you get me Lisa Brooks?"

"OK. I'll call you back," Witt said, and hung up.

Just as Jensen disconnected from Witt, an unmarked sedan pulled up. Three men in suits got out, each with police badges around their necks. The one Jensen assumed to be the in charge was about forty-five years old, with close-cropped salt-and-pepper hair. He gave direction to the detectives with him and immediately zeroed in on Jensen and Gabriel.

"My name's Detective Lankford. You the DHS guys who called this in?" he asked.

"Yep. Special Agent Lee Jensen. This is Gabriel Marx." They quickly shook hands. Lankford then stood very close to Jensen, a ploy to exert dominance over him.

"My chief told me that you'd be poking around here," Lankford said. "I told her that would be a bad idea, but she's the boss. Just do me a favor, OK? Stay clear of my men. We are professionals at this kind of thing, and I want to clear this case as fast as possible."

Jensen had worked with a lot of detectives, and this was about what he'd expected. His strategy was to say yes until he had to say no. "Absolutely. You're in charge. We are going to focus on our little piece of this."

"And what little piece is that?"

"We're interested in what Adnan—uh, the deceased has been working on in his lab."

Lankford grunted. "OK, but I'm not opening up the deceased's lab until we've cleared this scene. Got it?"

"Got it, Chief," Jensen said.

Lankford smirked, turned on his heels, and walked away.

"What do you make of him?" Gabriel asked.

"He's a close talker," Jensen said with a laugh.

CHAPTER TWENTY-FOUR

Washington, DC

"GO AHEAD, BROOKSY, MAKE MY DAY."

Jensen and Lisa Brooks were sitting in a darkened corner of her office while she scanned the contents of Adnan's tablet. She was looking for anything that matched a list of file extensions and keywords that Gabriel had provided them. She was also scanning the list of IP addresses Adnan had been visiting and comparing them with a database of known terrorist-related sites.

"He's been using a Tor browser for some stuff, so not sure we're going to find much in terms of his web browsing," she said.

"That hides the IP addresses he's connecting to, correct?"

"Yeah, it uses what we call an onion-routing system. It involves multiple layers of encryption and instruction designed to shield the original IP address from detection. It then randomly bounces them around the world using a peer-to-peer network of relays run by individuals. The result is that it's virtually impossible to figure out where web searches or messages originate from."

"Perfect," Jensen said.

"Damn, Lee, don't tell me you give up that easy," she replied.

Even in the macho world of Homeland Security, Lisa Brooks stood out. She looked like an athlete (she'd played hockey at Dartmouth and had a scar on her chin to prove it) and smelled like a guy (she'd started using her dad's Old Spice deodorant as a teen and never switched). She was Lee Jensen's kind of agent.

Brooks certainly hadn't started her career with the goal of becoming a computer specialist; in fact, she'd resisted becoming a member of DHS's internal "geek squad" as long as she could. But after she was injured in a training accident on the southern border, she'd been temporarily reassigned from the Houston Field Office to DHS Headquarters. There her bachelor's degree in computer networking caught the attention of the human-resources department, and she was "encouraged" to accept a lateral transfer to the technology and surveillance group—one of the few times that the huge bureaucracy that is Homeland Security got a personnel move correct. That was seven years ago, and Brooks was in the midst of a very successful career.

As the scan completed, she said, "It looks like he uploaded two files last night at 7:14 p.m., one to a blockchain and another, much larger one to an Amazon cloud account. That was his last activity."

"How do you know that he uploaded to a blockchain?" Jensen asked.

"He used a special browser called Blockstack to upload a rather small file to something called the SMRA block."

"The what?"

"SMRA as in S-M-R-A."

"Does that mean anything to you?"

"Not really, no."

At that moment, Gabriel walked into the office. "Does S-M-R-A mean anything to you?" Jensen asked him. "Some kind of bug acronym maybe?"

Gabriel thought about it for a moment. "No," he said. He picked up his iPhone and Googled it. "It's not a word. Or at least not an English word. Maybe an acronym?" He read from the search results. "Society for Magnetic Resonance Angiography? Social Media Research Association? I'm guessing not."

The three were quiet for a moment. Finally, Jensen asked, "So he uploaded a small file to a blockchain and a large file to Amazon. What does that tell us?"

"We can't really know for certain until we access them," Brooks said. "But my guess is that he's stored an encrypted file at Amazon and he uploaded the key to that file to this S-M-R-A blockchain."

"Why would he do that?" Jensen asked.

"It fits how the blockchain works. The blockchain isn't really meant to store actual files. It's a distributed database with an open ledger where all transactions—like digital currency and contracts—are managed and recorded by everyone, making everything transparent."

"That sounds like the opposite of secure to me."

Brooks laughed. "I guess it depends on the kind of security you are looking for. If you want personal privacy, then it's not a good solution. But if you want to ensure nobody can cheat the system, then it's a brilliant solution, because no central authority controls the data. You share it with only those who are in the chain, and everyone knows what's there."

Jensen thought for a moment. "So how does it work? And pretend you're talking to your mother."

Brooks sighed. She was used to having to dumb down technology for her coworkers. "Do you remember Napster?"

"Sure," Jensen said. She looked at Gabriel, who just shook his head.

"Well, Napster was one of the original dot-com companies in the late nineties. It used a peer-to-peer network to allow people to share music without having to pay for it. Basically, people connected to other people's computers to access the music they had available, bypassing the music companies. It ultimately got shut down because the rights owners sued when they couldn't control the distribution of their content."

"OK, but what does that have to do with—"

"Cool your jets. I'm getting there," she said, cutting Jensen off. "The blockchain is also a peer-to-peer concept that doesn't rely on a third party to validate or control the data that is being shared. But unlike Napster, the blockchain is totally secure because you must have a private, cryptographically created key to access only the blocks in the chain you own. In this case, others in the S-M-R-A blockchain have a key to access the block that Adnan added to the chain."

"And we think that block contains the encryption key to the Amazon file," Jensen said.

"Bingo," said Gabriel. "But my understanding is that it's almost impossible to break into, since the blocks are distributed all over the world and there is no central server to hack into. isis has been using this for its communication and funding for the past several years for just that reason."

Brooks paused of a second. "Yes, it's super hard to hack into. But that doesn't mean it's not still vulnerable. For us to know what's in that Amazon file, we need the encryption key that's in the blockchain. And we can get that if we can find another member of the chain. So that's where we need to focus."

"So we start with his known associates and work out from there." Jensen then turned to Gabriel, who'd been looking at the other material they'd taken from Adnan's house. "You come up with anything?"

"Nothing of value. We need to get into his lab."

Just then Jensen's phone buzzed. "Yes? Ok, we'll be right down." He hung up.

"Witt's got our warrant. Let's go."

CHAPTER TWENTY-FIVE

Manassas, Virginia

WHEN THE CARAVAN OF SUVS carrying the DHS team arrived at the BRL parking lot, they were greeted by a cluster of Prince William County and Manassas police cars, along with a couple of vans and more than half a dozen detective sedans. Someone had also called the media, and the local Fox television station was setting up a feed.

"Everyone wants their fifteen minutes of fame," Jensen said as he got out of the car. He knew that this was certainly the biggest crime committed in the area in the past decade, and he was certain that the local authorities were going to want their piece of the action. So he'd asked Witt to call the chiefs of both police departments to make sure they didn't screw up his investigation. Now he was going to see just how much juice the secretary of homeland security had.

Gabriel, Jensen, Brooks, and four other agents approached the scrum of police outside the entrance to the building. The DHS team had put on blue windbreakers with "DHS Police" stenciled on the back. When Detective Lankford saw them, he immediately called out. "You two, Jenkins and Marx!" he said.

Not knowing if he was purposely butchering his name or not, Jensen said, "It's Jensen."

"Right, Jensen. You two go with Detective Carlson. He's going to start in the lab proper and then work his way back to the victim's office."

"I don't think so," Jensen replied. He handed over his warrant. "This is a warrant issued by a federal judge that gives DHS the right to search the lab of the deceased. Do you have a warrant, Detective?"

Lankford smiled. "I sure do," he said, handing it over to Jensen.

Jensen skimmed the particulars. "This warrant says nothing about the lab. It's a general search warrant for the deceased's 'office work area.' An office is an office. A lab is a lab. They're not the same."

"Bullshit. This warrant is valid for the lab, which is where the deceased worked. Furthermore—"

"Detective! Sorry to interrupt. The chief's calling," a police officer said, handing Lankford a cell phone.

Lankford was irritated, but he took the phone. All Jensen and Gabriel could hear was Lankford's half of the conversation, which was more of a series of grunts with a few groans thrown in. Finally, Lankford hung up without a word. He then turned and called out, "Carlson!"

"Yes, sir?" A detective, dressed in a blue jacket and gray slacks, walked over to the group. He looked to be about thirty-five years old and was still in good shape; the years of long days and donuts as a detective hadn't yet taken a toll on him.

"You are going to accompany these gentlemen into the building. You're to stay with them at all times. I want you to carefully watch and record anything they find that you even remotely think could be connected to our murder case." Lankford then turned to Jensen.

"My chief says you win this round, Jenkins," he said, again getting Jensen's name wrong. "But she also said that the agreement she made with your boss is for us to shadow you. So that's what we're gonna do. Are we clear?"

Jensen tried to suppress a smile over the slap down. "Yep," he said. He turned to Gabriel and the others in his team. "Let's go."

They entered the BRL as a group, with the two detectives in tow, and were immediately met by an armed guard. "Can I help you?"

"Yes, you can get out of the way," Jensen barked, flashing his badge. "We have a federal warrant to search these premises."

The guard, a slender man about thirty years old, worked for a private security company and quickly gave way. "No problem, no problem," he said.

Jensen pushed to the front desk. "Who's in charge here?"

"I am," a man said, emerging from a side office. "I'm Dr. William Simons. What is this about?"

"Dr. Simons, we have a warrant to search the lab and office of Dr. Adnan Mishner," Jensen said.

"Adnan? Has he done something wrong?" Simons asked.

"We're not sure yet. That's why we're here."

Simons looked thoroughly confused. "I'll call him now. I'm sure he would want to be here."

Jensen looked over to Detective Carlson, clearly wanting him to address Adnan's murder. "Sir, Dr. Mishner is dead," Carlson said. "He was murdered last night."

"What? How? Where?"

"He was found at home," Carlson said. "That's all I'm able to discuss. We are conducting an investigation, obviously."

Simons looked at the warrant and at Jensen. "Why Homeland Security? Isn't this a matter for the police?"

This time Carlson looked at Jensen. "We are looking into Dr. Mishner's work here at the lab," Jensen said. "That's all I can tell you. Can you please show us the way to his office?"

Simons glanced one last time at the warrant and handed it back to Jensen. Then Simons said, "Right this way."

They followed Simons down a series of hallways to a set of double doors with a sign above that read, "Entomology Vector Research." Simons put his face up to a screen next to the door so his irises could be scanned, and a solenoid buzzed, automatically opening the lock. "We use all biometric security here," he said as he opened the door to a lobby area. It was furnished Spartanly with a worn couch and coffee table. "That's the lab itself," he said, pointing to a pair of large double doors with a biohazard sign attached. "It's a Biosafety Level Two facility, meaning to gain access to the inner area you must wear personal protective equipment including Mylar suits, gloves, and face masks. Our safety protocol requires that a staff member accompany you inside, and not more than two visitors at a time may enter."

"Why is that?" Jensen asked.

"It's because they are working with pathogens that may make you sick," Gabriel interjected. "I worked here a number of years ago with Dr. Mishner. I'm familiar with the lab and how it works."

Simons looked intently at Gabriel to see if he remembered him. "When was that?"

"Early 2020," Gabriel said.

Simons thought for a moment. "I remember that project very well. Caused quite a stir among the faculty. They didn't much like supporting U.S. policy in Afghanistan."

"Where's the office?" Jensen said, interrupting the jaunt down memory lane.

Simons motioned to a hallway with a half-dozen doors off it, most of them closed. "Adnan's office is the third on the left," he said as he moved down the hallway. He used a key to unlock it. As he pushed the door open, his breath caught. "Oh my," he said.

Jensen took a half step into the office. It was a mess; papers were everywhere, and the desk's drawers were turned over onto the floor. The dock for Adnan's computer was there, but there was no PC. "Did Dr. Mishner use a BRL computer?"

"He did, but only in the lab and only to run his experiments. We all use our own devices now and store everything in the cloud. So he likely used his tablet for everything else."

Jensen grunted. That was disappointing because they'd already scanned Adnan's tablet. It made it even more critical that they get into his Amazon cloud account. "OK, thanks, Dr. Simons. We'll take it from here."

Simons started to say something but then thought better of it. "Call me when you finish," he said, handing them the keys. "I'll call Dr. Bower and have her come over to accompany you in the lab." And with that, he left.

Jensen watched Simons walk down the hall and then turned to Brooks. "I want you and Gabriel to get into the lab. We need to know if there is anything of value on the computer in there. I'm going to stay here with Detective Carlson and go through the office. Or what's left of it."

As Brooks and Gabriel went to ask Dr. Simons to call Dr. Bower, Jensen started picking up the overturned drawers. "Someone either broke in, or Adnan was looking for something in a hurry," he said. "Given the security what are the chances that someone broke in here?"

Carlson looked around. Poking his head out into the hallway, he noticed surveillance cameras. "I'll go check out the camera feed. That should tell us something."

"Go," Jensen said. He then started sorting through the materials in the office. Most were academic papers that Adnan had written for various journals. It appeared that he'd been looking through his own work from the time he'd written his PhD dissertation to the last set of articles he'd written for publication in various scientific journals. There were also photographs mixed in. One of Adnan at a microscope, one of him in front of a genetic sequencer, and one of him high-fiving a colleague. There were also a few pictures of Adnan in Afghanistan.

Jensen was running his hands inside all the drawers to see if anything had been missed when his fingers caught the edge of a photo. It had become lodged in a crevice on the underside of the desk. With some effort he managed to work it free. "Well, hello there," he said to himself. It was a picture of a young woman. She was smiling at the camera and was wearing a tank top that showed her slender arms while accentuating her large breasts. She was striking. As he studied the image, he realized that he recognized the setting as Adnan's house. Turning the photo over, Jensen could see that it had been printed on a home printer. There was no date. Rather than put the woman's picture with the others, he slid it into his jacket pocket.

By the time Carlson returned, Jensen had finished sorting through the papers. "Got video?" he asked.

"Yep," Carlson said, proffering a CD of the footage. "They've got quite a high-def system here." He took out a small spiral notebook from his pocket. "Adnan was in the lab all day and then entered his office at 4:30 p.m. the day of the murder and left at 6:00 p.m. No one else came or went after that. When he left he was carrying a briefcase."

"What about his body language?" Jensen asked. "Was he rushing?"

Carlson thought for a moment. "He looked pretty frazzled. His hair was mussed. He wasn't running or anything. But he seemed stressed."

"So he was the last in and out. That's not a surprise given what I've found," Jensen said. "This is all Adnan's work," he said motioning to the papers and photos on the desk.

Carlson looked at the material and picked up one of the photos. "What do you make of it?"

"I think he left here knowing he wasn't coming back and wanted to remind himself of the brilliant career he'd had."

"So you think he knew he was gonna get killed?"

"Maybe. Or maybe he thought he was leaving town and not coming back."

Carlson nodded. Seemed plausible to him. He took pictures with his phone of everything that they'd found. He knew Lankford would want to know what they'd come across. "Now what?"

"We'll pack all this up and do a deeper dive back at DHS. And I'll make sure you get a complete accounting of it. Now let's see what's going on in the lab."

CHAPTER TWENTY-SIX

Manassas, Virginia

When Gabriel and Brooks arrived at the entrance to the lab, they were met by a tall, striking redheaded woman in a white lab coat. She wore a blue dress over black tights and ankle-high black boots. She put out her hand and said, "I'm Dr. Bower. I work in the infectious disease wing. Dr. Simons said you need an escorted tour of Vector Research?"

"We don't need a tour. I worked in VR for a time, so I know the lab well," Gabriel said, a bit more stridently than he'd intended. "What I mean is, we need an escort per regulations."

Dr. Bower looked at Gabriel curiously but finally said, "OK. You'll need to suit up." She presented her face to the scanner next to the lab door, and a light turned green; she then pulled the door open. "Follow me," she said.

They entered a holding area off which there was a small locker room. Gabriel immediately went in and took one of the white Mylar suits off the wall. It was like a big version of the onesies that babies wear and included attached booties.

"Anything my size?" Brooks asked Dr. Bower.

"I think so," she said, pulling open one of the cabinets. "Here's a female medium," she said, handing a suit over to Brooks. "This should fit."

They quickly suited up and put on gloves and face masks that shielded their eyes and mouths. Then Dr. Bower read them the standard rules and regulations. "Are either of you suffering from any immunosuppressant diseases such as HIV?"

Both Brooks and Gabriel shook their heads. "OK. You are about to enter a BSL-2 lab that deals with agents that are potentially hazardous. Most of the infectious agents are behind biological safety cabinets, which are essentially glass-enclosed boxes with built-in gloves for handling materials inside. But you are better off being safe than sorry. So treat everything as if it has cooties." Dr. Bower smiled and put on her own mask. "Follow me."

They proceeded to a large interior door made of stainless steel with a small window in the center. On it was a big sign that said, "BSL-2 Lab: Restricted Access," along with a big orange sign that said, "Biohazard." Bower approached a security screen, where she punched in a code. "The iris scanner doesn't work well with these shields on," she said in a muffled voice. In an instant the door opened, and they walked into an air lock; the door to the lab itself couldn't be opened until the outer door to the air lock was sealed tight. Once they were all in, a green light flashed indicating that it was safe to proceed. With a whoosh, the lab door, under negative pressure to ensure that no air would escape, opened inward.

The lab looked exactly as Gabriel remembered it. There were parallel workbenches that ran the length of the room on top of which sat microscopes, genetic sequencers, and autoclaves. On the far wall were floor-to-ceiling cabinets that contained test tubes, lab glass, and other vessels for specimen sampling and testing. And on the near wall was a line of biosafety cabinets (BSCs) that looked to be empty. "This is the main work area where the experiments are set up," Dr. Bower said. "For DNA work, physical samples of bacteria and viral agents are handled in the BSCs, and then they are genetically sequenced and analyzed at the bench. We then slice and splice new code snippets into larva DNA, and we then incubate the larvae in our vector tanks. They stay in the tanks until we are done with our experiments, we deploy them, or they die from natural causes."

"Wow, this is unbelievable," Brooks said. "I had no idea. This is like science fiction!"

"It's science, but it's not fiction," Gabriel said. "Let's check out the computer."

Brooks nodded and went over to the terminal on one of the benches. She powered it up and motioned for Dr. Bower to come over. "Can you use your credential to sign in?"

Bower hesitated. She saw it as a violation of professional ethics to access her colleague's lab computer without his knowledge. But she had also clearly heard Dr. Simons tell her to "cooperate fully and give them access to any information they require." So she reluctantly reached over the put in her password.

Brooks did a quick scan of the system and directory and opened up a lab folder with a list of the agents in the sequence database. She motioned Gabriel over for him to take a look.

Nipah
Dengue fever
Ebola
Rift Valley fever
Yellow fever
Zika
Malaria
Japanese encephalitis
West Nile virus
Sandfly fever
Crimean-Congo haemorrhagic fever
Lyme disease
Typhus and louse-borne relapsing fever

"Dr. Bower, can you take a look at this?" Gabriel asked.

Bower came over and looked at the screen. Her face suddenly showed confusion. "What is this?"

"It looks to me like a shopping list for some pretty gnarly pathogens," he said.

"I—I don't know where these came from. This lab doesn't work with most of these. Lyme disease and sandfly fever are the only ones approved for a BSL-2 lab like this one. The rest of those are restricted to BSL-3 and -4 labs."

"You run a BSL-4 lab, correct? Any chance these sequences could have come from there?"

"No chance. We have twenty-four-hour surveillance, and someone is in the lab 24-7."

"Could they come from anyplace else?" asked Brooks. "Isn't there a public database where scientists upload genetic sequences for research?"

"It's called GenBank," Dr. Bower answered. "The answer is yes and no. GenBank has sequence data for some of these diseases, but not all of them and they are not always complete. To really ensure quality and efficacy you want to use your own sequence data."

"And accessing GenBank creates a trail, correct?" Gabriel asked. "So if you were concerned about secrecy that wouldn't be the way to go."

"I guess not," Bower said, a hint of confusion in her voice.

Gabriel nodded and asked Brooks to copy the folder and upload it to a cloud account set up for this purpose. In thirty seconds it was done.

Gabriel then went into the room that housed the vector tanks to see the lab's current insect inventory. To his surprise most of them were empty; there were no Mediterranean fruit flies and thus no direct link to the Florida citrus attack. Just as it seemed he'd reached a dead end, Gabriel noticed one tank at the back of the room filled with *Aedes taeniorhynchus*, more commonly known as the black salt marsh mosquito. Gabriel remembered the lab as focusing on a wide variety of insects, including many rare and obscure species from around the world. The presence of a single tank with a fairly common mosquito such as the black salt marsh seemed odd to him, and he made a mental note to ask Dr. Simons about it.

Gabriel returned to the main lab room and raised his index finder, circling it as if to say, "Wrap it up," and proceeded back into the air lock. He waited for Brooks and Bower to join him; as soon as the door to the lab shut tight, blue-hued lights turned on, bathing them in high-intensity ultraviolet light that in seconds killed off any bacteria they might have picked up on their suits.

Once they were back in the locker room, Brooks asked, "Well?"

Gabriel didn't want to speak in front of Dr. Bower, so he simply said, "Pretty much as I remembered it. I'd like you to help me review those computer files when we get back to the office."

Dr. Bower put her suit in an airtight hamper and motioned for Gabriel and Brooks to do the same. "I'll show you both out."

Jensen and Detective Carlson were waiting for them with Dr. Simons in the lobby. Jensen could tell from Gabriel's face that they hadn't found the smoking gun they were looking for. But he'd wait until they got into the car to discuss this.

"Did you find what you were looking for?" Dr. Simons asked.

"Not really. But I do have a few questions," Gabriel said. "When was the last time you had medflies in the lab?"

Simons looked at Dr. Bower and then at Gabriel. "I'd have to check. Sometime last year, I believe. Why?"

"Just curious," Gabriel said. "If you could find out, we'd appreciate it."

"OK. What else?"

"I noticed that the vector tanks in there were empty with the exception of the one holding the black salt marsh mosquito. Do you know why the inventory is so low?"

"I wasn't aware that the tanks were empty. The last time I was in there they were full."

"How long ago was that?"

"A month ago. Six weeks, max."

Gabriel thought for a moment. What had Adnan been up to? "Do you know what kind of work Adnan was doing on the black salt marsh?"

Simons shrugged but looked over at Dr. Bower. "I believe he was working with the infectious disease team on something."

"That's your team, right, Dr. Bower?"

"Yes," she said. "To say he is working with my team is overstating it. He has been asking a lot of questions about how viruses are transmitted through the blood to the gut and salivary glands, particularly in mosquitoes. He says that he is preparing for a research project looking at why mosquitoes don't transmit HIV and Ebola but do transmit Zika and West Nile."

Gabriel was trying to digest what he was hearing. "Given that Adnan's lab doesn't work with those kind of pathogens, does that seem strange to you?"

Dr. Bower shrugged. "I guess it is. I didn't think much about it. We don't really pry into our colleagues' research projects."

Gabriel nodded.

"OK. We're done here for now," Jensen said. "Thanks for your cooperation, Dr. Simons."

"It's not like I had a choice," Simons said. "But you're welcome."

🐜

In the car on their way back to DC, Gabriel was quiet. He was thinking through what he'd seen—and not seen—in the lab. Jensen, sensing that Gabriel was troubled by something, said, "Uh oh. I know that look."

"It's not adding up," Gabriel said.

"How so?"

"First, Adnan had complete sequences on his system for diseases that his lab doesn't work with—Zika, dengue, Ebola. I believe those had to come from GenomeX."

"If that's true, there's our connection to Lebedev."

"But the lab was empty of vectors. Except for the black salt marsh."

"And that matters because why?"

"Because the black salt marsh mosquito doesn't really transmit diseases the way *Aedes aegypti* or *Culex pipiens* does. It doesn't fit with the work that Adnan would do at the BRL. It's weird."

"'Weird'? Now there's a scientific term," Jensen said with a laugh.

"Something's not right but I don't know what. How about his office?"

"You saw there were papers everywhere. When I sorted through them, it was like a career retrospective. Papers he'd written, photos of his work, even a few pictures of him in Afghanistan."

"Why did he turn the office inside out? Was he looking for something?" Brooks asked.

"He was," Jensen said. "He was looking for this." He took out the picture of the woman. "This was stuck in a crevice under the desk."

Gabriel took the picture and whistled out loud. "Too beautiful for Adnan. But that sure looks like his house in the background. Who is she?"

Brooks grabbed the picture. "Why would he want this so badly that he'd trash his office? I mean, she's hot, but it's just a picture," said Brooks.

"Because he didn't want us to find it," Jensen answered.

CHAPTER TWENTY-SEVEN

Washington, DC

BY THE TIME THEY GOT BACK TO DHS HEADQUARTERS, Witt was waiting for them. He'd been pacing his office like a caged cat, hoping that the search of Adnan's house and the lab would break the case open. Jensen had been cryptic on the phone: "We have a clue. It could be significant. I'll update you when we get in." When Witt heard the word "clue," he'd immediately thought of the board game he'd played as a kid. "Great, he's bringing me a candlestick," he said to himself when he hung up the phone. "Maybe he'll bring the rope too, and I can hang myself."

As Jensen, Brooks, and Gabriel walked toward the elevator in the underground garage, Witt's assistant met them. "The secretary is waiting for you in his office," she said. Gabriel looked at Jensen and raised an eyebrow.

They rode the elevator to the eighth floor and made a straight line for the double doors of Witt's office. Without knocking, they walked in.

"Did you bring your candlestick?" Witt asked, coming around from his desk.

Jensen looked confused. "What?"

"Never mind," Witt said. "Whaddya got for me?"

"Two things. We found the link between Lebedev and Adnan," Jensen said, telling Witt about the sequences they'd found and their belief that they came from GenomeX.

"Can we prove that, or is it an educated guess?"

"It's an educated guess. But it makes sense given what Lebedev accessed at GenomeX."

"OK," Witt said. "What else?"

Jensen pulled out the picture he'd taken from Adnan's office and handed it to Witt. He then went through the search and what they'd found in detail.

"Do we know who she is?"

"Not a clue. I discreetly showed it to a few of the staff at the BRL, and they'd never seen her before. But that's definitely Adnan's house in the background of the photo."

"OK. Let's get her picture loaded into SPARK as soon as possible. It's a long shot, but maybe we'll find a match. If she's applied for a visa or traveled abroad over the past several years, she'll be in it."

Jensen nodded. "That's going to take time. The last facial recognition search I did with SPARK took three days to complete."

"I'll fast-track it. But let's keep moving," Witt said. "What's our next step?"

"First thing we do is get over to GMU and pick up Lebedev's trail. We need to find out whom he worked with, whom he drank with, where he hung out, and whom he fucked."

Witt nodded. "What are we looking for?"

"Anything and everything that ties him to this plot."

"OK. I'm still waiting to see if the CIA can find something out about his ties to Chechnya. If we can link him to a specific terrorist group there, we might have a better idea of who he was working with here." Witt then looked at Gabriel. "You look pretty beat. You doing OK with all this?"

Gabriel smiled. "Yes, sir."

Witt studied him. "I promised your wife I wouldn't strong-arm you to stay on this longer than you want to. You still in?"

"All the fucking way in," he said, and then added, "sir."

Gabriel's enthusiasm was mostly real. But that night, as he got his first rest in the last thirty-six hours in a tiny hotel room across the street from DHS Headquarters, he struggled to get the image of Adnan out of his mind. Gabriel had not seen death like that since Iraq, and even then, it had usually been nameless, faceless Iraqis whose bodies were grotesquely twisted by the violence that had befallen them. They had seemed like no more than roadkill, random detritus littering the streets. That was the sad reality of war. This—this was something different.

His relationship with Adnan had been brief but intense. They'd worked closely in a lab for a few months, shared a tent in Afghanistan, gotten shot at together, and then separated as quickly as they'd come together. Gabriel hadn't really liked Adnan very much and remembered feeling relieved when their mission in Afghanistan was over. In particular, Gabriel had thought Adnan was hostile to America and was very angry about the war in Iraq. Had those been the musings of a potential jihadist? Or of a disaffected academic who hated George W. Bush? Gabriel didn't yet know.

But this he did know: the list of pathogens he'd found in Adnan's lab represented a tremendous threat to the country. And that wasn't even counting the danger of KPC, which, if synthesized in a mosquito, could create a deadly carrier of antibiotic-resistant bacteria. Gabriel realized that the work he and Adnan had done in Afghanistan had helped to start Adnan down this path, and Gabriel felt partly responsible for it.

CHAPTER TWENTY-EIGHT

Red Bluff, California

THE SMALL HOSPITAL IN RED BLUFF was quiet that Sunday morning when Mary Mills carried her young daughter Sally into the ER. Sally had been unable to eat dinner the night before and was complaining of "seeing two of everything." Mary had thought it was just fatigue, and so she had put her daughter to bed. But at 4:00 a.m. Mary had awoken to the sound of her daughter throwing up. When Mary asked her if she wanted a sip of water, her daughter couldn't speak.

The ER staff, led by Dr. Barton Sewell, immediately knew they were dealing with some kind of neurological problem, but they had no idea what it was. They intubated Sally to clear her airway, gave her a CT scan, and started to run tests on her blood and were able to stabilize her. But it was clear to Dr. Sewell that the little girl was seriously, even gravely, ill.

"Mrs. Wells, can you tell me what Sally has had to eat or drink over the past twenty-four hours?" he asked.

"She had a breakfast of cereal and then ate a normal lunch yesterday of bread with almond butter and honey," Mary said. "It's her favorite sandwich. But she didn't eat dinner because she wasn't feeling well."

Dr. Sewell wrote down what he'd just been told. Red Bluff was in California's almond country, and almond butter was a staple. "How old was the almond butter, and was it refrigerated? Sometimes it can go bad," he asked, even as he knew this was no case of rancid nut butter.

"It was fresh. I'd just bought it that morning from one of the stands outside Addison's." Addison's Farm was one of the largest almond growers in the area.

"Anything else you can tell me?"

"Not really. She got sick so fast. Is she going to be OK?"

Dr. Sewell, who'd worked at Red Bluff Community Hospital for more than twenty years, was worried but tried not to show it. "We're doing everything we can, but we don't have the right equipment here. She needs an ICU with capabilities to handle what looks like some kind of toxic poisoning, and we need to get her to UC San Francisco Medical Center. I'm going to order up a helicopter to transport her."

Back in Atlanta at the Centers for Disease Control and Prevention, Director Ken Smythe was looking at disturbing reports coming from throughout central California. Over the past thirty-six hours, there had been multiple cases of what appeared to be food poisoning with a set of suspiciously familiar symptoms: double vision, muscle paralysis, acute nausea, and high fever. The pattern looked a lot like how the outbreak of botulinum toxin had started on the East Coast, and this worried Smythe a great deal.

Smythe keyed his headset and said, "Call Secretary Witt's mobile phone."

The phone rang on the other end of the line with no answer. Smythe hung up, and he pressed the speed dial for Witt's office number. "Secretary Witt's office," said a cheery voice.

"This is CDC Director Smythe calling for the secretary."

"Yes, sir. I'll connect you."

The assistant got up and knocked on Witt's door and opened it without waiting for a response. "Mr. Secretary, I have Dr. Smythe on the line."

Witt looked up from the report he was reading. Oh, shit, he thought. He picked up the phone.

"Dr. Smythe, what can I do for you?" Witt asked.

"Mr. Secretary, we're starting to get reports coming in from California that look strikingly similar to the ones from the Florida citrus attack. Seven cases of toxic poisoning of unknown origin, including four cases of paralysis and one death."

Witt's stomach sank. This was what he feared. "Damn it! What do we know about it?"

"Not much at the moment. They are all centered in Red Bluff, California, which is almond-growing country. One of the reports indicated that a patient had ingested almond butter just before she got sick."

"Almonds? Seriously? Do they grow on trees? I must admit I have no goddamn idea where almonds come from."

Smythe laughed. "Don't feel badly; I didn't either. I had to ask my staff. Apparently they grow on a tree in the form of a drupe, which is a fancy name for a shell with a seed inside. That seed is the nut."

"God, I just remembered my grandmother used to have bowls of nuts—walnuts, pecans, and almonds—in the shell, with one of those nutcrackers. I loved that thing."

"Mine did too."

"Did the others get sick after eating almonds?"

"We're looking into that now. I just dispatched a team out to California to check things out. I'll let you know as soon as I hear something back. It could be nothing. But given Florida, I think we should be prepared for the worst."

"OK, Ken. Thanks. I'll wait to hear from you." Witt hung up. "Goddamn it!" He then punched in the number for Lee Jensen.

CHAPTER TWENTY-NINE

Fairfax, Virginia

AS WITT DIALED, JENSEN AND GABRIEL WERE SITTING in front of a bank of monitors at the George Mason University registrar's office. They were looking at Antonin Lebedev's academic record. Jensen was tempted to let his phone go to voice mail, but then thought better of it. Their investigation was moving quickly, and he didn't want to miss anything.

"It's Witt," he said as he punched the screen with his index finger. "Yes, sir?"

"I just got off the phone with the CDC," Witt said. "They are tracking another potential attack, this time out in California."

"Shit. What kind of attack?"

"The symptoms are similar to Florida. This time they think it might involve almonds."

"Almonds? As in the nut?" Jensen asked, looking at Gabriel.

"Almonds, as in the nut."

"We're gonna need a bigger boat," Jensen said.

Witt got the *Jaws* reference. "Yep. I'm going to brief the president again shortly. But we should expect that the FBI will be all over this by morning."

"OK, boss."

"What have you found out about Lebedev?"

"Looking at his academic record, it's clear he was a top student. Pretty much earned straight A grades across the board. His thesis was entitled 'The Use of Blockchain in the Communication and Analysis of Genomic Sequencing.'"

"Sounds like our guy."

"Yeah. And get this—his thesis advisor was a professor named Abdul-Azim Bashera."

"Sounds like an Arab to me. What do we know about him?"

"Nothing yet. But I've got Brooks doing a deep background check on him now."

"Good. Keep me posted. And keep digging," he said and disconnected the line.

"What's that about almonds?" Gabriel asked.

Jensen told Gabriel about what the CDC had reported, and as he did, Gabriel's face visibly darkened. "Uh oh. I don't like that look," Jensen said.

"Fucking genius," Gabriel said. "Almonds are the perfect vehicle for this kind of attack. They're a staple ingredient in hundreds of foods, and you can poison virtually the entire crop of the world's almonds in one fell swoop."

"Huh?"

"California grows and exports eighty percent of the world's almond supply—or at least it did before the tariff wars hit the market. But whatever it is now, it's still a huge component of California's agribusiness. So not only do you sicken a lot of people; you cripple the economy at the same time."

Jensen pondered that for a minute. "What kind of insects would be used in an almond attack?"

"Aphids, spider mites, whiteflies. Lots of different species."

Jensen was looking at the time on his phone when it started buzzing. It was Lisa Brooks. "Whaddya got for me?" he asked, putting her on speakerphone.

"Plenty," she said. "Abdul-Azim Bashera came to GMU in 2020 from Turkey, where he was teaching at the American University in Ankara. A Professor Ian Campbell, who at the time was the chair of the Computer Science Department at GMU and who was doing a sabbatical year in Ankara, recruited him. Bashera had arrived in Turkey in 2007 as a refugee from Iraq. His application for employment at the American University says he earned his PhD from Baghdad University and worked for the Coalition Provisional Authority during the occupation. After the CPA disbanded, he wrote that he faced persecution from Shi'ite factions. So he fled to Turkey."

"That makes some sense given the fact that the Shi'ites pretty much took their revenge on the Sunnis during the insurgency," Gabriel said. "Al-Sadr's death squads were pretty damn effective. I was in Iraq during that time. Jensen here was too."

"Well, I contacted a friend I have at State, and he did some digging for me on their database of Iraqis who worked for the CPA. There is no record of him."

"Interesting. How good was their record keeping then? Seems to me it was a shit show under Paul Bremer," Jensen said.

"My contact seems to think they were pretty thorough in vetting Iraqis who worked for the CPA. But, of course, he might have slipped through the cracks."

"Or changed his name," Gabriel said.

"Or lied about his working for the CPA," Jensen added.

The three were quiet for a moment. "What now?" Brooks asked finally.

"Look, if we go after Bashera head on, we're going to tip our hand and he may run," Jensen said. "I'd like to know more about him before we do that. Do we have a photo of him?"

Brooks said, "We do. It's in his immigration file."

"It wouldn't hurt to run his picture by a guy at the CIA that I know," Gabriel said. "We were in Iraq together, and he was responsible for inter-rogating high-value prisoners in the Baath Party we were capturing. You remember the deck of cards?"

"Hell yes, I remember," Jensen said. "Hussein was the ace of spades."

"Right. There were photos of all the Baathist leaders of the Iraqi government on a deck of playing cards. This guy knew all of them. If Bashera was a part of the Hussein regime or working for any of the insurgency groups, he'll likely know him."

"That's worth a try. In the meantime, I'll keep digging into Bashera's records," Brooks said.

"Good," Gabriel said. "Text me his photo, and we'll reconvene in a few hours."

CHAPTER THIRTY

Langley, Virginia

GABRIEL AND LEE JENSEN STOOD before the CIA Memorial Wall, commonly referred to as the "Wall of Stars." There were 132 stars carved into an expanse of gleaming white Alabama marble, each representing a CIA employee killed in the line of service. And underneath the stars, like a sentinel encased in steel and glass, stood the Book of Honor, which, where possible, listed the year of death and name of the deceased. Of the 142 stars, only 105 have names; the other 37 are for people who worked in the shadows and remain secret even in death.

Jensen traced his finger across a page in the Book of Honor until it rested on the name Mark Spalding. "He was a good dude. When we were running nightly raids against al-Qaeda in Iraq, Mark was a rock. His intelligence was always right. I never lost a man when he was involved. It got so I didn't trust anybody else."

"What happened to him?" Gabriel asked.

"One of the informants he was using put on a suicide vest and blew himself up. Killed Mark instantly. Fucking haji. That was a sad day. I was already back in the States when I heard."

Gabriel was about to say something when he felt a presence behind them.

"The bug boy returns," Sam Gaddis said with a laugh. He and Gabriel shook hands.

"I thought for sure they'd have put you out to pasture already," Gabriel said. "When are you going to retire, anyhow?"

Gaddis laughed again. He was a stout man with a white beard and short gray hair in his midsixties. He wore a corduroy sport coat that looked as if it had been bought in 1972 and an open-collared shirt. On his feet was a pair of tan desert combat boots like the ones Gabriel had worn in Iraq, proving an old agency adage that you can take an operative out of the field, but you can't take the field out of the operative. "Shit, twice I've put in my papers, but they won't let me go. ISIS screwed up my retirement plans."

"I bet," Gabriel said. He then introduced Gaddis to Jensen. "Is there someplace we can talk in private?"

"Sure," Gaddis said. They badged in and entered one of the secure meeting rooms on the ground floor. Once they were settled, Gaddis asked Gabriel, "Are you working with DHS now?"

"Sort of. I'm helping out on a case that involves, you know, insects."

Gaddis raised an eyebrow and smiled. "Interesting. Does that have anything to do with orange juice from Florida by chance?"

Gabriel smiled back. There was no use in pretending. Sam Gaddis had helped train him for the Afghan mission and knew all about the capabilities of genetically modified vectors. "Yep," Gabriel said simply.

"I thought so. How can I help?"

Jensen passed his phone displaying a picture of Bashera across the table. "Does this guy look familiar?"

Gaddis stared at the photo for a good minute. "Jesus, you look at enough of these Arabs, and they all look alike. Maybe he looks familiar. Who is it?"

"He says his name is Abdul-Azim Bashera," Jensen said. "He teaches computer science at George Mason University. Came here from Iraq via Turkey. Only we can't find any record of his time in Baghdad."

"Who'd you ask? State?"

"Yep."

"Shit, State couldn't find its own ass with both hands."

Gabriel and Jensen both laughed. "That's why we're here. I was hoping you might be able to ID him," Gabriel said.

"Did you say he got out via Turkey?" Gaddis asked.

"Yes, that's what we understand. He became a professor at the American University in Ankara," Gabriel said.

"No shit? The American University? Now, that's rich," Gaddis said, irony in his voice. He looked again intently at the photo. "Getting out via Turkey is significant. It took cash and influence to get the Kurds in the North to look the other way and allow passage. That's not cheap. So whoever he is, I'd bet he's important."

Jensen and Gabriel looked at each other. Gabriel then asked, "Do you have any records . . . ?"

Just then Gaddis had a glimmer of recognition. "Can you guys hang out here for a bit? I want to go upstairs and look at our database. I think I might be able to find this guy."

"Hell, yes. We can hang out," Gabriel said.

"This is the beginning of a beautiful friendship," Jensen said with a slight Bogart accent.

Gaddis looked at Jensen and then at Gabriel. "Huh?"

"Never mind him," Gabriel said. "We'll wait."

"OK. I'll be back," Gaddis said, this time with a slight Arnold Schwarzenegger accent.

All three of them laughed.

⚜

Gaddis's trip into the archive was an emotionally charged return to the most exciting and frustrating time in his life. He had led the first CIA team into Iraq well before the 2003 invasion; working in the North with the Kurds, he had led a campaign to soften up the Iraqi troops in that area so they'd surrender rather than fight the Americans, an effort that had largely worked to perfection.

But he had also lobbied unsuccessfully to influence the occupation strategy, encouraging the Coalition Provisional Authority not to disband the Iraqi army and indiscriminately purge the government of technocrats and experts that were needed to keep Iraq from falling apart. Ultimately, as history recorded, that effort failed. But as a result, Gaddis's team was charged with chasing down the former Baath Party leaders from Hussein's government who had escaped capture after the US invasion.

As Gaddis paged through files containing images of Hussein's henchmen, he was transported back to those days when the public was clamoring for heads on platters, and the Bush administration was publicly measuring its success via its deck of cards. Gaddis's team had tracked, arrested, interrogated, and killed much of that deck. But a few had gotten away, melting into the wind and through Iraq's porous borders. The idea that Bashera might be one of them was tantalizing to Gaddis. He could feel his pulse quicken, as if he were back in the fight.

Then, clicking on the next-to-last file, he found himself staring at a color image taken by the Iraqi Ministry of Information. The man in the photo wore an olive-green suit with a red tie and had a bushy black moustache instead of a full beard. But the cheeks were similarly pockmarked, and the eyes were the same—black like the night, irises bleeding into the pupils to form single dark masses. In that moment Gaddis felt that same sense of euphoria he'd felt when hunting in Iraq, a sense of anticipation, a feeling that he was about to crack a case wide open.

CHAPTER THIRTY-ONE

Langley, Virginia

GADDIS ENTERED THE GROUND FLOOR CONFERENCE ROOM carrying a manila folder, which he dramatically threw down on the table. He then sat down looking like a cat that had finally caught the canary. He was smiling, wondering how long he could keep them in suspense. Finally, he couldn't hold it in any longer. "Abdul-Azim Rahman."

Gabriel looked at Jensen and then at Gaddis. "Who?"

"That's your guy's real name," he said, opening up the folder. He pulled out the photo and tossed it across the table. "He was Hussein's top computer expert."

Gabriel picked up the photo and stared at it. He then compared it to the photo on Jensen's phone. "It sure looks like the same guy."

"It's the same guy, and we have a ton of info on him. And you aren't going to like what you hear," Gaddis said, picking up the file. "Rahman was born in Samarra, Iraq. His father was a shopkeeper. He was apparently a wiz at school, because he was sent to the Baghdad Military Academy at the age of twelve. From there he joined the Iraqi army, went to Baghdad University, and studied computer science. Got his PhD at the age of twenty-five and promptly went to work for the Ministry of Technology. He was the four of diamonds in our deck," Gaddis said, tossing a photo of the card over to Jensen.

"Jesus," Jensen said. "How in the hell did this guy get away?"

"Wasn't that hard. You guys didn't get to Iraq until later—'07 or '08, right? It was a mess then, but nothing like the clusterfuck under Bremer. He disbanded the entire army and Baath Party over a weekend. They all scattered like cockroaches in the light. We were damn lucky to get the ones we did."

"What else do we know about him?" asked Jensen.

Gaddis silently removed another picture from the file. "This is your guy when he was working for Abu Musab al-Zarqawi, the head of al-Qaeda in Iraq."

"You're shitting us, right?" Gabriel asked, looking at the photo. It had obviously been taken from a drone. The resolution wasn't good, but it did look a lot like Bashera.

"You sure that's him? Kind of hard to tell," Gabriel said.

"It's him," Gaddis said. "And it all makes sense. Many of the high-ranking Baathists turned into Sunni insurgents and fought the Americans and the Shi'ites. You remember the chaos in '05 and '06? It was basically a civil war. Al-Qaeda in Iraq was the most brutal of the bunch, but not the only one. You know, we couldn't figure out how al-Zarqawi was able to avoid detection for so long. We finally killed him in 2006, but damn he was good at hiding from us. Now I think I know why."

"Why?" Gabriel asked.

"The main weakness all these groups had was that we could track their SIGINT—their cell phones and emails. Al-Zarqawi was an exception. He had a bulletproof communication system."

"And you think that Bashera—uh, Rahman—was the reason?"

"I'd bet on it. Hussein was a buffoon in many ways, but the Iraqi regime had very good SIGINT capabilities. Rahman obviously took those with him to al-Qaeda."

"Motherfucker," said Gabriel. "So how do you think he ended up in Turkey?"

"My guess is that when we dropped those five-hundred pound bombs on al-Zarqawi in June of 2006, Rahman saw the writing on the wall. We found Zarqawi using intel gathered from a high-level member of al-Qaeda in Iraq who had been captured alive by the British Special Air Service. So it wasn't Rahman's fault. But there was a leadership purge after al-Zarqawi died, and everyone was suspect."

"So he became Abdul-Azim Bashera and ended up in Turkey."

"Yep. If Rahman had cash—and you can bet he did—he'd have had no problem getting a new passport and safe passage."

"OK, so let's summarize this," Gabriel said. "We have a professor of computer science at GMU who used to work for both Saddam Hussein and al-Qaeda in Iraq. We have a murdered entomologist with Egyptian roots who clearly knew how to weaponize insects. We have another computer scientist who studied under Rahman at GMU and who has disappeared with the genetic sequences for a host of antibiotic-resistant bacteria. And his brother was an Islamic terrorist to boot. And we have her," he said, motioning to Jensen to produce the picture found in Adnan's lab. Jensen handed it to Gaddis.

"Ever seen her before?" Jensen asked Gaddis.

"I wish. But, no."

They sat in silence for a few moments. Finally, Jensen said, "OK, we need to get eyes on Rahman. I don't want him to suddenly disappear. We also need to see if we can get access to his computer. I'll call Witt and see if he can get us a warrant," Jensen said.

"Call him? You can ask him. He's upstairs," Gaddis said.

"He is?"

"I thought you knew. He's meeting with Director Maddox right now."

CHAPTER THIRTY-TWO

Langley, Virginia

THE SEVENTH-FLOOR SUITE OF OFFICES of the director of the Central Intelligence Agency was significantly more luxurious than Witt's office at Homeland Security. Though DHS was far newer, and far bigger, Witt's department got stuck with a hodgepodge of furniture from the alphabet soup of agencies it had been created from—Secret Service, FEMA, US Coast Guard, INS, and a handful of others. The D/CIA, on the other hand, had leather couches facing a wall of original artwork, and a highly polished ebony conference table that you could see your reflection in.

"Thanks for coming over, Jason," Anne Maddox said. She was in her midfifties, with blond hair and bright blue eyes. She wore a jet-black suit and a cobalt-blue blouse set off by a string of luminescent white pearls. She'd been a career operative in the CIA's Clandestine Service and had spent her career overseas in some of the world's hairiest spots, including Beirut, Islamabad, and Cairo. And even though she'd become a political animal and was thus looking to promote the agency and its interests, Witt thought of her as a straight shooter.

"How's your son doing? He's what? Nineteen now?" she asked. Maddox had never married and had no kids, and she was always interested in other people's children.

"Nate, yes. He's nineteen and a sophomore at Maryland."

"Has he chosen a major yet?"

"Political science. You'd think by now he'd want to be as far from politics as possible. But somehow he's caught the bug."

Maddox was quiet for a moment. "Oh, to be idealistic again."

Witt glanced at his phone and saw that Lee Jensen was calling again—the third call in the past five minutes. Witt dismissed the call and said, "I appreciate whatever you can give me on Lebedev."

"It's not much, I'm afraid," she said, picking up a folder from her desk. "He landed in Moscow's Sheremetyevo airport on an Aeroflot flight from JFK on Saturday, which is now five days ago. He cleared customs and then got on a bus to Grozny and was picked up at the Chechen border three days ago after we alerted the Russians we were looking for him. From there he was brought back to Moscow. We've requested through our ambassador to speak with him, but so far they aren't cooperating."

"Fat chance. The FSB will never let us get to him. Poor bastard."

"He's probably in Lubyanka right now with a car battery clipped to his genitals. All their interrogation techniques are enhanced," Maddox said, her voice trailing off. Witt knew that this was a sore spot for the D/CIA, who'd run a number of CIA dark sites where high-value targets from Iraq were taken for—then legal—enhanced interrogation. When President Cooperman nominated Maddox for D/CIA, she had undergone a brutal grilling from Democratic—and some Republican—senators about her role. It had left wounds that were still fresh.

Just then Maddox's assistant entered the room. "Director, Sam Gaddis is here with an Agent Jensen from Homeland Security and another gentleman."

"Were you expecting a visitor?" Maddox asked Witt.

"No, he's leading this investigation," Witt said. "But I didn't know he was here."

"Well, I've known Sam Gaddis for twenty years, and we've worked together in more than a few shit holes. If he's here, it must be important." Maddox motioned to her aide to show them in.

As Gaddis led the group in, Maddox and Witt stood. "Director Maddox, this is Lee Jensen and Gabriel Marx. Gabriel is our bug expert," Witt said.

"Bug expert. That does sound intriguing. Someday I should like to hear more about that. Unfortunately right now we're short on time."

Witt raised his eyebrow at Jensen signaling for him to proceed. "Yes, ma'am. Agent Gaddis here has moved our investigation forward significantly today by identifying this man," Jensen said, handing her the picture of Abdul-Azim Rahman. Jensen then recounted the dossier Gaddis had on Rahman, including his role in al-Qaeda in Iraq.

"So Abdul-Azim ends up in Turkey after al-Zarqawi is killed," Maddox said. "How does he get pulled back into al-Qaeda? Or does he? Who is he working with?"

"A few minutes ago I chatted with Stan Baker," Gaddis said. "Baker was our station chief in Istanbul for years. He wasn't familiar with Rahman but did say that under Erdogan, ISIS has had a very active cell in Turkey and has pretty much displaced al-Qaeda. So his bet is that Rahman's working with ISIS."

Jensen attempted to string it all together. "So we know Rahman worked for al-Qaeda and now possibly ISIS; he teaches at GMU under an alias and was Lebedev's thesis advisor. We also know that Adnan worked at the BRL, which is a part of GMU. But what's Adnan's connection to Rahman?"

"That's the piece we need to figure out," Gabriel said. "And I bet it has something to do with our mystery woman."

"What woman?" Maddox asked.

Witt showed Maddox the photo found in Adnan's office. "We're doing a SPARK search now. Hopefully we'll know who she is soon."

"What does the CIA know about Lebedev?" Jensen asked Maddox.

Maddox recounted what she'd told Witt earlier about Lebedev being in the hands of the Russian FSB and their interrogators. She then asked, "So my question to you all is this: What are they going to extract from him?"

Jensen motioned for Gabriel to take the question. "I think there's a very real chance that the Russians are going to end up with the keys to a very dangerous weapon of mass destruction. Lebedev is either carrying a genetic sequence to engineer highly infectious antibiotic-resistant bacteria or knows where that sequence has been hidden. Either way, we have to assume that the Russians are going to get their hands on it."

Maddox nodded. Turning to Witt she asked, "Have you told the president that yet?"

"Nope. But I'm going over to the White House now. Before I came to see you, I got word from the CDC that they think there's been another attack, this time in California. So I'm full of good news."

Maddox reached into her desk drawer and pulled out a bottle of scotch. "This is thirty-year-old Famous Grouse. It was the only scotch my daddy ever drank. And he passed that on to me." She poured a couple of fingers into a set of crystal tumblers. Handing one to each person in the office, she clinked her glass against Witt's. "L'chaim."

Jason raised his glass, admiring the caramel colored liquid. "Mud in your eye," he said, and he downed the glass, the warmth filling his chest.

CHAPTER THIRTY-THREE

Washington, DC

JUST BEFORE DINNER, President Jennifer Cooperman sat in the solarium on the third floor of the White House Residence, watching a YouTube video of her daughter's most recent concert in Budapest. Cooperman had kicked off her shoes and had a glass of California Chardonnay in her hand. Her daughter was a violinist touring with the London Philharmonic Orchestra, and the piece she was currently playing—Tchaikovsky's Symphony no. 1—was one of Cooperman's favorites. The president had few moments alone like this, and she cherished her chance to steal away and connect with her daughter's work. The lights were off, and she was sitting in the dark, with only the glow from a rising moon filtering through the solarium's floor-to-ceiling windows.

"Jen? Are you in here?"

Cooperman reluctantly opened her eyes. "Yes, Jonathan. I'm just resting."

Her husband of thirty-one years came and sat next to her. "Tchaikovsky always reminds me of that summer we spent in Zurich. We only had three CDs, and that was the one we listened to the most. Remember?"

Cooperman smiled. They'd spent a summer in Switzerland when Jonathan had done a medical internship at the ETH university. They'd had little money then and lived in a small flat overlooking the Sihl River in the Niederdorf, an old part of the city with cobblestone streets. It had been one of the best times in their lives, when things were simple. "I remember," she said wistfully. "Those were great times."

Jonathan put his arm around her and pulled her close. Since she'd won the White House, they'd been in perpetual motion, with little time for each other. As the first "First Man" in the nation's history, he'd been a curiosity to the world. His schedule was packed with events, and he'd volunteered to chair a committee on health care. That had quickly turned out to be a political hot potato that he regretted taking on, and he'd had spent the past year working to minimize his role. He hated Washington and longed to return to California.

She began to snuggle into his arm when the phone next to the couch rang. "Should I answer it?" she asked, half in jest. She then reached over and picked up the receiver. "Yes?"

Cooperman listened for a few seconds. She then said, "Thank you" and hung up the phone without another word.

She melted back down into her husband's arms. "Jason Witt's on his way over. Can I pretend that phone call didn't happen? I want to stay right here."

He kissed her on the top of her head. "I wish. But a president's duty is never done."

"Shit," she sighed, moving to get up. "Don't wait on dinner for me, honey. I'll eat when I get back." With that she slipped on her blue Jimmy Choo pumps and headed for the elevator.

By the time Cooperman got down to the Oval Office, Jason Witt was waiting for her.

"Sorry to bother you at dinnertime, Madam President," Jason said. "I was just over with the D/CIA, and I wanted to update you on the bug case."

"We should probably give it a name at this point, don't you think? Something catchy historians will find compelling. 'The Poisoned OJ Caper' or 'Case of the Vicious Vector' or something like that."

Witt wasn't sure if the president was joking or not, but he dutifully smiled.

"Sorry, I shouldn't make light of this."

"Yes, ma'am. Unfortunately, we can't call it the Poisoned OJ Caper because it's no longer just about orange juice. In fact, the CDC is now investigating a possible new attack out in California."

Cooperman was suddenly no longer in a light mood. "What kind of attack?"

Witt recounted the discussion with Dr. Smythe on the apparent botulism cases in California and also updated her on what the CIA had uncovered about Lebedev and the Russians. "I hope to have confirmation of what we are dealing with in California by morning."

"Jesus, this thing is getting worse by the minute."

"Ma'am, that may not actually be the worst of it," he said carefully.

Cooperman's stare bored into Witt, and it suddenly seemed very warm in the Oval Office. "And?"

"And, we think that Lebedev was carrying with him the genetic code to genetically modify a vector that can carry and transmit a so-called superbug, an antibiotic-resistant bacteria capable of infecting humans."

"A bug that carries a superbug. Carl Sagan once said, 'The sword of science is double edged.' Boy, was he right."

"Yes, ma'am," Witt said.

"Are you telling me this could be weaponized against us?"

"Yes, ma'am. It could be. I don't know when—that would depend on the Russians' genetic engineering capabilities. But eventually we have to assume that it could be used against us or other Western targets.

Cooperman let that sink in. After a moment she asked, "So now what?"

"My team is running down some leads that I'd like to pursue before we call in the cavalry," Witt said, and told the president about the link to GMU, the presence of a known al-Qaeda and possibly ISIS operative and the mysterious woman who had yet to be identified. "Can you give me more time to work this?"

Cooperman stared at Witt as her mind raced through the endless risks and rewards of what he was suggesting. On the one hand, if they could keep this under the radar, she'd have an easier time continuing with her oft-stated position that the nation was safer than it had been under the previous administration. On the other hand, if it blew up and it were disclosed that she had sat on the information, she'd probably get impeached.

"OK, since we don't yet have confirmation on what's occurred in California, I'll give you more time," she said. "But as soon as we know it was a deliberate attack, I'm going to blow the lid off this. Are we clear?"

"Yes, ma'am. Thank you."

CHAPTER THIRTY-FOUR

Washington, DC

"WHAT IS ISAMO?"

Gabriel Marx and Lisa Brooks sat side by side in a small conference room at DHS Headquarters. They were going back over the layers of Abdul-Azim's life in America compiled through academic, immigration, and banking records. There was a line in his record that said he was a "faculty advisor to ISAMO."

"I looked it up. It's nothing." Brooks referred to her notes. "It stands for International Society for Structural Multidisciplinary Optimization. It's a computer science organization he belongs to."

Gabriel thought through that. "Is that right? Wouldn't that be I-S-S-M-O?"

Brooks's face went white. In her haste she had obviously mistyped the acronym. She immediately typed in the correct letters. The result left her feeling cold: Islamic Students against Mideast Oppression. "Oh, shit!" she said.

Gabriel quickly scanned the web page and clicked on the Washington, DC, chapter link, which brought up a picture of the Islamic Center of Washington. As he scrolled down, he read the mission statement out loud:

ISAMO is a student-led organization dedicated to protesting the occupation and oppression of Muslims by the imperial powers of the West: America, Europe, and Israel. ISAMO is focused on three activities:

The education of Muslim students about the plight of their brothers and sisters in the Mideast.

The creation of a safe and welcoming environment for students who wish to learn about the Koran and its teachings.

The organization of protests and active dissent against those who oppress Muslims throughout the world.

For more information or to attend our weekly meeting, please contact our faculty advisor, Professor Abdul-Azim Bashera, at aabashera@gmu.edu.

"Bingo," he said.

Thirty minutes later, Gabriel and Brooks were standing in front of the reception desk at the Islamic Center of Washington. Brooks took out her badge and discreetly showed it to the young bearded man who greeted them. His eyes looked at the badge, and for a split second, Gabriel could see fire in the man's eyes.

"How can I help?" he said in perfect, British-accented English.

"We'd like to speak with whoever is in charge here," Brooks said.

"That would be Dr. Habib," the man said.

Brooks waited a beat for the man to continue. When he didn't, she said, "Can you please tell him that we'd like a word?"

The man started at her and for a moment contemplated what to do. He then picked up a phone and pushed a single button. He spoke in Arabic to whoever answered on the other end of the line and then hung up. "He'll be right out."

Brooks and Gabriel stepped away from the front desk and looked around at the soaring atrium as Muslims streamed in the front doors for afternoon prayer. After a moment a diminutive man in a traditional Islamic robe walked up. He was in his early sixties with a well-trimmed salt-and-pepper beard and wore wire-rimmed glasses that would have looked at home on John Lennon. "You wanted to speak with me?" he asked, also with a slight British accent.

Brooks again discreetly showed her DHS badge. "We'd like to talk with you about a student group that meets here called ISAMO."

"Again? I've already had this conversation with the government," he said looking around. "Let's go into my office."

Once they were in Habib's office, Gabriel asked, "Who in the government did you speak with?"

"The FBI," Habib said. "They were here a month ago asking questions about ISAMO. Someone had complained that the group was teaching hatred of the West and the Jews. I told them that I don't tolerate such talk. They asked some questions and then left."

Gabriel now wondered if the FBI was already on Abdul-Azim's trail. "Did they ask about Professor Bashera?"

"Yes. But they seemed more interested in a few of the students in the group. In particular a young woman."

Brooks took out her phone and showed Dr. Habib a picture of the mystery woman. "Is this her?"

Habib looked at the image. "Yes, that's her."

"What did you tell them about her?" Brooks asked.

Habib was about to answer when he stopped himself. "What is this about?"

"We are conducting an investigation into a possible terror plot involving the man you know as Abdul-Azim Bashera and possibly some members of ISAMO."

"*Ya Allah!* That can't be! We are against jihad here!" Habib exclaimed. His face was suddenly filled with worry. "I've worked hard here to ensure that we work in the name of peace between Islam and the West . . ."

"I'm sure you have," said Brooks. "And we know you would want to avoid something terrible that might be linked to this mosque."

Habib blinked a few times and then nodded. "Yes, of course."

"Do you know who this woman is?" Gabriel asked, pointing to the picture.

"I don't," Habib said. "I told the FBI that as well. She was obviously a member of ISAMO, but I never met her."

"I find that hard to believe, Dr. Habib," Gabriel said.

"We have more than three thousand members and hold events every day. I can't possibly know everyone who comes here!"

"But you've seen her."

"Yes, I'm sure I have seen her," Habib said.

"Why are you sure of that?"

Habib looked down at the floor, and his face flushed. "I remember her because when I saw her, I thought she was the most beautiful woman I'd ever seen."

Gabriel knew that was a difficult thing for Habib to admit, and he immediately decided it was true. "That's not a crime, Dr. Habib."

"*Samhny ya Allah*," Habib said. Forgive me, God. "It is not a crime, no. But it is not something I am proud of. I've been married for thirty-six years," he said, with true contrition in his voice.

Gabriel worked to get the conversation back on track. "So you've seen her but don't know who she is. Have you ever seen this man?" He opened a picture of Adnan on his phone.

Habib studied the image. "I don't think so, no."

Gabriel tried to hide his disappointment. "Do you have video surveillance here?"

"Yes, we have a full system inside and outside the building. We installed it after 9/11. The only place we don't have it is in the prayer room. That would be an affront to Allah."

"How long do you keep the data? We'd like to view the footage just before and just after the weekly ISAMO meeting going back a few months. Can you help us with that?"

"Yes, of course," Habib said. "We keep the data for a year. Come, I'll show you where it is."

They walked into a back room where a uniformed man sat before a bank of monitors. Habib said a few things to him in Arabic, and the man gave up his chair. Brooks sat down in it. "How does this work?"

The security guard reached down and touched the screen, bringing up a menu. Brooks could feel him leaning into her and could smell his cheap cologne and was immediately grossed out. "Thanks, I think I can handle it," she said, pushing his arm away and forcing him to straighten up. She clicked on the list of cameras and selected the main entrance view. "Where are the cameras that view the room that ISAMO meetings are held in?"

"There is no camera inside the room since it's technically in the prayer wing. But there is a camera that points to the hall outside and the door." Habib asked the guard in Arabic what camera it was. When he replied, Habib translated. "It's camera twenty-two."

Brooks clicked on camera 22 and then clicked on the calendar. Once she was confident she could run the system, she turned to the guard. "You can go now."

The guard puffed out his chest, and the look on his face told her he wasn't happy about being dismissed by a woman. When he didn't move, she looked at Habib, who got the message. In Arabic, he tersely said something to the guard, who left in a huff.

"OK, let's start two months back and work forward." She switched to the camera on the front entrance, clicked on the first date, and selected the playback for 4:00 p.m., ninety minutes before the scheduled start of the ISAMO meeting. She then selected triple speed and hit Play.

For twenty minutes they watched the ebb and flow of people coming and going from the mosque. There was a noticeable pickup at the top of the hour when prayer time ended, and then it slowed to a trickle. Then they noticed a white self-driving sedan pull up and a man get out carrying a briefcase. He was dressed in a traditional Muslim tunic and had wavy hair and a full beard. Brooks immediately slowed the playback down so they could study him as he walked up the front steps and approached the camera location. Just before he got to the front door, he looked up, allowing the camera to catch a glimpse of his face before he put his hands up, as if shielding his eyes from something.

"That's him. But that was strange. Was he trying to shield his face from the camera?" Brooks asked?

"I don't think so," said Jensen. "It's almost like he didn't want to see something."

Brooks put on the second camera feed and cued the time to correspond to Abdul-Azim' arrival. They got a vivid view of him entering the room where the ISAMO meeting was held, as well as of a dozen young men and women. But no one who resembled either Adnan or the mystery woman.

They cued up the feeds from the following two meetings that month and again identified Rahman but no one else. "Maybe we should go further back?" suggested Gabriel.

Brooks nodded and then selected the same time on a date from four months prior. After ten minutes, Gabriel said, "There he is!"

He pointed at the screen as a man walked quickly up the steps; he was slender and wore a backpack. Brooks, who'd never met Adnan, said, "You sure?"

"Goddamn, I'm sure," said Gabriel. "Freeze it there. Can you zoom in?"

Brooks put her fingers on the screen and moved her forefinger and thumb outward, zooming in on the image. "That's him all right," said Gabriel. "Keep going. Let's see what he does." She restarted the video, and they watched Adnan approach the camera at the building entrance and stop. He turned around and faced the street and waited. By the camera clock, another six minutes went by.

And then they saw her. Walking up the steps came a young woman wearing a hijab tightly wound around her face. You couldn't see her face clearly, but Gabriel immediately knew that it was their mystery woman. She approached Adnan, but they didn't touch or speak; Adnan then opened the door for her and followed her into the mosque.

"That wasn't a very warm greeting," Brooks said. "If they were involved in a relationship, wouldn't they hug or something?"

"No," said Dr. Habib. "That would be an offense to Allah, for an unmarried man and woman to openly show affection, especially on the steps of a mosque."

Brooks nodded, and she switched the feed to the second camera, which showed them coming into the hallway. Just as they reached the entrance to the room where the ISAMO meeting was taking place, a few other students came out of the door they were about to enter, causing their mystery woman to stop short. Adnan pressed up against her from behind. "There!" Gabriel said.

You had to look carefully because it was a very small movement. But as Adnan pressed into the woman, their hands touched, their pinkies interlinking, showing affection. They were definitely a couple.

Gabriel turned to Dr. Habib, who had also seen the movement and seemed to be embarrassed. "Is that her?"

"Yes," he said, staring at her face, which now filled the screen.

CHAPTER THIRTY-FIVE

Fairfax, Virginia

AFTER THEIR MEETING AT CIA HEADQUARTERS, Lee Jensen had no trouble getting Witt to give him carte blanche on the investigation into Abdul-Azim Rahman. Jensen ordered 24-7 surveillance on Rahman's home and office and procured an emergency warrant to tap his cell phone and search his computer. Given the fact that Rahman was a computer expert, Jensen had no illusions about how hard that would be. But he trusted that Lisa Brooks would give Rahman a run for his money.

By 8:00 p.m., Jensen, Gabriel, and Brooks were packed like sardines inside a van outside of the Computer Science Department, joined by a DHS operative named Jim Sullivan. They were watching real-time video surveillance from Rahman's house just a mile from the GMU campus; there were lights on in the living room, and a drone overhead provided a full view of the modest three-bedroom home. Their goal had been to confirm that he was at home, and they'd even used an agent dressed as a pizza delivery driver to knock on the door, pizza in hand; when Rahman answered, the driver was apologetic that he'd gotten the wrong address. The agent reported Rahman was wearing a traditional long dressing gown and was clearly irritated by the disturbance.

"It will take Rahman at least fifteen minutes to get here, so let's not rush the search," Jensen said. "Brooksy, I'm hoping you can get into his computer and get access to that blockchain. That's the key."

Brooks nodded. She'd assembled every advanced tool that DHS had to break passwords and access personal computers and hoped they would do the trick. She also knew it was frequently the case that the more sophisticated the user was, the more chances he or she took on basic security things like passwords.

Quietly, Brooks and Sullivan slipped out of the van. She was dressed like a college athlete in a GMU soccer sweatshirt, and she carried a backpack and wore her hair in a ponytail. Sullivan, who had been chosen for this job because he was twenty-eight years old but looked as if he were still in high school, was dressed like a typical college kid, wearing sweatpants and flip-flops despite the chill in the air. Their instructions were to go through the front door and walk by security as if they belonged there; if stopped, they were to say they were going to the computer lab on the third floor. As they approached the entrance, they hung back a bit to slide into the wake of a large group of students who were entering the building and followed the pack all the way to the elevators.

Once they got off the elevator on the fourth floor, Brooks made a quick search of the hallway and found it empty. She approached Rahman's office door and pushed down on the handle to confirm that it was locked. She then squatted down as if looking for something in her bag while Sullivan calmly slipped a pick into the door's lock. Within ten seconds the lock clicked and the door gave way. Sullivan immediately walked back toward the elevator to keep watch on the hallway while Brooks slipped inside the office.

Keeping the office lights off, Brooks turned on a penlight and made her way to Rahman's desk. She reached under the desk and powered up the computer, a Dell tower that looked at least five years old. It was one of the ironies that made this job much easier than it might've been: academic institutions were notoriously behind the times in terms of the technology they used for email and office work, and even though Rahman taught computer science, that work was done more in the virtual world of the cloud or on sophisticated dedicated servers than on desktop computers like this one. This was the weak link, and Brooks hoped to exploit it.

Once the computer was booted up, Brooks slipped what was known as the Cypher Generator, a proprietary device the size of a thumb drive, into the USB slot and turned it on. A series of lights flashed, and a preprogrammed sequence of passwords were rapidly entered into the computer. These passwords had been compiled by a DHS team that had scrubbed Rahman's bio, looking for the kinds of references that most people typically turned into passwords: names, places, associations, hobbies, dates. In Brooks's experience it worked 80 percent of the time. If it didn't work, she was going to break into the system's motherboard BIOS and find the password by brute force. The downside of this approach was that it would leave a trail that would be unmistakable to anyone who next signed on to the computer, tipping Rahman off to the hack. That was something they hoped to avoid.

Brooks watched as the small device worked its magic, generating hundreds of password combinations in less than a minute. Suddenly the screen went from blue to white, opening up the GMU splash page. Brooks smiled and sent a quick text to Jensen: "We're in."

※

At that very moment, Jason Witt was in his SUV headed home after an eighteen-hour day when his cell phone rang. It was a blocked number.

"Witt."

"Jason, Ken Smythe here."

"Shit," he said. He knew that if Smythe was calling at this hour, it was likely bad news.

"Yep, it's not good. We've got twenty-five cases confirmed and two fatalities, including a young girl. The FBI has been able to trace almost all of the cases to the consumption of locally made almond butter, pies, nut mixtures, and breads."

"FBI?"

"Yep, they're all over this case already."

Witt's mind was racing. "Who's the SAIC out there?"

"Brian Sanderson out of the Sacramento Field Office. Know him?"

"By reputation. Old school from what I hear."

"You can say that again," Smythe said.

"What'd he tell you about the case?"

"Not much, really. Said that he thought it might be linked to the Florida case and that they believe it might be terrorism."

Witt was surprised by this but tried not to show it. "So what now?"

"I'm going to brief the president right after I finish this call with you. I'm going to recommend to her that we shut down all almond exports and issue a global recall of all almonds and almond-based products immediately."

"She's going to love that."

"Can't be helped I'm afraid. You'll need to alert customs, obviously."

"Not a problem. We have a contingency plan for just this kind of thing, though it's never been used. Do we know what the source of the botulism is?"

"No, and I'm going to need help from you on this one. Farmers have been reporting a higher-than-usual mortality in their almond trees and a greater-than-usual incidence of blight caused by insects like spider mites. I could use some of your bug experts on the ground out there."

"You got it."

"Thanks. I'm going to call the president now. Wish me luck."

"You're gonna need it," Witt said, and hung up. "Fuck!" he yelled to himself. He then dialed Jensen's cell phone.

"Yes, sir?" Jensen said in a hushed voice.

"Why are you whispering?"

"I'm in a surveillance van, and it's pretty close quarters."

"OK. Listen, I just talked to Smythe at the CDC. They've confirmed botulinum toxin out in California, and they think it is a copy of the Florida attack."

"No shit?"

"Yeah, and that's not all. The FBI is all over this now. They are leading the investigation out in California. So they know a shit ton more than we thought they did."

Jensen thought for a moment. After what Gabriel and Brooks had found out about the FBI at the DC mosque, there was no telling now what they knew. "I'd say our time is about up, boss."

"I know. But we're not stopping until the president orders us to," Witt said, weighing how blunt to be with Jensen. "If the FBI gets to Rahman, you can bet they'll Mirandize him."

"And he'll lawyer up."

"Yep. And that will make him useless to us."

"Well, boss, the good news is that I've got Brooks inside Rahman's office right now attempting to copy his computer."

Witt smiled in spite of himself. He knew that if they could access the blockchain, they'd remain in the game. "Be careful. And for Christ's sake, hurry up!"

Witt no sooner hit End Call on his iPhone than it rang again. This time he recognized the number.

"This is Secretary Witt," he said.

"Please hold for the president," an operator's voice said. After a moment Cooperman came on the line.

"Jason, I just got off the phone with Dr. Smythe at the CDC."

"Yes, ma'am. He said he was going to be calling you."

Cooperman was momentarily taken aback. "So you know what I'm about to say?"

Witt cursed himself for divulging that Smythe had already called him. Trust was the most important currency in DC, and he didn't want to ruin his relationship with the CDC. "I don't already know what you are going to say, ma'am. I only know that Dr. Smythe wanted DHS to provide support for him from our bug experts."

"OK," she said finally. "The attack in California has been confirmed, and I've put a call in to Director Timmons and the FBI. He told me that they've been quietly working this case for over a month."

"I'm surprised to hear that," Witt said. And he was.

"I am too. He hadn't wanted it to leak and so was waiting for confirmation before bringing it to my attention. I'm not entirely sure how I feel about that—but that's a conversation for another time. Right now we have to get the full force of the US government into this effort."

"Yes, ma'am."

"They have already linked the attack in Florida to an Islamic terror threat that the NSA picked up in a communication from Chechnya six months ago. It was unspecific, but the FBI has been working their sources. One of those sources belongs to a student organization that meets weekly at the Islamic Center here in DC—"

"ISAMO, yes, I'm aware of it."

"That's it. They had an informant in there for almost a year. He began to suspect that something was going on and reported it to his handler. They apparently honed in on the faculty advisor for the group."

Oh shit, Witt thought. "So how did they tie it to the attack in Florida?"

"I'm not sure. The NSA intercept said something about fruit, which at the time didn't mean anything. I guess they just put two and two together."

"I guess," Witt said doubtfully. He didn't believe in that kind of luck. There was more to this story.

"Director Timmons is moving on this now. He's taking down the faculty advisor and the other student members of that ISAMO group."

"Now, ma'am?"

"Right now."

"Yes, ma'am. Do you mind if I call you back, Madam President? I need to take care of an urgent matter."

Cooperman wasn't used to being put off but decided not to push it. "Sure, you know where to reach me."

"Thank you, ma'am." Witt hung up and speed-dialed Jensen. On the third ring, he picked up.

"Go," he said.

"The FBI is on their way to take down Rahman. If they catch Brooks inside, we are going to be out in the cold. Get her out now!"

"Fuck! OK, I'll call you back," Jensen said and hung up.

CHAPTER THIRTY-SIX

Fairfax, Virginia

LISA BROOKS'S PHONE STARTED BUZZING when she was in the middle of a complex command to ensure she got all of what was on Rahman's hard drive and browser data, including his Tor browser and block stack loader. This would enable them to emulate Rahman's computer as if Rahman himself were using it, thereby giving them access to his cloud accounts and other network data.

She was tempted to dismiss the call but then thought better of it. Looking at the screen, she saw it was Jensen. "What?" she said. "I'm in the middle of something here."

"Get out now. The FBI is on its way."

"Damn it! I need five more minutes to get this finished!"

"You don't have five minutes! Just take whatever you got, and get out!"

Just as Brooks was about to respond, she saw lights flashing in the parking lot. She moved to the window and peeked out through the blinds. There were a dozen cars and at least two vans pulling up to the entrance. "Too late, they're here!"

"Get out now, and that's an—" Brooks hung up, cutting Jensen off in midsentence. She crawled back to the keyboard and finished typing in the command she needed to complete.

At that moment Sullivan ran in from the hallway. "The police are here," he said in a loud whisper. "We gotta go!"

"It's actually the FBI," Brooks said, "and I'm not finished."

Sullivan moved over to the desk. "Are you shitting me? We get caught in here, and we're screwed!"

"I'm not leaving until this is done."

"Hurry the fuck up!"

Brooks didn't reply and watched the lights on her thumb drive continue to flash while it worked through the data. After thirty more seconds, it finished with a satisfying beep. She then carefully took the device out; rather than shutting down the computer, she put it into sleep mode. If it was off but the tower was still warm to the touch, they'd know that someone had just been there.

"Let's go," Brooks said, moving past Sullivan into the hallway. "Which way?"

Sullivan grabbed her hand. "This way," he said, running down to the stairway. They opened the door and could hear footsteps from below heading in their direction. They hugged the wall in order to avoid being seen from below and made it down to the third floor, where they ducked back into the hallway. That was the floor with the computer lab on it.

Brooks and Sullivan slipped into the lab, which at that point had roughly twenty students in it. They went to opposite ends of the room, turned on terminals, and pretended to be deeply engaged in their work. After about five minutes, the door opened, and a pair of FBI agents came into the room.

The agents didn't say anything, but they walked around, looking at each student. After a few minutes, they were apparently satisfied with what they saw and left. None of the students had even noticed them come in or leave, something that Brooks thought was strange.

Brooks took out her phone and texted Jensen: "We are in the computer lab. Mission accomplished. We are safe for now. We'll be here until the lab closes."

CHAPTER THIRTY-SEVEN

Washington, DC

THE NEXT MORNING, Gabriel, Lee Jensen, and Lisa Brooks crowded around the flat-screen display in her office. She was in the process of uploading Rahman's computer data onto a DHS server, a job that was almost complete.

"This should be the same as if we were sitting in front of Rahman's screen," she said. She opened up a new window, and they were staring at the GMU splash page.

"We have clearance, Clarence," Jensen said, trying to contain his glee. This was what they'd been waiting for.

Gabriel got the *Airplane!* reference. "Chill, Kareem. This is just the beginning. We still need to get into the blockchain."

"Gabriel's right," Brooks said. "Let's hope this works."

She opened up the block browser and typed "SMRA," the name of the block that they'd earlier identified on Adnan's computer, into the search bar. "Here goes nothing." She then hit Enter.

Instantly the SMRA block appeared. They browsed through the transactions looking for what was known as the "received time," the exact time

Adnan had uploaded the encryption key the night he was killed. "Here it is," she said, clicking on the associated block hash where the data was stored.

Up on the screen came a block of seemingly random numbers and letters. "OK, this is the key," she said. She copied the block and saved it to a thumb drive. She then took the thumb drive and placed it in a USB port connected to Adnan's tablet. Opening his Amazon cloud account, she pasted the encryption key into a window. Before she hit Enter, she looked at Gabriel and Jensen. "You guys feeling lucky?"

She didn't wait for an answer. Within seconds a file opened up on the screen. Brooks read it out loud:

There once was a merchant in the famous market in Baghdad. One day he saw a strange woman looking at him; he knew the woman was the Angel of Death.

Pale and trembling, the merchant fled the marketplace and made his way many, many miles to the city of Samarra.

But when at last he came to the city of Samarra, the merchant saw waiting for him the angel.

"Why did you look surprised when you saw me this morning in Baghdad?" the merchant asked the Angel of Death.

"Because," said Death, "I had an appointment with you tonight in Samarra."

Jensen and Gabriel looked at each other. Each had his own association with Samarra, a city in the Sunni Triangle in Iraq and the site of some of the most intense sectarian violence of the Iraq War. "Read it again, Brooksy," Jensen said. "Out loud."

Brooks read it again. Gabriel closed his eyes and tried to follow the story. When she was done, Brooks asked, "Where's Samarra?"

"Samarra is a city in Iraq," Gabriel said. "It's also the home of one of the holiest sites in Shi'a Islam. The al-Askari mosque is there. When it got blown up in 2006, it basically set off the civil war between the Sunnis and the Shi'a."

"It's a dark place. Full of religious symbolism," Jensen added. "The al-Askari mosque is a Shi'a shrine, but the Sunnis historically ran the city, just like they ran all of Iraq. Nobody knows who actually blew it up, but the Sunnis were likely behind it. After the invasion, the Iraqi government turned Shi'a, and the Sunnis have been in the government minority ever since. That's how ISIS came about. It was the Sunnis fighting back."

"How do you guys know so much about it?" Brooks asked.

Gabriel laughed. "We both spent a lot of time fighting bad guys in the Sunni Triangle."

Brooks nodded. "So what do you make of this—what is it? A poem?"

"I think it's more of a parable, actually," Gabriel said. "So, is that all there is in the file?"

Brooks scrolled down. "No, there's a huge file attached. Bunch of letters repeating."

"Let me see that," Gabriel said. "That's a DNA sequence." He looked at the metadata at the top of the page. "Shit. It's the sequence for KPC."

"Isn't that the one that Lebedev took with him out of GenomeX?"

"Yep."

"What is KPC?" Brooks asked.

"It's a Gram-negative bacterium that is resistant to antibiotics. It's basically a lethal superbug that can't be stopped."

"Jesus Christ."

"You can say that again," Gabriel said.

⚜

Gabriel hadn't intentionally avoided Brooks's question on what the parable meant; the truth is he wasn't sure. The essence of it was clear: man's death is predestined, and no matter what you do, when your time is up, it's up. But what else did it mean? That he did not know.

He spent the next few hours Googling "Samarra" and "merchant in Baghdad" and "death in Samarra" and found some more information about the parable. It was attributed to a play written by W. Somerset Maugham in 1933 and was an epigraph in a famous John O'Hara novel,

Appointment in Samarra. It was loosely based on a passage from the Babylonian Talmud in which King Solomon unwittingly sends two of his servants to their deaths.

All of which only brought up more questions. Wasn't the Talmud a Jewish text? Was this some kind of a message? A clue? Was this a message from Adnan? Or was it a feint, a way to confuse them? Or just another way of saying that the infidel was destined to die?

Fortunately, Gabriel knew just whom to ask.

CHAPTER THIRTY-EIGHT

Washington, DC

"WELL, BOSS, TO QUOTE GEORGE COSTANZA, we're no longer the master of our domain."

Jason Witt looked at Lee Jensen and smiled in spite of himself. He had just gotten a call from the White House summoning him to an emergency meeting of the FBI and the national-security team.

The jig was up.

"Get all the material you have, and be prepared to hand it over to the FBI. I want to share everything with them. And I do mean everything," he said pointedly.

Jensen said nothing at first. He knew that from both a moral and legal perspective, cooperation was essential. This was no time to play turf games. But he also knew that Witt was unlikely to drop the investigation completely, and he assumed that unofficially they'd stay on the case. But he wanted to hear it from Witt firsthand. "What's our play?"

"We're gonna cooperate. Let's see what the president says," he said.

Jensen waited for more. When Witt said nothing further, Jensen's mood sank. He hated the thought of giving up on this case. He was fully invested.

Then, just as he was heading out the door to the White House, Witt turned and said, "When I get back, we can talk about our next move."

Jensen grinned. "OK, boss."

🐜

When Witt arrived at the White House, he was escorted downstairs to the Situation Room, a high-tech conference room located in the basement. It was staffed 24-7 by the National Security Council and had the latest in high-tech, ultrasecure communication technology.

Witt entered the room and shook hands with the secretary of defense and the National Security Advisor and nodded to the chairman of the Joint Chiefs of Staff. He also noticed Ken Smythe of the CDC on the large screen at the head of the room, conferencing in from California. Witt had just found his seat when the director of the FBI, Mark Timmons, sat down next to him.

"Jason, I understand you've been working this case for the past several weeks without me knowing about it."

"We've been working the bug attack in conjunction with the CDC; that's correct."

"This is much more than a bug attack. You've stepped smack into the middle of a yearlong investigation into an ISIS cell at George Mason University. You almost screwed it up."

"Look, Mark, we've been following our leads, and I've been in full communication with the president. She gave us the go-ahead."

"Maybe. But that's done now. And I'm going to need everything you've got on this."

Just as Witt was about to respond, President Cooperman entered the room. They all stood.

"Take your seats, please," she said. "I've called this meeting because we have confirmation of a second outbreak of botulinum toxin in California. Director Smythe, can you update us please?"

"Yes, ma'am," Smythe said, his voice echoing from speakers in the ceiling. "We have verified four hundred cases of poisoning stretching from Red Bluff, California, to Sacramento. The poisoning occurred in almond-based products that were manufactured with locally grown almonds. We are now looking at data from across the country to see if any of these almonds were exported, which we believe they were."

"How many fatalities?" Cooperman asked.

"Sixty-five confirmed with another hundred fifty in critical condition," Smythe said. "We expect the death toll to rise significantly, possibly into the thousands, depending on how far and wide the almonds were distributed."

"Jesus," Cooperman said. "What do we know about the source of the toxin?"

Smythe lifted a vial. "This may not be easy to see, but we think there may be a link between the poisoning and these mites. Farmers noticed a dramatic increase in mite infestation about four months ago. While they damaged some of the trees, they didn't dramatically impact the harvest of almonds."

"What are we doing to verify that?"

"Secretary Witt has sent me two of his bug guys, and we are having genetic testing done at the CDC to see if the mites have been altered in the same way that the medflies were in Florida."

"Jason, any comment?"

"Until we have the results, we can't know for sure. But it looks consistent with what happened in Florida."

"Madam President," the director of the FBI said, "all this bug talk is interesting, but can we get to the root of the threat? This is a jihadist attack on the United States, and I want to make sure we have all the information we need to stop the next one."

Cooperman didn't like being interrupted. "Mark, I'm getting there. First, I want to make sure we are coordinating our response to the attack that has just occurred. That OK with you?"

Timmons turned red, and Witt suppressed a smile. "Yes, ma'am," Timmons said.

"Good. Jason, what are we doing about shutting down almond exports?"

"I have customs on it. They've impounded all shipments of almond products—almost five hundred SKUs—that were at ports ready for loading onto ships. The Ag Department is issuing a directive to all farmers in the affected areas to burn their crops wherever possible. The FDA has issued a full recall for all five hundred products as well, so those are being pulled out of the stores. And we have a national ad campaign about to start running asking people to check their pantries and dispose of any almond products produced anytime in the last four months."

"God, that's going to create hysteria on a massive scale. Not to mention crater our economy," Cooperman said.

"It will, but there is no other way, ma'am," Witt said.

Cooperman then turned back to Timmons. "Mark, what's the latest on the investigation?"

"We've been working a suspected ISIS cell at George Mason University for the past year, and we recently connected the murder of a Biomedical Research Lab scientist—a Dr. Adnan Mishner—with a radical student group called the Islamic Students Against Mideast Oppression or ISAMO. Mishner was an entomologist who worked on genomics and insects. His girlfriend was a woman who was one of the ringleaders of the ISAMO group. She disappeared after Mishner's murder, and we haven't been able to locate or identify her yet. But we have identified the ISAMO faculty advisor, Abdul-Azim Bashera, who is a computer science professor who emigrated to the US from Iraq via Turkey. We've taken him into custody."

Witt made a motion attempting to get Cooperman's attention. "Yes, Jason?" she said.

"Ma'am, Bashera's real name is Abdul-Azim Rahman. We've identified him as a former Baath Party member and computer specialist for Saddam Hussein and"—Witt looked at Timmons and could see his face reddening—"later al-Qaeda in Iraq, where he personally worked with al-Zarqawi before he was killed."

"Really?" Cooperman said. "Director Timmons did you know this?"

Timmons looked as if he'd seen a ghost. "No, ma'am."

Cooperman nodded. "I suggest you and Jason here get together and compare notes," she said. "Have you learned anything from this man Rahman?"

Timmons sighed. "No, ma'am. He's got a lawyer and is refusing to talk."

The secretary of defense almost came unglued. "You Mirandized him? Are you fucking kidding me?"

"No, I'm not fucking kidding you," Timmons growled back. "This is the United States. That's what we do when we arrest people."

"Jesus Christ! You should've sent him to Guantánamo!"

"That's enough!" Cooperman said, stopping the SecDef from saying something he might later regret. "What's done is done. Let's move forward." She then turned to Jason Witt. "Jason, you and your team have information that will be important to the FBI, and you will cooperate fully with Director Timmons and provide whatever assistance you can."

"Yes, ma'am."

"This investigation now belongs to the FBI," Cooperman said. "If they need help from DHS or the CDC or FDA—or any other agency for that matter—they'll ask for it. Is that clear to everyone?"

"Yes, ma'am," they all said in unison.

"Good." Cooperman then turned to the secretary of defense and the chair of the JCS. "Now, let's talk about some military options. I want to make sure we send a message to ISIS that this attack will not go unanswered."

CHAPTER THIRTY-NINE

Langley, Virginia

"WELL, I CAN RELATE TO THIS. Samarra almost killed me too."

Sam Gaddis read the parable again and then closed his eyes. He was thinking about that week after the al-Askari mosque was blown up, and the shit storm that had rained down on him and his team. It was the bloodiest week of the bloodiest year in Iraq. It left an indelible impression.

Gabriel was sitting at a table in Gaddis's office, a small space tucked away on the fifth floor of CIA Headquarters. On the walls were pictures of Gaddis sporting a thick beard and a kaffiyeh around his neck, kitted up with an M4 submachine gun, in various locations around Iraq. One picture was of Gaddis and General Stan McChrystal, who at that time was head of Joint Special Operations Command and was leading the hunt for Abu Musab al-Zarqawi. In an irony not lost on Gabriel, it was McChrystal who had called in the airstrike that killed al-Zarqawi, sending Abdul-Azim Rahman first to Turkey and then to George Mason University, where he was in the best possible position to do damage to America.

"What was it like working with McChrystal?" Gabriel asked.

"Fantastic. He's a relentless motherfucker. I loved the guy."

Gabriel just nodded. It conformed to what he'd heard from others who had worked with McChrystal and JSOC. "So what do you think it means?" Gabriel asked, pointing to the paper on Gaddis's desk.

"I think it's a message that we—the infidels—are destined to die. But the Samarra reference is interesting because of what the city represents."

"Well, I know what it represents for me," Gabriel said. "But what's the bigger picture?"

"Samarra was one of the capitals of the Abbasid caliphate that came to power in the eighth century. It was the seat of Islam during the early years of what is known as the Golden Age of Islam."

"What was so golden about it?"

"It was kind of like the Renaissance. A period when science and technology advanced, and when culture flourished."

Gabriel obviously looked confused, because Gaddis then said, "I know, seems counterintuitive, right? Islam being associated with science and culture."

"Radical Islam sure doesn't have that connotation," Gabriel said. "So is it weird that Samarra would be the reference they used?"

"Not really. isis and the radical jihadists see the golden age as a time when Islam was ascendant, and when the original battle between two visions of Islam, those of Ahl al-Hadith and of the Mu'tazilites, was in play. The Ahl al-Hadith were the fundamentalists who took the Koran literally, including all the stuff about killing nonbelievers. The Mu'tazilites were more liberal and saw reason and logic as more important than what was written in the Koran. In the end the Mu'tazilites won out, but as we've seen, the Ahl al-Hadith are still a major strain of Islam and are the inspiration for Salafism."

"At the risk of oversimplifying this, the Salafists are the Neanderthals of Islam—the anti-modernists who want to return to the Dark Ages. Women in bondage, honor killings, death to the nonbelievers, etc."

Gaddis said, "That's about right."

Gabriel pulled another paper out from his bag and handed it to Gaddis.

"I did some research and found that Somerset Maugham's version of the parable was inspired by a passage in the Babylonian Talmud," he said, handing it over to Gaddis. "Basically it goes like this: King Solomon meets the Angel of Death and asks why he looks sad. The angel says he's been sent to take away Solomon's two Cushite servants. So Solomon sends the servants away to the city of Luz where Death supposedly can't go. Then the next day Solomon finds Death and asks why he looks so happy. And Death answers, because you sent them to the very place I was to meet them."

Gaddis looked at Gabriel and then looked down at the paper.

"What I don't understand is why Islamists would use a story from the Talmud," said Gabriel. "I thought the Talmud was Jewish."

"Actually, the Babylonian Talmud originated in Iraq. Most people don't know that Islam and Judaism came largely from the same place and have many shared elements."

"So what do you think the Solomon reference means?"

"I'm not sure—and I'm certainly no expert on this. I know that Solomon was the son of King David and was revered in both the Talmud and the Koran. He's a symbol of wisdom and power. Maybe the message is that not even someone as powerful as Solomon can avoid the Angel of Death when death is ordained."

"And that even the powerful Americans will not be able to escape jihad?"

"Maybe," Gaddis said with a slight shrug.

"There has to be more to it than that."

"I actually know a guy who can help us figure it out," he said, pulling out his iPhone and searching his contacts. When he found what he was looking for, he texted it to Gabriel.

Gabriel looked at his phone when it buzzed. "Rabbi Yossi Rafaeli. Who's that?"

"He's probably the foremost Talmudic scholar in the United States. He was in Iraq doing research when I was there. I first met him at the bar at the Al Rasheed hotel in Baghdad. We became drinking buddies. He's a crazy bastard. You'll love him."

"He's in New York?"

"Yep. I'll tell him we're coming."

"We're coming?"

"Hell yes. I'm bored out of my mind. And I love New York," Gaddis said.

CHAPTER FORTY

New York, New York

THE MAZER SCHOOL OF TALMUDIC STUDIES at Yeshiva University was a modern building on the corner of Amsterdam Avenue and 185th Street. A mix of steel, concrete, and glass, it was an incongruous home for a school that studied the ancient foundation of the world's oldest monotheistic religion.

Gabriel and Sam Gaddis had taken the bullet train from Washington's Union Station and arrived at New York's Penn Station in less than two hours. It had taken almost that long to get from Midtown up to northern Manhattan, and Gabriel had spent the time in the back of the self-driving Uber longing for Claire and the serenity of the Russian River Valley. He'd be happy when this was over and he could go home.

When they arrived at the entrance to the Mazer School, they were met by a pair of guards standing just inside the double glass doors; they were wearing bulletproof vests and were armed with semiautomatic pistols in quick-release holsters. Behind them sat two other uniformed guards operating a standard metal detector and X-ray machine like you'd find in any airport. This was no ordinary college campus.

When Gabriel and Gaddis made it through the security phalanx, they were met by a young man in a plain white shirt, wearing a yarmulke. He sported a beard, and his hair was styled in the traditional *payot*, with side curls cascading down the side of his face. "Mr. Gaddis?" he asked in Hebrew-accented English.

"That's me," Gaddis said.

"Rabbi Rafaeli is in his office. He asked me to get you."

"Mazel tov," Gaddis said. "Let's go."

The young man smiled at the bit of Gentile humor and led them into the elevator and up to the fourth floor. On the walls of the elevator hung posters of Talmudic passages and images of Jerusalem. "How many students are part of the Mazer School?" Gabriel asked.

"There are about two hundred who specialize in the Talmud as a part of their degree program at Yeshiva," the young man said. "We learn about the original texts and commentaries and about Halakah, which is Jewish law."

"And what do you want to do after you graduate?" Gabriel asked.

"I want to become a teacher," the young man said as they exited the elevator. They walked down a narrow carpeted hallway to a partially open office door. Next to the door there was a small sign in block letters: "Rabbi Yossi Rafaeli, Eli Bloom Chair in Talmud and Jewish Philosophy."

Gaddis pushed open the door and said, "You still owe me a glass of wine, Rabbi. And not that Manischewitz crap."

Rafaeli grinned and stood from his desk. "You do have the memory of an elephant, Samuel. That was fifteen years ago!"

"More, actually," Gaddis said, enveloping Rafaeli in a bear hug. "Damn, it's good to see you."

"And you as well," Rafaeli said, grabbing Gaddis's hand. Gabriel could see that this was a real bond, like the kind that developed between men when they risked their lives together.

"Yossi, this is Gabriel Marx. I've known Gabriel almost as long as I've known you. He was with the marines in Fallujah and Ramadi. We did some good work together."

Rafaeli grasped Gabriel's hand. "Any friend of Samuel's is a friend of mine." Rafaeli had a firm grip and rough hands. They were not academic hands but rather those of a man who knew work.

"Pleasure to meet you, and thank you for your time today," Gabriel said.

Rafaeli waved the thank-you away. In a lowered voice, he said, "Samuel and I did a lot of drinking together in Iraq, and he bailed me out more than once when I found myself in a bit of trouble."

"Shit, a bit of trouble?" Gaddis said. "That's putting it mildly. Yossi here once got himself trapped inside some ruins in the Sunni Triangle, caught between Sunni and Shi'a death squads. I had to get the SEALs to bail him out."

Rafaeli laughed. "Yes, well, it all worked out OK."

Gaddis smiled. "We drank an awful lot that night."

Gabriel smiled too at the reminiscences. "Sounds like fun," he said.

"Strangely enough it was," Rafaeli said. Looking around at his office, he said, "I never felt more alive."

"What kind of work were you doing in Iraq?" Gabriel asked.

"My research then had to do with finding the source of some of the Talmud's tractates or books. Some of them hail directly from the areas in Iraq that were in what Samuel likes to call Indian country."

"More like the Little Bighorn," Gaddis said.

After a moment, Rafaeli said, "So I understand you have a Talmudic question for me."

"More like a puzzle, actually," Gabriel replied. He reached into his bag and took out the passage, handing it to Rafaeli.

"Ah, Sukkah 53a," he said, and read aloud:

There were once two Cushites who attended on Solomon, and these were Elihoreph and Ahyah, the sons of Shisha, scribes, of Solomon. One day Solomon observed that the Angel of Death was sad. 'Why,' he said to him, 'art thou sad?'—'Because,' he answered him, 'they have demanded from me the two Cushites who sit here.' [Solomon thereupon] gave them in charge of the spirits and sent them to the district of Luz. When, however, they reached the district of Luz they died. On the following day, he observed that the Angel of Death was in cheerful spirits. 'Why,' he said to him, 'art thou cheerful?'—'To the place,' the other replied, 'where they expected them from me, thither didst thou send them.' Solomon thereupon uttered the saying, 'A man's feet are responsible for him; they lead him to the place where he is wanted.'

"What does it mean?" Gabriel asked.

Rafaeli took off his reading glasses and smiled. "That's not a simple question. The Talmud is full of symbolism that is open to interpretation. It's why I have a job," he laughed. "Can I ask how you came across this?"

"It's related to a clue we received in an investigation we are working on. 'The Appointment in Samarra.' Do you know it?"

"Yes, of course. And you are right that this is where Maugham's version came from. He modernized it and made it more dramatic. But its roots are here," Rafaeli said, pointing to the paper Gabriel had given him. "Solomon sends his servants to their death even as he attempts to save them by sending them to Luz."

"Why Luz? And what is it?"

"In the Talmud it says that by tradition the Angel of Death had no power in Luz, which is the name of an ancient Canaanite city. So Solomon sent his servants there so they'd live. The verb form of Luz means to turn aside. The noun form means almond tree."

"Almond tree?"

"Yes, that's right."

"I'll be goddamned!" Gabriel said, looking right at Gaddis. And then Gabriel realized what he'd done and immediately said to Rafaeli, "Sorry."

"Don't be sorry. I've heard far worse, especially from him," Rafaeli said, nodding at Gaddis.

"So is this about Solomon being powerless to stop fate?"

"In one respect, yes. But it's also Solomon rejecting responsibility for their deaths when he says, 'A man's feet are responsible for him; they lead him to the place where he is wanted.'"

"So he's sort of holding up his hands saying, 'Not my fault'?"

"Yes. But there's a passage just before this one that I think provides important context to the verse you have," Rafaeli said, getting up to look at the bookshelves that lined the back office wall. He reached up and brought down a leather-bound book with gold lettering on the spine. He opened it up and quickly found what he was looking for. "Here's the verse before the one you've brought," Rafaeli said.

It was taught, Of Hillel the Elder, It was said that when he used to rejoice at the Rejoicing at the place of the Water-Drawing, he used to recite thus, 'If I am here, everyone is here; but if I am not here, who is here?' He also used to recite thus, 'To the place that I love, there my feet lead me: if thou wilt come into My House, I will come into thy house; if thou wilt not come to My House, I will not come to thy house, as it is laid, In every place where I caused my name to be mentioned, I will come unto thee and bless thee.'

He moreover once saw a skull floating upon the face of the water. 'Because,' he said to it, 'thou didst drown others, they have drowned thee, and they that drowned thee shall be drowned too.'

"A skull floating upon the face of the water. That's a pretty stark reference," Gabriel said. "Is there significance to it being in water? And what's the water-drawing?"

Rafaeli paused, trying to find the right words. "In the Talmud, water is a central part of the Sukkot, a celebration that marks the end of harvest. During Sukkot there is what is known as the Simchat Beit Hashoeva, the celebration of the water-drawing. In this celebration water is poured over the altar of the Holy Temple signifying the sustaining of life."

"Who is Hillel the Elder?" asked Gaddis.

"He was one of the great early religious teachers in Judaism and one of the fathers of the Talmud itself," Rafaeli said.

Gaddis nodded. "So what's he saying here?"

"He's saying that if you come into my house, I will come into your house; if you stay out of my house, I will stay out of yours. Same thing with the skull floating in the water. If you drown others, you will be drowned, and those who drown you will also, in turn, be drowned."

"So it's an eye for an eye?"

"Yes, but it's also a message that your fate is preordained. That's what Solomon is saying when his servants end up dead in Luz. It was meant to be."

"Look, we are working on a case that I can't tell you much about," Gabriel said to Rafaeli. "But we believe that the 'Appointment in Samarra' reference is a coded message left by Islamic fundamentalists. Given the Talmudic roots of the parable, does that make sense to you?"

Rafaeli thought for a moment. "It seems hard for people to believe now, but Islam is one of Judaism's daughters. The Talmud itself is an oral history based on discussions in rabbinic colleges alongside the Tigris and Euphrates in what today is Iraq. The discussions took place between the third and fifth centuries, but the Talmud was still being compiled and collated two hundred years later. By then the area was under the control of the Islamic Ummayyad caliphate."

"So elements of the Talmud are influenced by Islam?" Gabriel asked.

"Yes. And so it's no surprise that Islam and Judaism share similar characteristics. They are both based on a divinely revealed text—the Torah for the Jews and the Koran for Muslims. Both texts are interpreted by means of an oral tradition, the Talmud and the Hadith, respectively. Each tradition contains legal and ethical material. The Jewish legal material is called Halakah and the Islamic Shari'a; both terms mean a pathway, or way to go."

"Fascinating stuff. Does that mean the anti-Zionism in the Arab world is more about politics than it is about religion?" Gaddis said.

"Well, for many Arabs it's more about politics," Rafaeli said. "But not for the Salafists, isis, al-Shabab, or the other Islamic fundamentalists. For them it's very much about religion."

Gabriel nodded. It was starting to make sense. The association of Luz and almonds had hit him like a shot of adrenaline. He was starting to believe that Sukkah 53a—the source for "The Appointment in Samarra"—was the roadmap for the attacks, the instructions for the cell to carry out its plans. The almond attack had already happened. What was next? And how did the orange juice attack fit into it?

"Rabbi, anything about oranges in the Sukkah?" he asked. "Or Sukkot? Or in the story of Solomon?"

Rafaeli considered the question. "Oranges were widely grown in ancient Mesopotamia, so they are certainly part of the Babylonian Talmud. But not specifically in Sukkah 53a. There are etrogs in the water-drawing ritual, however. Those are as close as it gets."

"Etrogs? What's that?" Gabriel asked.

"It's a citrus fruit that is held in the hand during the Sukkot ritual."

"Citrus? Like an orange?"

"More like a lemon than an orange."

Not a perfect match, Gabriel thought. But it still might fit. He then stood and offered his hand to Rafaeli. "Thank you very much, Rabbi. This was most helpful."

Rafaeli shook Gabriel's hand and gave Gaddis a hug. "Anytime, my friend. And don't be a stranger," Rafaeli said to Gaddis. "It's been too long. Next time you are in New York, you come to dinner at my home. We can get drunk and tell stories about Iraq."

"You got it, Yossi. And thanks," Gaddis said with real emotion in his voice.

A few minutes later standing in the elevator, Gabriel said, "The pieces are starting to fit for me."

"How so?"

"That passage in Sukkah isn't just about fate. It's also about cause and effect. Isn't the entire Islamic fundamentalist movement about getting the US out of the Middle East? Wasn't that bin Laden's major gripe? That we are in their house? And that as result, they are going come into our house to try and destroy us?"

"Yes," Gaddis replied. "Bin Laden hated that we were in Saudi Arabia during the first Gulf War propping up what he saw as a corrupt regime. From there it just grew into a larger movement against our presence in the Mideast. But to really hurt us—to really punish us—they ultimately had to come to America."

"Well, they're here."

After a moment Gaddis asked, "Ever heard of the three warnings in Islam?"

"No."

"There's a saying in the Hadith about snakes," Gaddis said. "Muhammad says when you see a snake in your house, you should warn it three times. If it returns a fourth time, you should kill it."

"And?"

"And three warnings. The first warning was the oranges. The second warning was Adnan's very gruesome murder after you showed up to talk to him. And the third warning was the almonds."

"Those weren't warnings. Those were attacks."

"Shit, Gabriel. What was the damage? A couple of hundred sick and a few dozen killed? Some crops ruined? Those weren't real attacks. I think those were warnings."

Gabriel looked at Gaddis. "I hadn't thought about it that way."

"Well, think about this: In 1993 al-Qaeda bombed the World Trade Center. Six Americans killed. That was warning number one. In 1998 they bombed the US embassies in Africa. A couple of hundred killed, mostly Africans. That was warning number two. In 2000, they hit the USS *Cole* in Yemen. Seventeen sailors killed. That was warning number three. And then on 9/11, they killed the snake. Three thousand dead."

Gabriel stared at Gaddis for a moment before replying. "And?"

"And my bet is that whatever's next, it's going to be the snake killer. And I believe the clue is in there," Gaddis said, pointing to the bag that held the printout of the passage from Sukkah.

Gabriel shook his head in wonder. "Ironic, isn't it? The key to a twenty-first-century threat can be found in a book written in the fifth century."

"That's one word for it," Gaddis said.

CHAPTER FORTY-ONE

Washington, DC

"HER NAME IS HANIYA RAZAVI," Jensen said, holding up her picture. The SPARK search had finally come through. "She came to the United States from Pakistan on a student visa in 2019. Studied computer science at GMU and then entered their grad program."

"That fits," Gabriel said.

"I just passed that info off to the FBI," Jensen said. "She's now officially on their most wanted list."

Gabriel was sitting in Jensen's spartan office at DHS Headquarters. Gabriel had just briefed Jensen on what he and Gaddis had uncovered in New York. Gabriel had been racking his brain about the Talmudic passage, trying to see the clue to the next attack. So far, he was at a loss.

Just then an agent popped his head in the doorway. "Lee, the secretary wants to see you." Then turning to Gabriel, he asked, "Are you Marx?"

"Yes."

"Nice!" the agent said. "I was sent to track you down as well. I was about to call your cell. He wants to see you too."

"Show time," Jensen said.

When they arrived at Witt's office, they found him on the phone. Though they could hear only one part of the conversation, it was clear that Witt was getting chewed out. After a few grunts and an "OK" or two, he hung up.

"God, what an asshole," he said.

"Don't tell me. The director of the FBI?" Jensen asked.

"The one and only. He's still pissed about us not bringing them in after the first sign of trouble. And he suspects we broke into Rahman's computer. How he figured that out I'm not sure. But he knows."

"I have no idea what you're talking about, Mr. Secretary," Jensen said with a smile. "Gabriel, do you know what Secretary Witt is talking about?"

"I haven't the foggiest idea."

Witt laughed. "Me neither. You guys want something to drink?" Jensen and Gabriel both shook their heads. "So whaddya got for me?"

Gabriel updated Witt on what he'd learned in New York from Yossi Rafaeli about the Talmudic origins of the "Appointment in Samarra" parable. He also explained to Witt the reference to Luz and the almond trees. "I don't think they're using the Somerset Maugham version as their vehicle. I think the message for the group was in the Talmud Sukkah 53a passage."

"Whoa, back up," Witt said. "You think that this was an intentional message? From ISIS?"

Gabriel realized he'd jumped ahead and needed to lay more groundwork for Witt. "Sorry, let me give you the context. Gaddis at CIA believes the parable itself was a way for ISIS to communicate plans to its operatives—sort of a coded message. Al-Qaeda often used coded portions of well-known writings to hide their plans—sort of a poor man's Enigma machine."

"Exactly," Jensen said. "After al-Zarqawi was killed in Iraq, their communications capability went to shit, largely because Rahman fled to Turkey. So they turned to using open communication with Koranic and other verses that had hidden meanings."

"And that's what you think this Samarra thing is?" Witt asked.

"Yes, sir. The Angel of Death in Luz and the killing of Solomon's servants relates to the poisoning of the almond trees. Gaddis also thinks that the almond-tree attack was the third warning," Gabriel said, explaining to Witt the Hadith story about Muhammad and the snake.

"So we've had three warnings now, and he thinks the next one is the big one? The one that kills the snake?" Witt said.

"Yes, sir," Gabriel said. "That's the theory. And if that's true, there is potentially another clue in the Sukkah about the next attack."

"Huh," Witt said. "Are you buying this, Lee?"

Jensen shrugged. "I talked to Gaddis, and he seems to think it makes sense. Besides, what else do we have got to go on?"

"Unfortunately, nothing," Witt replied. He then asked, "Why do you think Adnan uploaded this? Wouldn't his coconspirators already have it or know what it said? Makes no sense."

"That gets us back to blockchain," Gabriel said. "If there were others in the chain who needed the message, he'd need to upload the key"

"So there are more attackers out there," Jensen said.

"Probably," Gabriel said.

"Well, it's the FBI's problem now," Witt said.

Gabriel's heart sank. "So we're out?"

"Officially, yes. Unofficially, no. I've made arrangements with Ken Smythe at CDC to have you attached to their investigation out in California. That will allow you to go home for a bit and kiss your wife. And we can continue to monitor the investigation while working on whatever leads we still have."

Jensen looked at Gabriel and smiled. "There's no place like home, Auntie Em," he said. Then looking at Witt, he asked, "What about me?"

"Don't worry, Dorothy, you're going too. You can work out of the Sacramento Field Office. Just be careful not to get in the way of the FBI. The SAIC out there is a guy named Sanderson. He's a real prick."

Jensen nodded. "Got it."

"Good. Any questions?"

"What do you want us to do with the Talmud info and analysis? Share it with the FBI?"

"Yes. And write a short memo for the record. Let them know we think there's some message in it. They won't pay any attention, but at least we'll have tried."

"OK," Jensen said.

"But, Gabriel, you should keep working on it. Maybe you can find the hidden clue about the next attack."

Gabriel, who had no intention of stopping work on it, said, "Roger that."

CHAPTER FORTY-TWO

Outside Denver, Colorado

THE BROWN SHAG CARPET INSIDE ROOM TWENTY-TWO of the roadside motel just outside of Denver stank of cigarettes and stale beer, and though Haniya Razavi tried mightily to focus on her prayers, with each kneel toward Mecca, her senses were assaulted. After a few minutes, she decided to revel in the smell; inhaling deeply through her nose, she used it help fuel her rage at the fat, dumb Americans who lived like pigs.

Since almost decapitating her boyfriend, Haniya had been on the run. She had enacted the plan that she and Abdul-Azim had put in place, grabbing a prepacked suitcase that included several changes of clothing, $5,000 in cash, and a secret cargo disguised as a roll of toilet paper. Using the cash, she'd rented a car using a fake name and driver's license and gotten on the road. By the time Gabriel Marx and Lee Jensen were knocking on Adnan's door, she'd already been five hundred miles to the west.

Once her prayers were complete, she got into her car and drove into the city of Lakewood, about six miles west of downtown Denver at the foot of the Rocky Mountains. She had removed her hijab so as not to attract attention; she wore a gray jacket over a simple blouse and jeans, with her hair pulled tightly into a bun. She'd spent the morning looking for an internet café, but they had officially gone the way of the dodo and the public pay phone. So she ended up at the Lakewood Public Library, a modern single-story building with a rock garden at the entrance. She had been told by Rahman never to access the web using her phone and to use a "burner" for calls.

Walking into the library, Haniya found the bank of computers to the left of the check-out desk. The woman working at the front was busy with another customer and didn't look up when Haniya entered. Sitting down, she quickly opened a browser and logged into an email account that had been specifically set up for this purpose. She was looking for an email from Abdul-Azim—or, rather, the absence of one. If she got no email communication, she would know their operation had been compromised and he had been either taken into custody or killed. In that event she was to quickly move forward with their next attack.

"No new mail."

Quickly logging off, Haniya walked through the library and out the front door. She got into her car and immediately fired up the GPS. Locating I-70 West, she made her way to the interstate and plugged in her destination.

CHAPTER FORTY-THREE

Russian River Valley, California

CLAIRE MARX LAY BESIDE HER SLEEPING HUSBAND and lightly traced the curve of his shoulder with her fingers. His hair was tousled and too long, but his beard was neatly trimmed. Hanging around the federal government tended to smooth over rough edges, which was why most government workers were clean-shaven. Gabriel called it the "slow erosion of the self." It was one of the reasons he'd left the service.

But Claire knew there was another side to the story, and the moment Gabriel had walked in the door, she had recognized it in his eyes. An excitement she'd not seen before; as he recounted the frenetic pace of the past ten days, he'd grown more and more animated. He was wired on the adrenaline of the hunt and the chase for clues in the puzzle he was working on, and for an hour straight, he talked. And then, just as abruptly, he crashed onto the bed and fell deeply asleep.

Light was starting to filter through the windows, and Claire slipped out of bed and went toward the kitchen, trailed dutifully by Frankie. Any move toward the kitchen was reason for Frankie to wag his tail, hoping that food would miraculously appear in his bowl or something edible would fall to the floor. "C'mon, Frank," she said, as she opened up the back door to let him out to do his business.

Claire was something of a coffee aficionado, so the morning brew was a ritual. She carefully took out the beans, sourced from individual farms in Guatemala and delivered to her doorstep by an Amazon drone twice a week. She put the beans to her nose and savored the aroma of cherry and chocolate. She then placed the beans into a burr grinder that produced just the right amount and consistency for a perfect cup. Carefully scooping out the dark brown grounds into a copper filter, she filled the tank with cold water and hit Brew.

Out of habit she then fired up her tablet; she'd tried to break the habit of turning to an electronic device immediately upon getting up, but it was a battle she'd been losing. Everyday when Gabriel was away, she'd been scouring the news for information, first on the orange juice investigation and later on the almond scare. The news media had at first downplayed the significance of both events, but as the death toll had begun to mount, the reporting had become more and more dire. The headlines this morning were no exception: "CDC Reports 250th Death from Almond Toxin," "Recall Expected to Cost Industry More Than $2 Billion," "FBI Investigating Terror Links to Almond and OJ Poisonings."

When the coffeemaker finished brewing, Claire put the tablet down and poured her first cup. Returning then to the news, she made a mental note to ask Gabriel more about the FBI. From his rapid-fire delivery of events from the night before, she'd figured out that he was going to support the CDC on the almond investigation. But he hadn't said much about the FBI.

Just then she heard Frankie at the back door. Looking out the window, she also saw Gabriel's boss, Ed Collier, at the door. He had a small package in his hand.

"Claire, sorry to bother you so early," Ed said. "Is Gabriel up? I heard he was back."

"That's OK, Ed. How'd you hear he was back?"

"Charlie Thomas called to tell me about the Gulfstream V with 'United States of America' written on it that landed last night. Don't see that often at Sonoma County Airport." Thomas was the airport manager. "I figured it had to be your husband."

"Good guess," Claire said.

"This," Ed said, holding up the package, "arrived in the mail at the vineyard offices yesterday."

Claire took the package. It was addressed to Gabriel c/o Landmark Estates. There was no return address. "It's so light. Probably bugs," she said, smiling.

"Is he up?"

"Not yet. I'll have him come up to the big house when he's up and around."

"Great, thanks. Glad to have him back."

She closed the back door and put the package on the table.

CHAPTER FORTY-FOUR

Sacramento, California

LEE JENSEN had just sat down in a small café across the street from the California State Capitol building when his lunch "date" appeared at his table.

FBI Agent Joe Spiro looked around the small restaurant and sat down as well. "Could you have picked a more conspicuous place?"

"Hey, I just made the invite. You didn't have to come."

"You knew I was gonna come. And I know what you're doing too."

"Keep your friends close and your enemies closer."

"Exactly, only this ain't *The Godfather*, Lee. This is real life, and I don't want to get my ass in a sling. My boss is a piece of—"

"Shit?"

"I was gonna say 'work.' But that fits."

They both laughed in spite of themselves. "Look, can't a couple of old army buddies get together for a meal?"

"Normally, yes. But my boss's boss apparently hates your boss. So in this case our trip back to auld lang syne won't be much of a defense."

Just then their waitress came over for their order. "What can I get you gentlemen?"

"We'll both have the BLT and a Coke," Jensen said.

"Thanks, Dad," Spiro said.

"So what can you tell me about the almond investigation?"

"Whoa, no foreplay? That's it? Wham, bam, thank you, ma'am?"

"This is a quickie. We can do foreplay postcoitus," Jensen said, laughing at his own humor.

"God, you are so lucky that I like you. We're pretty much all hands on deck now. We've got teams scouring surveillance logs and footage from Sanger to Mount Shasta and everywhere in between. We're also working with the CDC and Ag to quarantine every almond tree—do you have any idea how many acres that amounts to? I had no freaking idea how big the almond business is."

"Any movement on the girl?"

"Not yet. We put out a BOLO to all law enforcement. That bitch is going to be famous inside of twenty-four hours. Unless she grows whiskers, she'll have a hard time hiding from us."

Jensen grunted. He knew that despite the modern tech the government now used, finding a single person in a country of 330 million people was a long shot. They'd have to get lucky to find her. "Have they been looking at the Samarra reference and Talmud info we gave you guys?"

"Beats me. Sanderson kicked it over to research in the Counterintelligence Division as soon as he got it. He's a cops and robbers guy. Not the intellectual type."

"Hard to believe the FBI could have an SAC who is that old school. The world operates on data and analysis now."

"Apparently Sanderson and the director have a bromance going. Not sure what that's about, but that's what I hear."

"Jesus," Jensen said. "You guys are missing the key to the whole thing. The clue is in all that stuff we gave you."

The waitress came over with their food and placed it down on the table. "Need anything else?"

"Extra mayo?" Spiro asked.

The waitress nodded and went away. "That stuff'll kill you," Jensen said. "This lunch is gonna kill me. I might as well enjoy it."

⁂

Jensen and Spiro shook hands at the table and left the restaurant separately. When Jensen got to his car, he dialed Gabriel's cell phone. A voice, groggy with sleep, answered after the fourth ring.

"Hello?"

Jensen looked at his watch. "This is your wake up call, pal."

"If that's a movie reference, skip it. I'm too tired."

"OK, I won't go all Gordon Gekko on you. I just had lunch—it is lunchtime, by the way—with a buddy of mine at the FBI. Got some good intel."

Gabriel yawned and poured himself some coffee from the pot Claire had made him before she left for work. "Like what?"

"Like they kicked up the Samarra parable stuff to research. God knows where that is now. It doesn't seem like Sanderson the G-man was too impressed with the analysis we did."

"We did?"

"OK, fine, Rabbi Marx. You did."

"What else did he say?"

"They are hot on this case as we knew they would be. Put out an all-points be on the lookout on our girl Haniya. But she could be long gone by now. So not sure what that's going to do for us."

Gabriel took a sip of coffee. "She's not gone. She's the snake killer."

Jensen didn't necessarily agree with that conclusion but didn't press it. "When are you going to start working with the CDC?"

"As soon as I get a shower and a change of clothes. I'll be in the town of Hooker tonight—about ten miles outside of Red Bluff."

"OK. I'll finish up a few things and then meet you there. We can grab a beer at The Hooker."

"Is there a bar there called The Hooker?" asked Gabriel.

"Hell if I know. But if there isn't, there should be."

Gabriel laughed and hung up. He'd slept so deeply that he didn't remember Claire getting out of bed, which was unusual for him. In fact he couldn't remember the last time he'd slept as well. Perhaps there was something to Claire's theory that he needed a mission in life.

Just as he was about to get up to refill his coffee cup, he noticed a note from Claire and a small brown package on the table. He picked up the note and read it:

Hun —

Ed brought this by early this a.m. Came a couple of days ago to the winery. He misses you and I told him you'd visit him in the big house today.

L— Claire

Gabriel picked up the package and felt how light it was. It had been sealed with Scotch tape and looked as if a five-year-old had wrapped it. Turning it over, he noticed no return address. He carefully slipped his finger under the cardboard's edge and pulled it open.

Inside was a small bundle wrapped in newspaper. When he unspooled it, a small glass vial fell out and onto the table. It had a black cap and looked just like the containers you would find in any lab.

Picking the vial carefully up from the table, he moved it into the light. Inside, slightly distorted by the thickness of the glass, was a lone insect lying dead at the bottom.

He was suddenly completely awake.

CHAPTER FORTY-FIVE

Hooker, California

GABRIEL WASN'T SURPRISED that there was no bar called The Hooker in Hooker. In fact the only bar in town was a dive called Dynamite, and that's where Gabriel found Lee Jensen. He was sitting at the bar drinking a Budweiser from the bottle. Bob Seger's "Turn the Page" was playing, and a group of roughnecks were playing pool at the back of the room. Though Gabriel was too young to swear by it, he figured this was probably a very authentic 1970s flashback. All that was missing was a haze of cigarette smoke.

Gabriel pulled up a stool and put the package he'd received in front of Jensen.

"What's that?" Jensen asked.

"Open it."

Jensen pulled out the newspaper and unspooled it from the vial. Holding it up to the light, he said, "God, you and your bugs."

"That's not just a bug, Lee. That's a message."

Lee peered again at the vial and then immediately looked over at the bartender, a fifty-something woman with too-blond hair and a leather vest that showed more than anyone likely wanted to see. When the bartender came over, she looked Gabriel up and down and said, "What can I get you, handsome?"

Gabriel smiled and said, "I bet you say that to all your customers."

She laughed and looked around the bar. "Not all of them, honey."

"Beer. But not what he's drinking. Something more substantial."

"Fat Tire on draft?"

"Perfect," Gabriel said.

When the bartender left, Jensen said, "What message is that?"

"This vial came to the vineyard, addressed to me, several days ago, in a plain box with no return address."

Jensen looked at Gabriel and waited for the punch line. When it didn't come, Jensen asked, "And?"

"And it came from Adnan."

"How the fuck do you know that?"

"Because when we searched Adnan's lab, this was the only insect in the entire place. Besides, who else would it be from?"

"I don't have any idea. Don't all you bug guys send stuff to each other?"

Gabriel sighed. "Yes, but not like this. There's a protocol that we follow. It includes specific containers and background data and notes. And it's never sent anonymously."

"Huh," Jensen said, taking another swig of his beer.

"I think it's part of the message he was trying to tell us with the parable. I think it fits into one of the clues he's given us."

"Which one?"

"I don't know. Yet."

Just then the bartender returned with Gabriel's beer. "There you go, honey," she said.

"What is it?" Jensen asked, pointing to the vial.

"It's a black salt marsh mosquito," Gabriel said.

"The one we talked about after searching Adnan's lab?"

"Yep."

Jensen gingerly handled the vial and looked at its contents. The mosquito had white stripes on its legs and white spots on its body. "Looks nasty."

"It's nasty all right. It's also been genetically altered to transmit Ebola."

"How the fuck do you know that?"

"Because I ran it through the sequencer in Landmark's lab."

"We have to tell the FBI about it."

"First thing tomorrow I'm going to drop it off with Smythe and the CDC, and then we'll go see the FBI. Right now I want to finish my beer, and then we need to go back to the hotel together and take another look at the parable."

"OK, I'll go back to the hotel with you. But don't get frisky, pal. I'm armed, you know.

Gabriel lay propped up on one of the two double beds in the small motel on Hooker Creek Road. He had the Talmud passage in his lap and was rereading the notes he'd taken when he and Gaddis had visited Rabbi Rafaeli in New York.

Lee Jensen was sitting at the foot of the other bed, his back against it, drinking a beer and flicking through channels on the wall-mounted flat-screen TV. "Damn, I love this flick!"

Gabriel looked up and said, "What is it?"

"It's an oldie. It's called *Rudy*."

"Shit, every kid in Michigan watched that movie for motivation during football season. We hate Notre Dame with a passion."

"Well, don't ruin if for me. I'm a closet Golden Domer."

"Figures," Gabriel muttered, and went back to his reading. "Do me a favor, and keep the volume down. I'm working here."

"Whatever," Jensen said with a chuckle.

Gabriel read and reread the passage that Rabbi Rafaeli had given them, the one about Hillel the Elder that appeared just before the part with Solomon and Luz. He then said, "Hey, mute that for a moment. I want to read you this."

Jensen sighed and hit the Mute button.

"He moreover once saw a skull floating upon the face of the water," Gabriel read. "'Because,' he said to it, 'thou didst drown others, they have drowned thee, and they that drowned thee shall be drowned too.'"

"Who is he?" Jensen asked.

"'He' refers to Hillel the Elder, one of Judaism's most influential teachers and scholars."

"Read it again," said Jensen.

Gabriel did so and paused in thought. "What does that mean to you?"

"Coming from a grunt who barely got through college? It makes me think of an eye for an eye."

"What about the skull floating on the water?"

"Signifies death by drowning maybe?"

Suddenly a light went off in Gabriel's head. "Death by water. That's it."

Jensen could tell from Gabriel's face that something had clicked. But he wasn't following. "Come again?"

"Fucking brilliant!" Gabriel said, reaching over to the nightstand and picking up the vial. "Water is the key to this whole thing! Like all mosquitoes, the black salt marsh breeds in water—in this case saltwater tidal pools, inlets, and marshes."

"You realize that doesn't really help us much, right?"

"It actually does help us some. It tells us that we are looking for something along the coasts."

"What's the total coastline of the United States? Ten thousand miles? That's really narrowing it down, partner."

Gabriel was silent for a long moment. "We need to find the girl."

CHAPTER FORTY-SIX

Roseville, California

IF YOU DIDN'T KNOW the FBI field office outside Sacramento was a government building, you'd swear you'd walked into the headquarters of a tech company. It was all steel and glass with an angled, bow-like entrance designed to evoke a feeling of modern precision. Since 9/11 the FBI saw itself increasingly as a data organization, with vast databases of information covering virtually every type of threat to the United States, both foreign and domestic.

As Gabriel and Lee Jensen walked into the building, they were hit with a wave of welcome cold air from the building's AC that flooded the modern, light-filled lobby. It was an impressive entrance. "Your taxpayer dollars at work," Jensen said under his breath.

"I wonder what J. Edgar would think of these digs," Gabriel said.

They walked over to the reception desk, where a uniformed officer greeted them. "May I help you gentlemen?"

Jensen took out his badge and said, "We're here to see Agent Sanderson."

"Can I see your IDs please?" the officer asked.

Jensen handed over his DHS ID, and Gabriel took out his California driver's license. The guard looked at Gabriel with suspicion, but wrote his name down on her sign-in sheet and handed the IDs back.

"Is he expecting you?" she asked.

"No," Jensen said.

"Can I tell him what this is in regards to?"

"No," Jensen said again.

The guard stared at Jensen for a moment and then picked up her phone. She dialed a number and said, "I have two gentlemen here for Agent Sanderson. An Agent Jensen from DHS and a civilian." She paused to listen. "No, they don't have an appointment."

Jensen held his hand out and motioned for the guard to give him the phone, which she reluctantly did.

"This is Lee Jensen from DHS. Please tell Agent Sanderson that Secretary Witt's on the phone at this very moment with the director of the FBI, and he's going to be mighty pissed to find out that someone's cock blocking us from providing information that is critical to the case the FBI is working on."

Jensen listened to the answer and then said, "Thank you," and handed the receiver back to the guard.

After another few seconds, the guard hung up, handed Jensen and Gabriel visitor badges, and said, "Someone will be right down to get you."

"Well, thank you so much," Jensen said with more than a hint of sarcasm in his voice. He then turned to Gabriel and smiled.

"Let's hope that works with Sanderson," Gabriel said.

"Don't hold your breath," Jensen said.

A young woman in a gray suit and purple blouse walked up. "You from DHS?"

"Yep. I'm Lee Jensen, and this is Gabriel Marx."

The woman nodded and, without offering a hand or introducing herself, said, "Follow me please."

They took the elevator to the third floor and were escorted to a bare conference room with a view of the parking lot. "Agent Sanderson will be right in," she said. And without another word she disappeared down the hallway.

For the next ten minutes, Gabriel and Lee stood next to each other facing the window, watching cars roll in and out of the parking lot. Neither of them knew what to expect from Brian Sanderson.

"Funny, I was just on the phone with the director," Sanderson said, entering the conference room. "He says he hasn't spoken to your boss in a few days."

"Huh. I must've gotten my signals crossed," Jensen answered. "And anyhow, the only reason we're here at all is because Secretary Witt insisted that we share what we have with you. If it were up to me—"

"You'd be running your own investigation. I know. That's what the director told me."

They squared off across the table for what Gabriel thought was an eternity. Finally, Sanderson broke the stalemate. "I've got ten minutes for you. My cock-blocking assistant tells me you have information on my case."

"We do," Jensen said.

Sanderson waited for more. "And?"

Gabriel took that as his cue. He took out the material he'd compiled and started to explain the package he'd received the previous day. Before getting to the meat of it, he was interrupted.

"A mosquito?" Sanderson asked. "As in the bug?"

"That's right. *Aedes taeniorhynchus* to be exact," Gabriel said.

Sanderson laughed. "Is that a joke?"

"It's no fucking joke, Sanderson," Jensen replied.

"OK, take it easy," Sanderson said. "And where's this mosquito now?"

"I gave it to the CDC this morning so they could run more tests," Gabriel said.

"That's evidence in this case and should have been given to us."

"I'm sorry. Did I miss the sign downstairs for the genetic testing lab?" Jensen asked.

Sanderson didn't like being questioned and turned a shade of red. "Why would I need that?"

"Because," Gabriel answered, "the mosquito in that vial carries the Ebola virus, which could kill off most of the people in this building."

Sanderson stared at Gabriel and decided he was telling the truth. "How the fuck do you know that?"

"Because I tested it myself in the lab where I work."

Sanderson was silent for a moment as he ran through the ramifications of this disclosure in his mind. "Where did the mosquito come from?"

"We don't know," Jensen said, preempting Gabriel before he could answer.

Sanderson looked straight at Gabriel. "Do you have a guess?"

Gabriel paused. He felt he had no choice but to tell Sanderson what he thought. "My guess is that it came from Adnan Mishner. I think he was having second thoughts."

Sanderson shook his head. He didn't buy it. "So what else do you have besides the bug?"

"We have this," Gabriel said, pulling out the Sukkah passage from his bag. He pushed it across the table.

"More ancient Jewish crap? Seriously? I sent all this to our research folks already."

"Agent Sanderson, this isn't crap. Let me explain to you why I think this, combined with the mosquito, is a critical clue to our case."

"You mean my case."

Gabriel ignored the last bit and took ten minutes to explain to Sanderson the three warnings, the significance of the water reference, and the possible link to the mosquito. When Gabriel was finished, the room was quiet.

"That's quite a hypothesis. Let's say it's true. What does that tell us? That we should be on the lookout for mosquitoes and water? That's hardly actionable intel."

"Maybe not. But it's a lead. What other leads do you have?" Jensen asked.

"We have plenty. We're interviewing every farmhand from Reedley to Redding, as well as running down every ISIS and al-Qaeda lead in our database."

"That's searching for a needle in a haystack and you know it," Jensen said.

"Whatever we got is better than a fucking mosquito and some hunches based on thousand-year-old passages from the Torah."

"It's the Talmud, not the Torah," Gabriel said.

"Whatever," Sanderson said. "It's a hunch built on conjecture surrounded by wishful thinking."

Jensen could see that the meeting was about over. "By the way, any news on the BOLO and the girl?"

"Not yet," Sanderson said. "You guys got anything else for me?"

Gabriel shook his head. This was a dead end.

"Great," Sanderson said. "My staff will show you out."

CHAPTER FORTY-SEVEN

Roseville, California

"HE'S RIGHT," Gabriel said as they drove away from the FBI building. "It's not much to go on."

"He's a dinosaur whose time has passed. Sanderson's investigating this like you would back in 1995. Gumshoe interviews aren't going to crack this baby open. And he clearly isn't taking our 'ancient Jewish crap' seriously."

"Would you if you were him? The hunches of a civilian?"

"If that was all I had, then fuck yes I would. Do you know how many cases have been cracked because someone had a hunch?"

"No, how many?"

"Plenty," Jensen said with a laugh. Gabriel couldn't help but smile. He knew that Jensen was trying to make him feel better, and he appreciated it.

Gabriel was quiet the rest of the way back to the DHS offices. As they were pulling into the parking lot, he said, "I'm going to head up to Red Bluff and meet with Smythe's team. I can't just sit around here and wait for the other shoe to drop."

"OK. I'll keep a lookout for anything on the girl. If I hear anything, I'll call you."

In Gabriel's mind there was little else to do but keep himself busy and hope the BOLO would produce results. On the drive up to Red Bluff, he listened to Nina Simone, her smoky voice filling the cab of his truck. Gabriel loved blues, and Simone was one of his favorites. In college he'd taken a music appreciation class and written a paper on Simone's life as a black woman in America during the civil rights era; her music was infused with themes of racial tension and protest, and since she had been more a devotee of Malcolm X than she had been of Martin Luther King, her lyrics were tinged with anger. It was that tension in her voice, a frustration and passion for change, that Gabriel was most attracted to.

And frustration perfectly fit his mood.

Pulling off Interstate 5 into Red Bluff, Gabriel entered the small town from the east and drove through the downtown district just after midday. The town, named for the rouge-colored bluffs nearby along the Sacramento River, was an historic throwback to the California gold rush. Like so many Central Valley towns in a state known primarily for technology and tourism, it seemed like a place that time had forgotten.

The CDC had set up its operation in the parking lot of the post office. It included three ultramodern trailers built for mobile interventions just like this one that housed everything from a command center with the most sophisticated communication technology to a mobile kitchen capable of feeding up to a hundred people three square meals a day. These trailers were a reflection of how the combination of climate change and an increasingly interconnected global population were changing the nature of world health. Viruses and bacteria, particularly from Africa and Asia, were hitching rides on jet airplanes and taking root in the West at breathtaking speed. A century ago it might have taken a hundred years for a deadly new virus to make the leap from Africa to North America, now it was happening in a matter of days.

Gabriel walked into the command trailer and found Ken Smythe sitting at a small conference room table. He had been shuttling back and forth between Atlanta and California for the past several days and was visibly worn.

"Anything new?" Gabriel asked as he pulled up a chair.

Smythe looked up from the printout he was reading. His normally pleasant face with the quick smile was drawn and serious. "Unfortunately, yes," he said. "We confirmed your findings from that mosquito you gave me. An Ebola sequence has been inserted into its cells. That mosquito was bred to spread the virus."

Gabriel's face showed that he wasn't surprised. He said, "We've got a huge problem on our hands."

"Are you restating the obvious, or is there something else I should know?"

"Yes, there's something else. The black salt marsh is a pretty rugged mosquito. It's normally found in brackish water, salt marshes, tidal flats, and lots of other places inhospitable to other mosquito species. Its range until the last decade has been along the East and Gulf Coasts. But with global warming, its range has greatly expanded. And because it's not known for transmitting disease, it won't raise much suspicion when it shows up and starts infecting people. Basically they've created a very effective weapon of mass destruction."

"Great," Smythe said. He then remembered something. "By the way, did you happen to notice the newspaper that vial was wrapped in when you gave it to me?"

"Not really, no."

"Huh. Well, I did. Take a look," Smythe said, handing the wrinkled paper to Gabriel. He smoothed it out and found an ad for solar-powered drones on one side. Flipping it over, he noticed a large color picture of an Asian man in a white coat standing in front of GenomeX's headquarters. The caption said, "Dr. Ed Nomura is leading GenomeX's cutting-edge research into genetic-based therapies."

"I'll be damned. I actually met Nomura as a part of the investigation. Lebedev, who was the source of the type I botulinum toxin, worked there, and he's connected to Rahman, Adnan, and GMU in a multitude of ways. I wonder if there's more to the story than we know."

Smythe laughed. "There's always more to every story than we know."

"Look, if the black salt marsh was a message, maybe so was this newspaper clipping."

"What kind of message?"

"Well, GenomeX is in Redwood City, just on the border of Silicon Valley. That's a pretty fat target."

"Jesus. I've got to call the president."

Gabriel began to get up. "I'll be outside—"

"No, please stay. I'm going to need your help."

Gabriel sat down as Smythe swiveled his chair around and picked up the phone on the desk. He punched in a few numbers and said, "Dr. Smythe calling for the president." He listened for a few moments and said, "OK," and then hung up.

"She's in a meeting with the national-security team. They're going to video conference us in."

"You sure I should stay for this? I'm not really—"

"I'm sure. How often do you get to talk to the president of the United States?"

"Under the circumstances I wish I wasn't."

"You and me both."

The large screen on the wall suddenly came to life, and an image of President Jennifer Cooperman flanked by the secretary of defense, the national security advisor, FBI Director Mark Timmons, and Jason Witt appeared. In the corner Gabriel could see a smaller image of himself and Smythe. He was suddenly very self-conscious of his appearance and tried to smooth the front of his shirt.

"Dr. Smythe, who is that with you?" Cooperman asked.

"Ma'am, this is Gabriel Marx. He was assigned by DHS to help us on the almond investigation. He has information that's very pertinent to this . . . case."

Cooperman looked over at Witt. "Well, if Secretary Witt vouches for him here, then that's good enough for me."

"I do, ma'am," Witt said with a slight smile.

"So what do you have for us, Ken?" Cooperman asked.

"Ma'am, we've had a major development here. I'm going to ask Gabriel to explain what's transpired over the past forty-eight hours."

Gabriel cleared his voice. "Madam President, several days ago I received a package that had been mailed to me. . . ." He went on to recount what he'd received, how it intersected with the case that they'd been working on in relation to Adnan Mishner and the BRL, and what he'd done with it.

"That's a lot to digest," the president said. "What makes you think this came from one of the terrorists?"

"Ma'am, I believe that Adnan Mishner was having second thoughts," Gabriel said.

"Do you have any proof to back that up?" asked the secretary of defense.

"Sir, I was part of the team that searched Adnan's lab at the BRL. One of the mosquitoes that he had there in abundance—in fact the only mosquito he had there—was called the black salt marsh. It's the same species that was sent to me."

"And you think that's some sort of message?"

"Yes, sir."

"That's pretty thin, don't you think?" President Cooperman asked.

"Ma'am, I understand why you would say that. But there's another element that we've just confirmed that makes it virtually certain that the mosquito came from Adnan."

"And what's that?" Cooperman asked.

Gabriel looked over at Smythe. Gabriel was about to drop the bombshell and wanted to make sure Smythe was OK with it. When Smythe nodded, Gabriel plunged ahead.

"We had the mosquito I received tested by the CDC. And it's come back positive for the presence of Ebola virus.

"Oh my God!" Cooperman exclaimed. "Well, that doesn't say much for our security, does it? We had a terrorist working at a government lab handling Ebola and other deadly diseases?"

"Actually, we found that Adnan's lab wasn't working with Ebola," Gabriel said.

Cooperman looked confused. "You've lost me."

"When we searched the lab's database, we found a large number of genetic sequences for a host of viruses and bacteria that we are certain came from GenomeX courtesy of Antonin Lebedev."

"Including Ebola?"

"Yes."

"So you believe that Adnan sent you this salt marsh mosquito infected with Ebola as a clue. Is that about it?"

"Yes. Only the mosquito is not technically infected with Ebola. Rather it's been engineered to synthesize — and spread — particles of the virus to humans."

Cooperman again seemed confused. "I don't understand," she said simply.

"Ma'am, this involves a lot of complex genetics, but basically the sequence for Ebola — the DNA code as well as key viral proteins — were inserted into a chromosome of mature mosquitoes so they became a part of their cell structure. They essentially became carriers of the virus, which propagates inside of them but doesn't harm them. Then, when they lay their eggs, their offspring also carry the same DNA encoding. When the eggs hatch…"

"You have new mosquitoes capable of infecting people."

"Correct."

"I remember when Ebola popped up in Africa back in 2014," the chairman of the Joint Chiefs said. "I was CENTCOM commander then, and we looked closely at the risks to our troops on the continent. We also provided humanitarian support. I distinctly remember being briefed that mosquitoes didn't transmit Ebola. Is that not correct?"

"Sir, that's correct in the wild. In other words, there are clear indications that mosquitoes are not good hosts for Ebola, and a mosquito biting an infected person won't lead to the transmission of the virus to someone else. But that's not what we are dealing with here. This genetic modification is designed so that Ebola becomes a part of the mosquito's cell structure. That means it's everywhere inside the insect. Including its spit."

"Spit?" Cooperman asked.

"Yes, ma'am. Mosquitoes transmit viruses not through blood but through their saliva, which contains a natural anticoagulant. The mosquito actually injects its virus-filled saliva into you when it bites you. So this mosquito has been engineered to spread Ebola."

"Jesus," Cooperman said. "So how would they release these mosquitoes? Don't they need airplanes or helicopters and other equipment?"

"Unfortunately, they don't need any of that, ma'am. The nature of mosquito eggs is that they are tremendously durable. They can stay viable in a dry state—like dehydrated grains of rice, only smaller. They can be carried easily on filter or parchment paper. A box of coffee filters can carry a million eggs or more. They only have to be rehydrated in water at the right temperature, and they will hatch into larvae and ultimately become mosquitoes."

"So all the next attacker needs is a roll of toilet paper filled with eggs and water to unleash the Ebola virus?" asked the secretary of defense.

Gabriel looked at Smythe before replying. "Yes, that's about it."

"Ken, let's say they are successful at this," Cooperman said. "Can you tell us what this means from a public health perspective?"

"Yes, ma'am. Ebola is a virus that first appeared in the mid-1970s in Africa. There have been periodic outbreaks since then, most recently in 2017 and 2019 in the Democratic Republic of the Congo. Ebola virus causes a hemorrhagic fever that essentially breaks down the body's connective tissues. People who are infected come down with a headache, backache, and high fever and eventually suffer from total organ failure and uncontrolled bleeding. They literally bleed out. Mortality rates will range from fifty to eighty percent."

"Meaning it's a death sentence," said Cooperman.

"It's often fatal for the infected individual," Smythe said. "From a pandemic standpoint, it's actually far worse that that."

"Worse than being fatal?" the SecDef asked.

"Ebola is spread by blood and saliva and semen, either directly from person to person or on surfaces that are contaminated, and may be spread through the air. It's highly infectious. So if mosquitoes can start the fire, people will keep it going. It will turn into a massive, widespread conflagration in a matter of weeks."

"Impressive," said the chair of the JCS, more to himself than anyone else.

Cooperman heard what he'd said. "How so, General?"

"Just that it's impressive as a weapon, ma'am. It starts a chain reaction that, if it gets up enough speed, can feed upon itself."

"I'd say it's more diabolical than impressive. But I get your meaning. OK, Ken, what now?"

"From a public health perspective, all we can do is warn the public about mosquitoes and proactively work to keep people aware of the risk. We've been doing that in Florida, Louisiana, and other places in relation to Zika for the past decade. We can build on that. But until we find the source of the threat, there isn't much we can do to stop it."

"Director Timmons, what's the update on the search for the terrorists?" the president asked.

"Ma'am, we are continuing the search for the primary suspect in the case, a Haniya Razavi, and have issued a worldwide be-on-the-lookout notice. Our agents continue to work both the almond and citrus cases, and we are pursuing all leads associated with Adbul-Azim Rahman and ISIS."

"Jason, any update from DHS?" Cooperman asked.

"We have secured all ports of entry and exit and have ICE on the lookout. So far, nothing."

Cooperman nodded. "Do we have any idea where they will strike next?"

The room was silent. In for a penny, in for a pound, Gabriel thought. "Ma'am?"

"Go ahead, Gabriel," the president said.

"I think there may have been another clue in the package that was sent to me. The vial that contained the mosquito was wrapped in a newspaper from several years ago. It was a picture of a scientist at GenomeX."

"The company in California?"

"Yes, in Redwood City. We know Antonin Lebedev, who was the source of the type I botulinum toxin, worked at GenomeX. And we know that he studied under Professor Rahman at GMU, so there's a link between GenomeX and the university. Which also means there's a link to Adnan and the BRL."

"And?"

"And I have a hunch that this clipping means they are going to target Silicon Valley."

That made some sense to Cooperman. Silicon Valley was home to the top technology companies in the world and two of the three most valuable companies on the planet. An outbreak of Ebola in the tech sector would quickly cripple the US economy. "Where exactly would they attack us?"

"Ma'am, the Peninsula is full of water and has the San Francisco Bay on one side. Redwood City itself, where GenomeX is headquartered, is adjacent to marshes and deltas and plenty of water."

"Isn't the San Francisco Bay salt water? I thought mosquitoes only breed in fresh water."

"Ma'am, that's just it. I think they chose the black salt marsh because, as its name suggests, it thrives in salt water and can be found in tide pools, bays, and estuaries. I think they chose it because the San Francisco Bay is the target."

"With all due respect, you're just guessing," said Timmons. "It could just as easily be New Orleans, Miami, or Orlando."

"Yes, sir. It could be," Gabriel admitted.

"Do you have a better guess, Mark?" Cooperman asked the FBI director.

"No, ma'am. I'm just saying that we can't be sure of where they will strike. So we have to cover all our bases."

"True," Cooperman said. "But I think there's some logic in what Gabriel is saying. Make sure your men in Silicon Valley are monitoring the bay closely."

"Yes, ma'am."

"We'll reconvene tomorrow morning for an update. In the meantime, let's hope we get a break on this," Cooperman said. "Thank you, gentlemen," she said. The screen went dark.

Smythe looked at Gabriel. "Well, one thing's for certain. Nobody will ever call you shy."

CHAPTER FORTY-EIGHT

Livermore, California

HANIYA HAD CALCULATED HER FUEL usage down to the gallon and had been certain she'd make her destination without having to stop. Her training told her that the chances of being caught increased dramatically every time she left her car, and that included at self-serve gas stations. Even not having to speak to an attendant was no protection against HD cameras that would catch her image. By that point she had to assume that her face was plastered all over every police station and patrol car from there to Mexico City.

Even before she finished pumping the gas, Haniya instinctively knew that something was wrong. The attendant was staring at her from behind green-hued bulletproof glass; it was different from the usual male gawking. That she was accustomed to. This was more intent, more urgent. She made an effort not to look back at him, but she couldn't help herself. Their eyes met, and the man reached down and picked up his phone. Coincidence? She thought it unlikely. As the pump hit three gallons, she quickly decided she had enough to reach her destination. She replaced the hose and screwed in the gas cap, making sure that it clicked in securely. Then as nonchalantly as she could, she got behind the wheel and drove off.

Word of the sighting reached Lee Jensen almost immediately. He'd asked the Sacramento Sherriff's Office to call him if the BOLO got a lead, and so far this was the twenty-second time he'd been alerted. The twenty-one others had been false alarms. Some had been close and actually looked like Haniya; others had been so inaccurate that he was reminded again how wildly unreliable eyewitnesses were. People saw what they wanted to see.

So when this latest alert came in, Jensen was appropriately skeptical. "Is there video?"

"Yeah, we've got video," said the sheriff's deputy. "Let me send it over."

"Great, thanks," Jensen said. He waited the thirty seconds it took for the video to appear on his screen. He hit the Play button. As the video buffered, he said to himself, "Life is like a box of chocolates. You never know what you're . . ." He stopped in midsentence. He quickly picked up the phone and dialed Gabriel's number.

Gabriel picked up on the second ring. "Jensen, you won't believe who I just talked to."

"Never mind that. Where are you?"

"I'm on the I-5 just outside of Sacramento."

"We found her."

"No shit? Where?"

"Thirty minutes ago at a gas station in Livermore, California."

"Livermore? Fuck! I was right!"

"Right about what?"

"About GenomeX. Never mind. Let me bring up a map." Gabriel switched on self-driving mode and brought up a map of the Bay Area on his heads-up display. He traced his finger along Route 84, which ran through Livermore and turned into the Dumbarton Bridge. On one side of the bridge was the Don Edwards San Francisco Bay National Wildlife Refuge, and on the other side sat Bair Island and the marshes that made up Redwood Shores—just a stone's throw from Oracle, Facebook, and a dozen other high-tech behemoths.

"I'll pick you up in twenty minutes," Gabriel said, looking at his watch.

"Where're we going?"

"We're gonna say hello to our little friend," Gabriel said in his best Al Pacino impression.

CHAPTER FORTY-NINE

San Francisco Bay Area, California

LEE JENSEN SPENT THE FIRST HOUR of their drive from Sacramento getting an update from Gabriel on what he'd told the president. The second hour he spent working his phone. His first call was to Jason Witt.

"Boss, we've got a BOLO hit on Haniya Razavi. She's still on the run, but we think we know where she's going. We could use some help. Can you authorize ICE to direct the Drone Unit to put eyes over the Bay Area?"

"Absolutely. Can you narrow down a search area?"

"Yes, hold on. Calculating it now. I'll email it to you as soon as I have it," Jensen said, disconnecting the call.

"What's the Drone Unit?" Gabriel asked.

"Our eyes in the sky. Over the past decade the government invested beaucoup bucks on surveillance technology in tracking illegals. ICE has its own drone air force. Most people don't know this, but ICE is pretty much overhead in California, Texas, and Arizona 24-7."

"That's a pretty well-kept secret."

"You know what? The politicians in Sacramento know about it. They don't talk about it, because it's not part of their politically correct shtick. But they know about it."

"Doesn't surprise me," Gabriel said under his breath.

Jensen used his phone to send Witt the general coordinates of the area Gabriel had identified. Jensen also sent Witt the location of a Starbucks on Ralston Avenue just outside Redwood Shores, one of the prime potential targets for Haniya. The mobile drone team would meet them there.

"So what exactly are we looking for?" Jensen asked Gabriel. "I mean, the girl, yes. But how is she delivering her payload?"

"Vector vessels. Normally that's how insects are carried and delivered. The vessels can also be connected to projectiles that allow the canister to be delivered to more distant targets, like a mortar. That's what we used in Afghanistan. But she won't be using a vector vessel."

"Why not?"

"It's the brilliance of their plan," Gabriel said. He then explained what he'd told the president about how you can carry dehydrated mosquito eggs on rolls of paper.

"Death by toilet paper. Now I've heard it all," Jensen said. "It's going to be pretty hard to find her. She can slip that into the water pretty easily," Jensen said.

"Yep. But my guess is that she'll wait for dark and then spread it around to multiple locations to widen the impact. That movement is how we're gonna nail her."

"You know, I once went sailing on the San Francisco Bay, and the water was freezing. Isn't it too cold for mosquitoes?"

"It was for many years. But the summers are so warm here now that the shallow areas of the bay around inlets and marshes heat up to the point that they are well suited for mosquitoes like the black salt marsh."

"Huh. And do you think that Adnan would have known that?"

"Absolutely. Global warming has moved the range of many mosquito species to the north, and entomologists and health experts are tracking that trend closely. He would have known that it's made areas like San Francisco,

Seattle, and Chicago more vulnerable to mosquito-borne diseases."

Fifteen minutes later they pulled into the parking lot of the Starbucks. There were three plain black panel vans at the back of the lot, each with multiple antennae sticking into the air. "That's them," Jensen said.

Gabriel pulled into a spot next to one of the vans and looked over. A bearded man with a black ball cap was sitting in the front seat; his window was closed, and Gabriel could hear their engine running. The Bay Area had been in the grip of a heat wave for the past several weeks, and they needed to keep the air conditioning on. Jensen looked past Gabriel and said, "I know that guy," and got out of the truck.

"Jensen, I should've known it'd be you," the man said, shaking Jensen's hand.

"Who else would it be? Everyone else is at the spa," he said, slapping the man on the back in a friendly embrace. "Chuck, this is Gabriel Marx. He's working with us on this. Gabriel, this is Chuck Knox. Chuck is, among many other things, the great-grandson and namesake of the guy who coached the Los Angeles Rams in the 1970s. I know that because my dad was a huge Rams fan when I was a kid."

"Nice to meet you," Gabriel said. Knox was a strapping man with arms as big as most men's legs. His handshake was crushing. In the marines you got used to sizing up men in a split second, like the way dogs sniff each other. The longer you were in the military, particularly in combat, the easier it was to tell if the guy was a good dude or a douchebag. Gabriel instantly knew that he liked Chuck Knox.

"Come on around back," Knox said, leading them to the back of the van he'd been in. He knocked twice in rapid succession, and the door popped open, releasing a wave of cool air. Inside was a command center that looked like an airline simulator. There was a bank of monitors that surrounded three chairs, each with joysticks in front of them.

"Cool!" Gabriel said. He loved anything to do with airplanes and had a simulator of his own at home.

"This controls the four drones we have stored in the other vans," Knox said. "They're Fulmar fixed-wing micro-UAVs capable of twelve hours of continuous flight and a ninety-kilometer range. Should be perfect for this operation. And the best thing is that they are pretty quiet."

"Do they have cameras?" Jensen asked.

Knox laughed. "Yes, Lee, they have cameras. HD video and full infrared capabilities, meaning we'll be able to see heat signatures of people moving at night."

"Sweet!" Jensen said. He too was caught up in the gadget euphoria that had overtaken the group.

Knox turned to Jensen. "So what's the plan?"

"Beats me," Jensen said without a hit of embarrassment. Looking at Gabriel, he asked, "What's the plan?"

Gabriel gave Knox a quick overview of who they were looking for and what she was likely to be doing. Gabriel then moved over to one of the monitors, which already had Google satellite maps up. "We have four drones, and I think we should divide them this way. One should be over Redwood Shores," he said, using his fingers to zoom in. "This area is like a system of inlets with homes all in and around the waterways. It's a perfect target."

Knox got up to take a closer look. "That should be easy enough for us to cover. What else you got?"

Gabriel moved his fingers south to Bair Island, a marshy area along Bayshore Freeway. "This area is shallow and full of reeds and grasses, a great area for mosquitoes. It also has a marina where she may try and highjack a boat to better get around." He then moved the map east across the bay to the San Francisco Bay National Wildlife Refuge. "Let's get both of these covered as well."

"What about here?" Knox asked, pointing to an East Bay area north of the wildlife refuge.

"That's Eden Landing Eco Reserve. That's the fourth spot."

"OK, that works," Knox said. "How do you want us to split up to cover these? One team can cover the two areas on the west side of the bay because they're pretty close together. But on the east side, we're going to need two separate teams if we're gonna have a decent response time."

"Agree," Jensen said. "Gabriel and I'll take the west, and your guys can split up and take the east. OK?"

Gabriel nodded and Knox said, "Fine by me." He then looked at his watch. "It's now 16:55. We'll plan on having birds in the air by eighteen hundred hours."

"Roger that," Jensen said. "Anything else?"

"Yeah," Gabriel said. "The suspect here is a woman who will likely be carrying mosquito eggs wrapped in paper. They are dried eggs that, when submersed in water, will rehydrate and eventually hatch if the conditions are right. If she manages to get the eggs into the water, we are going to have to remove them quickly, or the whole area is going to have to be hit with insecticide."

"How fast is 'quickly'?" Knox asked.

"Good question. It depends on how fast the paper dissolves. Fifteen to thirty minutes, tops. I've got bags and gloves for your guys. Be sure they wear them."

"OK. We'll do our best," Knox said.

Jensen nodded and moved to exit the van. "You guys want coffee?"

Gabriel shook his head no. But Knox said, "Sure. Triple venti vanilla soy no-foam latte."

Jensen just shook his head and laughed. "One black coffee coming up," he said.

CHAPTER FIFTY

Redwood City, California

THE DOCKTOWN MARINA HAD ONCE BEEN AN ENCLAVE for funky houseboats and hippies, a throwback to a time when the Peninsula wasn't just for overpaid software engineers and tech executives. That was a decade ago, before Redwood City had decided that it could no longer abide the last vestige of cheap housing and free living in the increasingly tony area. So the houseboats were gone, replaced by the yachts of the rich and a few small sailboats used by a local sailing school.

Gabriel sat in his truck on a dark frontage road outside the marina, monitoring the radio traffic between Knox and his men. Knox and one other drone operator were set up in their van about a mile from Gabriel. Both of their drones were high above, one directly over the marina and one over Redwood Shores. The other van, with two more operators on board, sat across the bay running the drones above the National Wildlife Refuge and the Eden Landing Ecological Reserve. They also had two other team of agents with them, strategically placed so they could quickly react if the target was spotted.

After some discussion, Lee Jensen had ended up with another DHS agent to the north of Gabriel in Redwood Shores and was also sitting in a parked car among the waterfront townhouses and homes. Initially, Lee had been reluctant to separate from Gabriel, believing that they should stick together given the uncertainty of who and what they'd encounter. But Gabriel had argued that the distance between the marina and Redwood Shores was small and that it was critical to have coverage in both areas so they could react quickly. Jensen ultimately relented. "Try not to shoot yourself," he'd said when he handed Gabriel his extra service weapon. "I know marines have trouble with that sort of thing."

Now Etta James sang softly in the background as Gabriel watched and waited. Part of the reason he'd sent Jensen to Redwood Shores was that he'd wanted some time to think. It seemed like forever ago he'd been living a quiet life on the vineyard with his wife and dog, though in reality it had been only a week and a half. So much had happened during that time that he hadn't processed it all. One thing he was sure of: he loved the hunt, the sleuthing, the puzzle, and the excitement of cracking the case. He felt as if he'd stumbled into what he should be doing with his life, though he had no idea if he'd be able to keep doing it, or if he'd really want to if it meant moving to Washington, DC. He hated DC and everything it stood for; politics had become a blood sport, and even the agencies that were supposed to be above it all—the FBI, Justice Department, and even DHS—were infused with partisan infighting. Gabriel was not going to trade the vineyard for the swamp.

But he also knew that Claire was right about him and that he needed more than what he was getting from their life in the Russian River Valley. His nightmares and anxiety had disappeared since he had gone on this mission, and he knew this was not a coincidence. Something in his subconscious was calling out for a mission in life, and going back to the wine wasn't going to cut it for him. He'd need to find some way to get back in the game.

For the next several hours, he and the DHS team checked in with one another on the half hour. Knox was reporting some activity around Redwood Shores but nothing on the water itself. One young couple was apparently having sex on the deck of one of the boats and hadn't bothered to bring a blanket, but otherwise things were pretty quiet. So it was also across the bay at the wildlife refuge and the ecological reserve.

By 3:00 a.m. Gabriel was starting to think that maybe he'd gotten it wrong and that Haniya had another target in mind. He picked up his phone and called Jensen on his cell.

"You awake?" Gabriel asked when Jensen answered.

"I'm awake. This ain't my first rodeo, pal. Done my fair share of stake-outs. It's pure boredom punctuated by gnarly farts."

Gabriel laughed. "At least I'm by myself."

"Is she gonna show?"

"We still have three hours until daybreak," Gabriel said as if to buoy himself. "There's still time."

"There's definitely still time. Hang tough," Jensen said, and disconnected the line.

Just as Gabriel put his cell phone down, a voice, tinged with urgency, came over his headset. "We've got movement!"

Gabriel keyed his mike. "Whaddya got?"

"I've got movement at the marina! Single figure moving toward the boats, headed down the second line of slips. They're heading toward a large boat moored at the end of the dock."

Gabriel got ready to get out of the truck but waited to hear more. If this was someone who entered the boat and turned on the lights, it could be someone who lived on the boat or a boater getting an early start on the day. "Keep watching."

"Roger. They've disappeared now behind the boat. I'm repositioning now to pick up the visual again." The operator moved the drone around until he could see movement. "OK, I've got it. They're getting in a small boat and moving away from the dock."

Gabriel didn't wait for more information. He quickly got out of the truck, put Jensen's Glock into his jacket pocket, and ran toward the dock.

CHAPTER FIFTY-ONE

Redwood City, California

HANIYA, DRESSED ALL IN BLACK with a black backpack, had slipped into a dinghy and was quietly rowing toward Redwood Creek and a group of homes along the water. It was pitch black, and the water was warm and still. She had worn a black turtleneck and quickly began to sweat.

Her mission was to proceed along Redwood Creek, dropping the paper gently into the pools of water close to shore, among the reeds and plants that were thriving there. She intended to put out more than half the roll over the next two hours and then move to the west, under Bayshore Freeway, to get the payload as close to the Redwood City business district as possible.

As she rowed toward where she planned to begin dropping the paper, she recited prayers, reaffirming her mission and knowing that the end was near. Whatever happened she would soon be with Allah.

Gabriel sprinted toward the dock with the voice of the drone operator in his ear. "Head straight and then left down the gangway to that large boat, and I'll tell you when to stop."

Gabriel put his head down and pumped his arms and legs. He was acutely aware of his breathing because the microphone he was wearing made every breath echo in his ears. By the time he reached the boat, he was breathing heavily. "Look straight out from there," the voice said. "Do you see her?"

Gabriel peered into the darkness. He could just make out a dark form on the water, but she was moving steadily away from him. "I see her," he said. Without prompting he went to the adjacent boat and found an inflatable dinghy tied up at the stern. He jumped in and landed in several inches of water on the bottom, soaking his boots and pants. Untying the dinghy, he grabbed a single oar and set out after her.

"You're about three hundred yards behind her. Keep heading in the direction you are currently going," said the voice.

Gabriel kept paddling in a rhythm: one paddle on the left, two on the right, two on the left, one on the right. He'd spent summers on a lake in Michigan as a kid and knew how to get around on a boat.

Haniya stopped her own paddling and drifted the last fifteen feet toward a series of small ponds just adjacent to the creek. They had been built for the enjoyment of nearby residents and filled with turtles and koi fish, with benches and chairs arrayed around them. Coming to a rest at a small dock, she took off her backpack and unzipped it. Gently taking out the roll of paper, she took off the wrapper and unspooled a foot of it, tearing it easily with her hands. Then moving toward the pond, she gently submerged the paper in the warm water, allowing it to mingle with the reeds and grasses. Satisfied, she then repeated the same process with the other three ponds.

"The target's stopped and moving around just onshore," the voice in Gabriel's ear said. "Looks like she's on a dock of some sort. It's about a hundred fifty yards in front of you."

Gabriel continued his paddling, taking care to be as quiet as possible. He knew that sound traveled easily on the water, and he didn't want to lose the element of surprise.

"OK, the target's back on the water headed away from you. Looks like she's moving into the marsh area by the adjacent road. You're about a hundred yards away now."

Instinctively, Gabriel crouched down in his dinghy, making smaller and smaller movements. His speed slowed to a crawl.

⁕

Lee Jensen had heard it all on the radio and was racing down Bayshore Freeway toward the marina. His fellow DHS agent was driving, and Jensen was pressing him to go faster. They were following a Google map that clearly showed the road running adjacent to Redwood Creek, and that was where Jensen wanted to go. But they couldn't find the access road to it and ended up behind a tall fence that divided the road from the water. Jensen was fit to be tied.

"Knox!" he shouted. "Can you give me directions on how to get the fuck over there?"

"Hang on," Knox said, moving the drone around. "Turn around and head north until you get to Maple Street. Then you'll have to park and hoof it."

"Fuck!" Jensen yelled.

⁕

Gabriel was by then drifting silently forward, just ten yards from Haniya. He was prone on the floor of the dinghy with his gun in his right hand, his head barely peeking above the boat's edge. Just a few more yards, and he'd have her.

#

Haniya was oblivious to the threat behind her. Her prayers filled her mind, and she was totally focused on the task at hand. She'd methodically laid her paper trail down as she went, carefully submerging the eggs into the bath that would unleash a deadly disease on the infidel.

#

Gabriel's dinghy rammed into Haniya's with more force than he was expecting; caught off balance, Haniya fell hard into the water just as Gabriel launched himself onto her boat. Without anything to push against, Gabriel missed his landing and bounced off the side of her boat, dropping his gun into the pitch-black creek. He was now unarmed, and they were now both in the water.

Even before Gabriel could come up for air, she was on him. Trying to gouge his eyes out, grunting and shrieking, she pushed on his head and tried to force him under. Finding his footing, he braced himself on the bottom and grabbed her arm, twisting it as hard as he could. She then clawed at his face with every ounce of energy she had, drawing blood from his cheek. He was trying to grab her other hand when she was able to wrest herself free from his grasp.

In a single practiced move, Haniya pulled a Fairbairn-style knife from a scabbard secured to her forearm and took a big slash at him. The knife, a type favored by commandos, was six inches long and razor sharp. Gabriel could feel the blade cut into his jacket, splitting it open like a ripe watermelon. It raked his skin, and he started bleeding from a long cut on his chest. She then came back at him from the other direction with a big sweeping motion, but Gabriel was able to block it with his forearm while grabbing her wrist with his free hand. The knife was now suspended in midair, hovering over him like a bird of prey waiting to find a target.

It wasn't a fair fight. Though Haniya had been well trained, she was more than sixty pounds lighter than Gabriel, and he quickly gained the upper hand. As she started to weaken, Gabriel felt a change in the pressure she was exerting; rather than pushing against him, she was pulling him into her, moving the knife ever closer to her face. He immediately sensed what she was doing and tried to stop her.

But his feet were slipping on the slick bottom of the creek, and he couldn't get the leverage needed to stop her momentum. In an instant, Haniya plunged the knife into her neck, cutting through cartilage and bone, severing her carotid artery in the process.

"No! No!" Gabriel screamed into the night. He reached out to her in the dark, desperately trying to staunch the flow of blood, his hands trying to cover the wound in her neck.

But it was too late. Blood coursed out of her body, bleeding through his fingers in waves, timed perfectly with the beating of her heart. After a moment he began to feel the sting of his own wound, and released his grip on her. She then settled slowly onto her back, her eyes open, fixed on the night sky.

Like a skull floating upon the face of the water.

CHAPTER FIFTY-TWO

Russian River Valley, California

FOR MANY WEEKS AFTERWARD, Gabriel relived the events of that night in Redwood Creek. He couldn't get the image out of his mind of Haniya's blood on his hands, nor could he absolve himself of the guilt he felt. By letting Haniya kill herself he had forever lost the chance for the government to find out more about the plot and the plotters. He felt he'd let Witt and Jensen down, and he was having a hard time forgiving himself.

That others had been more sanguine didn't really make him feel any better; Witt had called him a hero and Jensen had been regularly sending texts with random inspirational movie quotes. Even the president had called to see how he was doing.

And then slowly, as if a curtain was being lifted, he began to make peace with what had happened. And, in what Claire thought was the best sign of all, he was starting to get antsy.

"So what now?" Claire asked one morning as they sat outside on the deck sipping coffee.

Gabriel, sitting on a deck chair overlooking rolling hills filled with pinot vines, knew it wasn't an idle question. He turned to her and said,

"Witt wants me to come back to DHS. Says that the threat isn't really over and the president is really worried about the Russians."

Claire waited a few moments, hoping Gabriel would continue the thought. When he didn't, she asked, "And?"

Gabriel was silent for a long moment. He turned to his wife and slowly smiled. "Do you think pinot goes well with borscht?"

EPILOGUE

One Year Later
Moscow, Russia

Antonin Lebedev stood before a bank of monitors inside the command center of the Russian biological weapons test facility on the outskirts of Moscow. One thousand kilometers to the south, a drone circled Klinkovo. It was classified on the map as a town but really wasn't more than a collection of low-slung buildings. But it had meaning to Lebedev, who'd spent summers on his grandfather's farm in another Chechen town not more than ten kilometers away. As he watched the screen, he wondered if they'd chosen Klinkovo as the place to test their new weapon just to spite him.

Probably, he thought.

He watched as the Russian military drone placed its crosshairs over the town's main building, a mosque housed in a converted warehouse. It was the de facto headquarters of the Revolutionary Islamic Regiment, one of Chechnya's main separatist groups. The RIR had recently carried out a brutal attack on Russian soldiers and hewed to a particularly virulent strain of Islamic radicalism.

Over a loudspeaker he could hear the drone operator counting down: "*Tri, dva, odin, ogan!*" Suddenly, a white mist filled the screen as a canister carrying more than a hundred thousand mosquitoes gently deposited its cargo over the town.

"Congratulations," said a man who had suddenly appeared next to him. Lebedev turned his head slightly and noticed that it was Vladimir Putin himself. "You have done us a great service, helping to ensure that Russia remains a great power. And there is much more to do. Can I count on you, Antonin?"

Lebedev turned his gaze back to the screen, and watched as the cloud of mosquitoes engineered to spread the virulent antibiotic-resistant bacteria KPC settled onto the town. He knew that within days the entire area would be infected with a deadly illness for which there was no cure. It sickened him deep inside. But in the interest of survival, he'd made a Faustian bargain.

"*Da,*" he said at last.

THE END

AUTHOR'S NOTE

This story is both fiction and science — but it's not science fiction. Everything described in these pages is possible today — the use of CRISPR/Cas-9 to modify the genome of insects to carry dominant lethal genes for population control has already been done. The technology to insert the code for bugs to synthesize a deadly toxin or disease is totally feasible. As technology improves and costs continue to come down this capability will become more widely available, making it a very real terrorist threat.

The character of Gabriel Marx is loosely based on a real person who, in the interest of his privacy, shall remain nameless. He is the brother of a good friend of mine, and while some of the details of his past have been changed around, he is a real "bug hunter" working for the DHS. I will be forever thankful for the inspiration he gave me for this story.

I also want to thank a few people who were helpful to me in getting this story on paper. First, I received invaluable editorial help from Tim Erickson, an avid reader who happens to be author Eliot Peper's go-to for story advice. He helped immensely in making the story better while giving me encouragement to press on. It would be hard to imagine publishing anything without Tim first reading it! Thanks also to my editor Katie Herman who did an amazingly thorough job of validating facts and story issues. And to my wife Juliet who read the manuscript so many times she could recite it in her sleep!

In addition, Dr. Ruben Flores provided insight into genetic engineering and CRISPR. The author and science writer Debora MacKenzie was kind enough to send me an article she wrote entitled "Run Radish Run" for *New Scientist* magazine that was inspiration for some of the plot points in the story. I am appreciative of their support but in no way are they responsible for any errors or omissions. Those are mine and mine alone.

I hope you enjoyed this novel. If so, please do leave a review on Amazon! Reviews are critical to the success of authors in this day and age. And please be sure to check out my other book, *The Two Gates* also available at Amazon.

CPSIA information can be obtained
at www.ICGtesting.com
Printed in the USA
JSHW030728080420
5014JS00001B/215